FEAR THE REAPER SERIES

KANE: TOOTH & NAIL

FEAR THE REAPER 1

MARK ALLEN

ROUGH
EDGES
PRESS

Kane: Tooth & Nail
Paperback Edition
Copyright © 2024 (As Revised) Mark Allen

Rough Edges Press
An Imprint of Wolfpack Publishing
1707 E. Diana Street
Tampa, FL 33610

roughedgespress.com

Paperback ISBN 978-1-68549-627-2
eBook ISBN 978-1-68549-626-5

Based on characters by Brent Towns.

KANE: TOOTH & NAIL

PROLOGUE

Ciudad Victoria, Mexico

Blood and bullets. Gunfire and guts. These days, it felt like that was all his life had become. War was hell, make no mistake.

Kane felt the weariness. He had begun to see the scars on his soul reflected in his eyes whenever he looked in the mirror. The price of being a warrior. Sometimes in order to protect the living, you started to feel dead inside. You brought it to the bastards, damn straight, but no matter how righteous the violence, it took its toll.

He lay prostrate on the roof of an abandoned church in a slum section of Ciudad Victoria, frequently rated as one of Mexico's most dangerous cities. He was dressed in black to blend in with the shadows, although the moon overhead glowed brighter than he would have preferred due to a lack of cloud cover. For some reason, he craved a smoke, even though he hadn't indulged in a cigarette in a long time.

Through a pair of night-vision binoculars, he studied the dilapidated warehouse across the way, surrounded by a fissured, weed-sprouting parking lot. He judged the distance from the church to the warehouse to be approximately three hundred meters—far enough away so he wouldn't be detected when the targets rolled in, close enough that he could close the gap quickly and crush them like human cockroaches. Because unless things took a pooch-screw turn and forced him to use a long-range option, this strike would be a close-quarters affair.

Kane glanced at the large cross that stabbed into the night sky from the top of the church's bell tower. Plotting bloodshed in the shadow of a holy place might have given some men pause, but Kane wasn't particularly religious. He had survived so long on the killing fields that it was easy to think his mission in life—to serve gunfire justice to the cartels—was divinely sanctioned. The reality was, he didn't give it much thought. He fought his wars for his own reasons, not because he believed them to be blessed by some higher power.

Clouds wisped across the face of the moon as Kane went over the mission parameters in his head for at least the hundredth time. Right now, the night was still and peaceful, but soon, it would be stained with blood.

This strike was a solo assignment, undertaken at the personal—and private—request of Hank Jones, the Chairman of the Joint Chiefs. His nine-year-old goddaughter Kristina—Krissy, he called her—had been abducted just outside a resort in Mexico while on a family vacation.

Kane remembered thinking the bastards who took her would have been better off slathering themselves in salmon guts and bitch-slapping a hungry grizzly bear.

"I want them dead," Jones had said. *"You hear me, Reaper?*

Not wounded, not in prison—dead. Get Krissy back, and kill every son of a bitch who had a hand in taking her."

"Understood. Does General Thurston know?"

"We can tell her when it's over. Right now, nobody knows but you and me, Reaper. Promise me you'll keep it that way."

Kane had promised. The reason remained unspoken between them, but he knew why Jones had sent him in alone, without the team's knowledge. This was an assassination, and while Team Reaper had gunned down hundreds of bad guys during their missions, they were not considered a kill squad. Even by nebulous black ops standards, specifically targeting foreign citizens for termination was dirty work. Kane had been asked to get his hands dirty but keep his team clean. He had agreed without hesitation.

He also knew Jones trusted him to pull the trigger when the moment came.

Using all the considerable sources available to him as Chairman of the Joint Chiefs, Jones had identified the abductors as child pornographers, bottom-feeders in the Zeta cartel, which specialized in kiddie snuff films. Just the thought made Kane's blood boil. The scumbags used various warehouses and out-of-the-way places to kill the kids while the camera rolled. No grainy film reels either; this was high-end slaughter, the carnage in crystal-clear 4K.

The sleaze merchants generally operated as a seven-man team: five men providing site security, one camera operator, and one sick son of a bitch—Ignacio "Igniter" Alvarez, whose calling card was murder by immolation—to commit the abuse and killing.

Not tonight, Kane vowed. Tonight, he would be the only one doing any killing.

A team of seven was child's play for a seasoned

warrior like Kane. Tonight, they would come to the warehouse, unaware that the darkness concealed a predator far more deadly than they. They would come, he would hunt them down, and they would die. No prisoners, just the way Jones wanted it. The kind of filth capable of committing horrific acts on innocent children did not deserve to keep sucking God's good air.

While Kane waited, he checked the SIG-Sauer M17 riding in a low-slung holster on his right thigh. The twenty-one round magazine was loaded to max capacity, and a cartridge bristled in the chamber. A suppressor threaded onto the muzzle ensured that no loud gunshot would be heard during this strike.

Still and silent, he felt the adrenalin pulsing in his bloodstream but kept it tightly leashed. He was about to charge into yet another snake pit and stare down the roaring throat of the evil hydra that would never truly die. More notches on his gun, more deaths on his soul, another bloody mile on the hard road he had chosen to ride. He was not haunted by all the killing he had done—everyone he had ghosted deserved it—but he did feel the burden of the lives he had taken.

How long could he keep going? Was there any kind of future for him beyond the blood and thunder? What might life look like after the bullets and the bodies and blitzes? Or maybe there was no "after" for him. Maybe for a warrior like him, the gunfire wouldn't die until he did.

Maybe the only way to survive on the killing fields without going insane was to forget the past, ignore the future, and just live for today.

Sufficient unto the day is the evil thereof.

He'd heard that scripture verse somewhere, and it

seemed to apply. Especially since he was lying on top of a church.

Headlights appeared on the potholed road that led to the warehouse. Seconds later, Kane heard the distant sound of the vehicle's engine. He quickly raised the binoculars and studied the scene three hundred meters away, painted in shades of green by the night-vision optics.

A cargo van pulled up to the ruined building, and five goons packing Micro-Uzis exited and performed a quick sweep. It was sloppily executed, about as half-assed as you could get, but these guys weren't pros, and they weren't expecting any trouble out here in slum country, especially since the turf was under the control of the Zeta cartel.

Kane intended to teach them the error of their ways.

Four of the gunmen remained outside, while one cleared the warehouse. Unaware they were being surveilled from a distant rooftop, they judged the area safe. Three of the men let their Micro-Uzis dangle from shoulder straps as they fired up cigarettes. The non-smoker slapped the side of the van, and a moment later, the door slid open. A thin, bespectacled man climbed out, holding a video camera in one hand and a tripod in the other.

Even through the scope, Kane thought the man looked tired, as if he were weary of all the horrific carnage he had seen through his camera lens. Not that Kane had any sympathy for the videographer. Hell, no. But if the man was tired of filming kiddie snuff flicks, Kane would be happy to put him down for a permanent dirt nap with a 9mm sleeping pill.

As the cameraman lugged his equipment into the warehouse, another man, this one wearing a leather jacket and sporting a buzz cut, emerged from the van with a body draped over his shoulder. Kane recognized Alvarez from the photos Jones had provided. He also recognized Krissy. Her long brown hair hung down and swayed from side to side as she was carried to the warehouse. Judging from her closed eyes and the way her limbs dangled limply, she had been drugged for the trip. If he didn't know better, Kane might have thought she was already dead, but there was no way they had killed her yet. They wouldn't get to that bit of nastiness until the camera rolled.

The thought made Kane grind his teeth. Any harder, and he would crack enamel. He terminated targets out of a sense of duty, not pleasure, but he would be lying if he said he didn't take some primal satisfaction in executing those who preyed on children. Predators who feasted on innocence deserved no mercy. Even if Jones hadn't requested it, this would be a corpse party all the way.

Kane shinnied down to the ground and ghosted through the darkness, creeping along the edge of the church, ducking through a hole in the mesh-wire fence surrounding the warehouse, and moving silently toward his target.

As he closed on the warehouse, Kane drew a Ka-Bar combat knife from its sheath, filling his fist with deadly steel as he hugged the deep shadows on the south side.

He needed to eliminate the sentries as quietly as possible without warning the men inside the warehouse, and razor-edged steel was the best tool for the job. Even suppressed pistols made enough noise to alert the other guards, and Kane knew any raised alarm would result in Krissy's immediate murder. He couldn't risk it, so the only option was close-quarter kills. Instead of headshots, he would go for cut throats.

Kane closed on the first hoodlum easily. The man leaned against the wall of the warehouse and studied his cell phone. As Kane crept closer, he saw the guy busily flipping through photos of nude women posed with bright-colored vegetables. The last image the sentry would ever see was a curvy redhead licking a zucchini.

The photo disappeared beneath a hot, splattering torrent of blood as Kane slapped a hand over the man's mouth and sliced his throat from ear to ear. His dying breath whooshed out of his severed windpipe.

Kane eased the convulsing corpse to the ground and wasted no time moving to intercept his next target. As he hugged the wall, he heard footsteps approaching the corner and the sound of someone whistling an out-of-tune rendition of Metallica's *Seek & Destroy*. Kane almost smirked; the gods of war were whimsical tonight, dishing out warped irony.

The man stopped whistling as soon as he stepped around the corner because it was really hard to whistle with seven inches of steel buried in your esophagus. Kane twisted the blade and ripped it out sideways. The man staggered backward with blood spurting from his slashed carotid, then tripped over a broken cinderblock and went down flat on his back. He wouldn't be getting back up.

Kane quickly made his way to the other side and finished off the other two sentries, leaving his knife coated in red right up to the hilt. He flicked the blood off the blade and shoved it back in its sheath. Three men still remained inside, but now it was time to go to guns.

Crack the front door, toss in a flashbang, double-tap the dirtbags, and rescue the kid. That was the plan. A simple hit-'n-git. The lethal version of knock-knock.

Silent as a shadow, Kane drew his Sig and circled back

around to the front of the warehouse. Two rickety metal steps led up to the door. Kane crept up the stairs, which threatened to buckle under his weight. When he reached the small landing at the top, he reached for a flashbang.

The door suddenly smashed open from inside, slamming into Kane's chest and knocking him off the landing. As he fell, he saw the last of the guards standing in the doorway, silhouetted against the backlight, raising his Micro-Uzi. The machine-pistol spat flame in a sustained, staccato burst of high-velocity hornets. Snarling a curse, Kane hit the ground and rolled as bullets chased him, blasting divots from the sunbaked concrete.

Using his momentum, Kane powered into a combat crouch and triggered a shot from his SIG that split the sentry's face wide open like a 9mm hatchet. Blood exploded everywhere as the guy fell back into the warehouse, heels drumming a death-rhythm on the floor.

Inside the shack, Krissy started to scream.

Kane stormed up the steps with the M17 leading the way. The night air cooled his skin, but beneath the surface, his blood burned hot. He kept his finger locked on the trigger, ready to unleash gunfire justice.

As he crossed the doorjamb, he saw the videographer cowering next to his tripod, the camera mounted and ready to roll. The guy looked like he was about to piss his pants. Fluorescent lights flickered overhead, the fly-speckled bulbs burning with enough wattage to chase the shadows out of every corner.

Someone had flopped a filthy mattress in the center of the large, open space. Iron shackles that looked like they belonged in a medieval dungeon adorned each end, secured to heavy bolts in the floor. A stainless steel table sat an arm's reach away, littered with instruments of torture, including knives, pliers, axes, and a pair of blood-matted chainsaws with clumps of hair tangled in the metal teeth. Beneath the table was a five-gallon jug of gasoline.

Kane again vowed that nobody would leave this place alive except for him and Krissy. Scorched earth, take no prisoners, blow 'em all to hell, and don't look back.

Ignacio Alvarez stood on the mattress with Krissy in front of him. She was a waif and he was a big man, built like a *luchador*, so she wasn't much of a shield, but the muzzle of the Glock he pressed behind her right ear made sure Kane kept his distance.

Kane aimed his Sig at the shivering camera operator and growled, "Let the girl go, or I'll kill this son of a bitch."

Alvarez shrugged. The Glock stayed tucked against Krissy's mastoid bone. "Go ahead," he said, his voice thick and accented. "That stupid *cabron* don't mean *mierda* to me."

"Have it your way." Kane blasted a bullet into the videographer's chest, drilling a hole in his heart. The impact smashed the sleazy filmmaker flat to the floor as if he'd been hit by a train.

Kane didn't know if the man had killed any kids, nor did he care. If he sat there filming while children were raped and slaughtered, he was no better than the scum-bags doing the dirty work. Bottom line, the bastard deserved the bullet.

Kane turned the Sig back on Alvarez. "Looks like you're the last man standing."

The Mexican sex-trafficker kept the Glock tight against Krissy's head. "Now what, huh?" the man growled. "It's just you, me, and this little *puta*."

This wasn't Kane's first standoff. No point in dragging things out. "Let's cut through the crap," he said. "We put down our guns and settle this man to man."

Alvarez snorted. "Do I look like *estupido* to you? Why the hell would I do that?"

"Because it's your only chance of getting out of here alive."

"You seem to have forgotten I've got the girl, gringo."

"And you seem to have forgotten I can put a bullet in your head."

"If you do, the bitch dies."

"Maybe," said Kane. "Maybe not. Sure, if I put one in your brain, it's possible your finger still pulls the trigger, and Krissy dies. Call it fifty-fifty odds."

Krissy whimpered at the announcement, and Alvarez smirked. "See, I knew you were bluffing."

"But," Kane continued, "if I let you walk out of here with Krissy, the odds are one hundred percent she dies. So unless you put down that Glock and go man to man with me, I'm going with the fifty-fifty odds and taking the shot." Kane's eyes glinted as cold and grim as the gunmetal in his fist. "Like I said, this is your only chance at walking out of here alive."

Alvarez seemed to be kicking it around in his head. Kane imagined a mental pinball machine in there, the steel ball getting batted back and forth between options. He waited, knowing what the answer would be. The Mexican really didn't have much choice, plus bloodlust burned brightly in his eyes. He wanted to go toe-to-toe with the man who had just wrecked his little empire. He was a predator, and predators fought back when wounded.

"Let's do it," Alvarez finally said. "But with one change of rules." He jerked his chin toward the table full of torture instruments. "We use chainsaws."

Chainsaws? Are you kidding me? He just shrugged and said, "Whatever. I'll kill you with a paperclip if that's what it takes."

"What I'm going to do to you, *bastardo*, will hurt way more than a paperclip." Alvarez sneered. "Guns down on three?"

Kane nodded.

The Mexican rattled off a three-count, and both men dropped their weapons at the same time. Alvarez shoved Krissy away so roughly that she fell on her face. She quickly scrambled to put her back against the wall.

"Stay," he snapped as if she were some kind of dog. "Don't you dare move." He then stepped over to the table and picked up a chainsaw. Through the blood and grime caked on the machine, Kane saw the word "Stihl" emblazoned on the side. He recognized that as a top-tier brand. Nothing but the best for butchering kids.

Alvarez moved aside and Kane approached the table, keeping a wary eye on his enemy to make sure he didn't try any funny shit. Not that he expected him to; Alvarez seemed eager for the battle, ready to clash steel against steel in mortal combat. A dangerous, lunatic fire blazed in his eyes.

Kane hefted the remaining chainsaw, a PowerKing, which was lighter than he expected. That meant it would be easier to maneuver in the upcoming deathmatch. The eighteen-inch bar jutted from the small but powerful machine, bristling with jagged teeth ready to rend and tear. Kane mentally reminded himself that if he fell victim to those unforgiving flesh-rippers, Krissy would be next. He could not afford to lose this fight.

Alvarez grinned, a blood-crazed madman clearly enjoying the moment. "*Amigo!*" he shouted. "Start your engine!" He cranked the starter cord, and the chainsaw rumbled to life in a billow of noxious smoke.

Kane glanced at Krissy. The little girl was stricken with terror. No surprise there. "Don't watch," he said. "You don't need to see this."

She nodded tearfully and turned her face against the wall.

Kane fixed his ice-cold gaze on Alvarez. "Time for you to die." He fired up his chainsaw and hit the throttle, making the steel teeth spin around the bar in a metallic blur.

The Mexican appeared convinced of his own immortality, not a shred of worry showing on his face. "Let's dance!" he roared, lunging forward and thrusting the Stihl toward Kane's face like a lance in a joust.

Kane dodged to the side, and the screaming teeth missed his head by inches. The thunder of the engine brutalized his eardrum. The Mexican tried dropping the blade in a vertical cut to catch Kane's shoulder, but he sidestepped out of harm's way.

Seizing the offensive, Kane swung the PowerKing toward Alvarez's flank, hoping to carve a gash through his ribcage and into the vital organs beyond. The sex trafficker jumped back, and Kane's saw cut through nothing but thin air.

He gritted his teeth and pressed the attack, slicing toward the Mexican's belly, going for a disemboweling strike. But Alvarez again hopped back, and the blow missed. Not by much, but that didn't matter. A mile or an inch, a miss is still a miss.

Sensing an opening, Alvarez raised his chainsaw overhead for a downward, chopping stroke that would split Kane's head from crown to chin.

Kane brought his own chainsaw up and blocked the

blow. The metal bars clashed together, steel teeth mangling each other in a harsh spray of sparks. Violent vibrations shuddered up his arms. Alvarez's brute strength pushed the screaming blades closer to Kane's face, muscles heaving with his herculean effort to kill his foe. His lips were peeled back from his clenched teeth in an animalistic snarl.

Rather than expend his energy repelling Alvarez's power, Kane rolled out from underneath the crisscrossed chainsaws. Robbed of a resisting counterforce, Alvarez lurched forward, stumbling as his Stihl slashed through suddenly-empty space. Moving with the lethal grace of a jungle cat, Kane spun behind the off-balance Mexican and prepared to drive the PowerKing's blade into the man's spine.

But Alvarez, holding his chainsaw in just one hand, flailed backward with wild desperation. Kane dropped to his knees and felt the Stihl's blade whip over his head with only millimeters to spare. But a miss was a miss, and the warrior seized the advantage.

Like a scene from a horror movie, Kane thrust the chainsaw up between Alvarez's legs. Shredded flesh and hot blood sprayed everywhere in a thick, wet slurry. The Mexican screamed like the little girls he had savaged as metal teeth ripped his groin into a ragged red ruin, and he fell to the floor, writhing in agony.

Kane rose to his feet, letting the bloodied chainsaw drop to the floor as he retrieved his Sig. Alvarez had deserved what had happened to him, no doubt about it. However, Kane was a soldier, not a sadist who took pleasure in his enemy's pain.

He fired a mercy bullet into Alvarez's skull and ended his misery.

Hot smoke curled from the muzzle of the gun as he

shut off both chainsaws, then walked over to where Krissy huddled against the wall. He could hear her frightened whimpers. "Come on, Krissy, let's get you home."

"*Hijo de puta!*"

Kane dropped into a crouch and spun toward the door as an angry voice filled the warehouse. The Sig snapped up, seeking target acquisition on this unexpected threat. His finger had the trigger halfway home, ready to pump out a whole lot of hollow-points.

The young Mexican kid standing in the doorway couldn't be any older than fourteen. The nickel-plated Browning Hi-Power .40 caliber pistol in his fist looked even newer.

Kid must have been waiting in the van, Kane thought.

The teen's face twisted with rage and grief. "You killed my brother!" he shouted.

Kane moved to put himself between the gunman and the girl. He kept the M17 locked on target but kept his voice low and calm. "Easy there, kid. I've got no fight with you." Even from here, he could see the boy's resemblance to Alvarez. Talk about a messed-up situation. He was standing over the body of the kid's brother, and the only way out, the only way to save Krissy, might be to kill the kid too.

The rage on the boy's face transferred to his gun hand, which shook badly. His whole body trembled, vibrating with shock, horror, sadness, and fury. "I've got a fight with you!" the teenager shouted, and even his voice quivered.

"I get it," Kane said. "Really, I do. I've had people taken from me, so I get why you're feeling raw right now. But believe me, your brother was doing some bad shit that couldn't be allowed to stand."

"I don't care!" the kid shouted. "He was *mi hermano*. I must avenge his death!"

Just like that, his hand stopped shaking.

Kane mouthed a curse. He didn't want to kill a kid. There had to be a way out of this standoff.

The boy's eyes narrowed. The knuckle of his trigger finger tightened.

Kane saw the signs. He was out of time.

Dammit!

The teen started to pull the trigger.

Kane beat him to the punch.

The bullet ripped into the kid's chest. He still managed to get off a shot, but he missed badly, staggering from the lethal impact. He stared at Kane, eyes wide in their sockets, full of shock and hurt and the horrified realization that his young life was over. Blood poured from the hole drilled in his heart. He grabbed at the wall to keep from falling but failed, sliding to the ground in a twitching heap.

"Stay here," Kane said to Krissy, then ran over to the fallen teen.

By the time he got there, death had glazed the boy's eyes as he stared into whatever waited beyond the business end of a bullet. Guilt tore a jagged wound across Kane's conscience. He could have sworn he saw accusation in the kid's dead eyes.

With a soul-weary sigh, Kane turned back to Krissy. She looked at him like she wasn't sure if he was a good guy or a bad guy. Right now, he wasn't sure himself. Yeah, he had killed some deserving scumbags tonight, but he had also killed a kid. He wasn't sure how that would balance out on the scales of justice.

He shook his head. Maybe he wasn't cut out for this anymore.

He gave the frightened little girl a reassuring smile.
"Come on, Krissy. Let's get you home."

As he guided her out into the night, the shadows
closed around them, the darkness outside mirroring his
internal darkness. Shielding Krissy's eyes as they stepped
over the boy's corpse, Kane felt a cold hollow carved into
his guts. He wondered if the feeling would ever go away.

Someone had to ride the blood and thunder. Someone
had to cross swords with the savages and cannibals who
preyed on the innocent. Someone had to carry the fight
into the gaping, tooth-filled maw of the beast. But what
price did the warrior pay? How many scars could a soul
stand?

Kane had once vowed to be that warrior.

Now, he wasn't sure he could do it anymore.

ONE

Even with the GPS guiding him, Kane drove past the sign for Wolf Pond Road. He glanced in his rearview mirror to make sure there was nobody behind him—there wasn't, just like there hadn't been for the last thirty miles—then hit the brakes on his Jeep Wrangler. He backed up until he could turn onto the unpaved, poorly-marked, dead-end dirt road.

Gravel crunched under the Jeep's tires as the road curved around the small body of water for which it was named. He saw a man and a boy down on the bank, wetting their fishing lines. They stared at him as he drove past. Kane raised his hand in a polite wave, but they didn't wave back.

"Friendly folks," Kane muttered. Maybe he should have checked the back of the *Welcome to Black Bog* sign he had passed a half-mile back to see if it said, *Now go the hell away*.

A mile farther on, he pulled up in front of the house at the end of Wolf Pond Road and parked the Jeep next to a rusting metal mailbox marked with the name E. Foxx.

As he climbed out of the Wrangler, the fresh mountain air hit him, laced with the scents of pines and cedars. Before he could really savor the crisp smells, the biggest Maine Coon cat he had ever laid eyes on raced around the corner of the house and charged at him. The loud meows coming out of the cat's mouth could have drowned out a dragon's roar. Thankfully, the Maine Coon's ears weren't pinned back.

Kane offered a non-threatening hand for the cat to sniff. Almost instantly, the meows changed to purrs. As he scratched the cat under the chin, a man came out of the house and stood on the porch. "Don't worry about ol' Doofus; his meow is far worse than his bite. He might break your foot if he happens to step on it, but that's about as dangerous as he gets."

"You named your cat 'Doofus?'" Kane asked.

"Trust me," the man said, "if you'd lived with that fleabag as a kitten, you would've named him 'Doofus,' too. Personally, I wanted to call him 'Dumbass,' but the wife took exception." Despite the insult, the affectionate gleam in the man's eyes when he looked at the Maine Coon made betrayed his true feelings.

The men sized each other up. Kane knew he cut an imposing figure at 6'4" with his broad shoulders and hard muscle. He judged the other man to be somewhere in his late fifties or early sixties. Hard to tell behind the full, bushy, mountain-man beard he sported. His blue jeans and red-black checkered flannel gave him the look of a logger, but the significant belly betrayed him as a man who enjoyed his beer. The guy sported a battered camouflage baseball cap perched slightly crooked on his head, strands of salt-and-pepper hair, heavy on the salt, poking out from underneath.

The man came down the stairs and walked over. "You John?" he asked.

"That depends," Kane said. "You Ernest?"

"Ernest Foxx, that's right," the man replied. "But only my ex-wife called me Ernest, and you'll note she's an ex. Folks who don't want to get on my bad side call me Ernie."

"Fair enough. I'm John, but most people call me Kane."

"Why's that?"

"Because it's my last name."

Ernie shook his head. "Round these parts, everyone calls each other by their first name. Except for the correctional officers over at the Black Bog Federal Prison." He waved a hand toward the west, apparently indicating the direction of the prison. "They always use last names. Must be a prison thing." He shrugged to indicate it didn't mean much.

Over Foxx's shoulder, Kane saw a large field of wild grass, at least ten acres, edged by pine and cedar trees. A soft autumn breeze rippled the grass like ocean waves. Nearby mountains loomed over the tranquil scene, some with peaks so high it looked like you could touch the clouds if you reached the summit.

"Nice place you've got here," he remarked.

"It suits me," Foxx said. "Peaceful and quiet, 'cept for when wife number two starts yapping at me." He shook his head in exaggerated regret. "Can't believe I was dumb enough to get hitched again after I threw the first one out."

Kane grinned. "The things we do for love, right?"

"Love?" Ernie snorted derisively. "More like good old-fashioned lust. Wife number two had a great ass at one point, before the Dorito- and doughnut-addictions set in."

"Well, peace and quiet are what I'm looking for." Kane hoped Foxx would take the hint and get down to business.

The old man nodded. "Of course, son, of course. Here I am, prattling on about my love life, and you probably just want to get up to the cabin, kick off your boots, and do…well, whatever it is you came all the way up to God's country to do."

"Just looking for a little R&R, that's all."

"You're not some kind of hooligan, are you? Running from the law?"

"Far from it," Kane said. "Just need to sort some shit out in my head, and looking to get away from the world while I do it."

Foxx nodded. "Well, you've come to the right place. The cabin's two miles back in the middle of nowhere, completely off-grid, and not a speck of cell service to be found."

"Perfect."

"Like I told you when we spoke on the phone a few days ago, I get payment in full up front." As Kane forked over the money, Foxx said, "I didn't use to be so rigid about that, but a few years back, a young Canadian couple rented the place, and I said they could pay on their way out. They ended up getting killed, and I didn't get a single red penny."

Kane asked, "What killed them?"

"Bear got 'em."

"A bear? A man-killing bear is kind of rare, isn't it?"

"Not as rare around here as you might think," Foxx replied. "You bring protection?"

"You mean, a gun?"

"I'm not talking about a rubber, son."

"Then yeah, I've got protection."

"Hope it's not some nine-millimeter peashooter," Ernie said. "When it comes to dealing with bears, bigger is definitely better."

Kane saw no reason to tell him about the Sig M17 tucked in the small of his back beneath his jacket. Knowing he would be hiking in some wild country, he had also brought along heavier firepower. No harm in telling Foxx about that. "I've got a forty-four mag with me."

"Rifle or handgun?"

"Handgun."

"With proper shot placement, a good-quality six-shooter will definitely get the job done."

"It's a semi-auto."

Ernie's eyebrows shot up. "Desert Eagle?"

Kane nodded. "Looks like you know a little something about guns."

"Hobby of mine. I do some collecting, plinking, that sort of thing. Got a whole reloading setup down in my basement." He waved a hand. "But enough about all that. You've got yourself a heavy-caliber bear deterrent, and that's all that matters." He reached into his pocket and pulled out a key, attached to a spent brass .223 cartridge.

Kane grinned. "What, no rabbit's foot?"

"A bullet will bring you more luck." Foxx handed him the key and pointed to a trail, not much more than twin ruts in the dirt along the edge of the field. "Follow that all the way out back, and you'll see a metal gate. Key opens the gate as well as the cabin. Once you're through the gate, just follow the path until you come to the cabin. It sits up on a hillock about two miles back. Once you cross Dribble Creek, you'll know you're almost there."

"I'll need to pick up some supplies," Kane said. He jerked a thumb over his shoulder. "Back to the main road and head north to get to town?"

"Vesper Lake is about three miles up the road," Foxx replied. "Closest thing we've got to a real town around here. If you're looking for Walmart, you came to the wrong place."

"Just somewhere to pick up the basics. Town must have some kind of grocery store, right?"

Foxx nodded. "Baldy's. It'll be on your right once you cross the old railroad tracks and roll into town."

"Baldy's?"

"Stupid name, I know. Double-stupid because the owner's got a head of hair that would make a lion proud."

"Strange little town you got here."

"Now there's an understatement," Foxx said. "Because, mister, you don't know the half of it. If you belly up to the bar down at Saws 'n' Suds, old Fred will fill you in on everything you need to know and a whole lotta shit you don't, if you let him keep yakking at ya."

"Good to know," Kane said. "Because my first impression is that the town doesn't care much for outsiders."

Foxx snorted. "Most don't, but you don't strike me as a man who cares much about what people think of you." He headed back to the house, saying over his shoulder. "Enjoy your stay, Kane, and I hope you get that shit in your head sorted out. You need anything, you know where to find me."

Kane gave Doofus a quick scratch between the ears, then climbed back into the Jeep.

As he drove along the edge of the field, the ruts gave the Wrangler's suspension a good workout. When he lowered the windows to let in the mountain air, he spotted a small group of whitetail deer in the far corner with their heads up, keeping wary eyes on him to make sure he posed no threat.

The trail dead-ended in a parking area of sorts, but he spotted the metal gate off to the side. He unlocked it and left it open, knowing he would be heading back into town after he got settled in at the cabin.

This trail was better maintained, any ruts or rough patches filled in with gravel. It was narrow, though, and tree branches frequently clawed the side of the Jeep.

He drove slowly, not just because of the terrain, but because that was what he needed—a slowdown. Mentally and physically, he needed a break from all the running and gunning, the *Go! Go! Go!* pace of life with Team Reaper. He needed to slow down, look inward, absorb what he had done, and learn how to live with it.

Some of his teammates had urged him to just keep pushing forward, get back in the saddle, and refuse to be broken. Good advice, and well-intentioned, but Kane knew that sometimes you just can't put the past in the rearview mirror and forget it. Sometimes, in order to move forward, you have to grapple with your demons. Otherwise, they just keep dragging you back.

And "refuse to be broken?" That might look great as an inspirational meme superimposed over a snarling wolf or something alpha-primal like that, but Kane knew what the others didn't fully grasp—he already *was* broken. Gunning down the boy had done something, taken something from him. Charging hell-bent-for-leather into another firefight wasn't the solution, not for him. He needed to slow down and figure out how to put the broken pieces back together.

General Mary Thurston, the team leader, had been slightly less than understanding.

"We're a covert, rapid-response strike force, Reaper," she had said when he'd informed her he needed a break. *"We hunt the bad guys, and since the bad guys don't take vacations, neither do we."*

"It's not a vacation."

"Call it whatever you want, but it means you're not going to be here for…how long did you say?"

"Not sure."

"How about I just deny your not-sure-how-long leave of absence? What would you say then?"

Kane's eyes had gone steely. *"I'd say that you're my leader, but you're not my damn boss, and I'm standing down until I feel like I'm ready to come back. I'm no good to my team right now. They deserve someone on their six who isn't all messed up in the head."*

"That kid tried to kill you, Reaper. It was self-defense. Why can't you see that?"

"I can see it. But I still have to figure out how to live with the fact that I put a bullet in a kid's heart."

Thurston had looked him dead in the eye. *"You ever going to be able to pull the trigger again, Reaper?"*

He had stared right back at her. *"That's what I'm going to find out."*

The team had seen him off with reassuring words and pats on the shoulder, telling him to take as long as he needed. Only Cara, who knew him better than anyone else, seemed to truly understand.

"Do what you have to do, Reaper," she had said after the others drifted away. *"Don't come back until you're ready."*

"And what if I'm never ready, Cara? What happens then?"

"Then you come back here and get me, and we'll ride off into the sunset together."

Thinking of it now, as the Jeep rumbled up the trail to Dribble Creek Camp, Kane smiled. God, he loved that woman. They had called it off months ago, but the emotions still simmered beneath the surface for both of them. Maybe someday, they would sort it all out.

He had driven from Texas to Maine, taking four days to make a trip that he could have completed in two if he had elected to push it. But "pushing it" wasn't part of his plan. He'd spent three days in Maine visiting his sister Melanie, who was still comatose following the death of their parents. He had also checked on Cara's son Jimmy.

During his stay in Maine, he had researched private, off-grid cabins. He had eventually settled on this place in the northern Adirondack Mountains of upstate New York, not too far from the Canadian border. A call to Ernie Foxx had confirmed the cabin's availability.

He passed a cedar swamp on his right, and a short time later, he came to Dribble Creek, conveniently marked by a wooden sign on the side of the road just before the bridge. It was a short bridge since Dribble Creek turned out to only be about twenty feet across at this point. The Jeep navigated it easily, then started up a sharp incline.

After a few switchbacks, Kane arrived at the cabin. He killed the engine, climbed out, and looked over the place he would call home for the next week.

As Foxx had stated, the cabin perched on of a hillock of sorts, flattened on the top like a mesa. The cabin sat off to the right, a single-story structure built from rough-hewn logs. He saw a propane tank for the lights and stove and a generator on a cement slab. A spacious deck jutted off the west corner to offer a spectacular view of the mountains on the other side of the valley. The fall foliage was near its peak, the woods a riot of orange, purple, and yellow, creating a truly breathtaking sight.

Off to the left was a lean-to covering neatly-stacked piles of chopped firewood. Beside it was a large stump with a double-bladed axe sticking out of it, as well as a gasoline-powered log splitter for those who preferred to let technology do the hard work.

Directly in front of him, next to a large picnic table, was an outdoor stone fireplace, complete with a ten-foot-high chimney that looked like it had been fashioned from large, water-smoothed rocks harvested from Dribble Creek. The fireplace was big enough to roast a buffalo.

On the farthest southwest corner of the hill's flat crest squatted an old-fashioned outhouse. Kane couldn't see the door from where he stood, but he would have bet dimes to dollars there was a crescent moon carved in it.

He grabbed his gear and hauled it into the cabin. Just inside the door was a mudroom of sorts, with boot racks, shelving, gun racks, and coat hooks, along with a couple of bunks. He dumped his gear on one of the bunks and stepped into the main room of the cabin.

More bunks, upper and lower, lined two of the walls. All told, the cabin could sleep ten comfortably. High on the vaulted ceiling, mounted deer heads gazed at him with glass eyes. A large table dominated the center of the room, ringed by eight chairs. A woodstove stood against the back wall, and off to his right was the kitchen area. A large picture window set into the western wall gave him a spectacular view out over the deck and down into the valley.

He unpacked his clothes and rolled out his sleeping bag on the bunk closest to the window, then fired up the woodstove to chase away the chill. While the cabin warmed up, he laid out his weapons.

He never went anywhere without his SIG-Sauer M17 —he felt damn near naked without it—and as he had told Foxx, he had also brought along a Desert Eagle .44 magnum. He knew most magnum handgun connoisseurs gravitated toward revolvers, but his time in the Marines, followed by his stint with Team Reaper, had acclimated him to favor semi-autos. Some guys had trouble handling a Desert Eagle hand cannon, but Kane was a big man, with big hands more than capable of handling the heavy beast.

His was the Mark XIX L6 model, eleven ounces lighter than most other models in the Desert Eagle lineup. It sported a hard-coat anodized black aluminum frame with a stainless steel slide and an integral muzzle brake, along with a picatinny rail beneath the barrel, to which he had attached a flashlight. All in all, it had plenty of power to tackle a bear should he be unlucky enough to cross one's path.

He had left his HK416 back at headquarters in El Paso—he couldn't see where he would need a full-auto carbine up here in the mountains—but had replaced it with a Beretta 1301 tactical shotgun, which made more sense for this trip. With its integrated BLINK gas-operating system, featuring a cross-tube gas piston, the Beretta cycled faster than any other semi-auto shotgun on the market.

He went outside, got a fire going, and sat on the deck as the sun sank behind the western mountains. Somewhere in the distance, a coyote howled; much closer, an owl hooted as it prepared to hunt in the twilight. Kane leaned his head back and gazed up at the moon as it materialized in the darkening sky, letting the calm roll over him.

Weariness from his road trip and the soothing warmth of the fire combined to make him drowsy. With nothing better to do, he closed his eyes, and sleep claimed him in less than two minutes.

His dreams were not peaceful.

He stood in the shower, letting the water pound him, rinsing away the dust and grime of the day. Steam rose around him, the vaporous heat creating a soothing fog.

Suddenly the glass door shattered, exploding inward, filling the shower with razor shards.

The boy he had shot stood in the bathroom, holding a sledgehammer. Blood oozed from the hole in his heart to spatter the floor, and the ghost-gray of death colored his face. When the boy opened his mouth to speak, maggots came out, falling like rain on the bloody floor.

"I'm sorry," Kane said over the pulsing hiss of the water that continued to flow from the showerhead. "I'm sorry I took your life away."

He tried to move, but his arms felt cemented in place. The hot water pouring down his body now felt like liquid chains holding him fast.

The boy tried to speak, but nothing came out but grunts and gurgles as blood seeped from the corners of his mouth. When he opened even wider, Kane heard a buzzing sound coming from his rotting throat, like a swarm of flies trapped inside him.

Reaper didn't fully understand what was happening, but he knew his sins had come home to roost.

The boy suddenly raised the sledgehammer high above his head and roared, "Die!"

Unable to move, Kane could only wait as the hammer descended to smash his head open like an eggshell.

Kane jerked awake, a startled *"No!"* trapped behind

his clenched teeth. The gruesome dream images scurried back to whatever subconscious corner of his mind had spawned them while real-time situational awareness rushed in to take their place. He wasn't sure how long he had been out of it, but full night had fallen; the moon was now master of the sky, the sun having surrendered for another day. The fire had burned down to a subdued glow, little more than a few flickering flames and red-glowing embers. Out in the forest, something screamed as it fell prey to a predator in the primal circle of life.

Kane pushed himself out of the chair, shaking his head to get rid of the last vestiges of the nightmare as he headed toward the Jeep. He knew that from a psychological standpoint, it was a bad sign his dream had taken such a symbolic turn. Shooting that kid had messed him up more than he cared to admit.

Washing down the guilt with some Jack Daniels seemed like just the thing.

Time to head into town.

TWO

Black Bog Federal Prison was hardly the crown jewel of the Federal Bureau of Prisons, which operated under the umbrella of the Department of Justice. The United States Penitentiary, Administrative Maximum Facility—or Supermax, as it was more commonly called—out in Florence, Colorado, generally grabbed the headlines when reporters needed a story about a badass prison.

Black Bog Federal Prison, on the other hand, usually flew well under the radar. It was old, having been built in 1980, originally designed as a campus for Winter Olympics hopefuls who came to the region to train before being retrofitted into a correctional facility. It was located in the middle of nowhere, high in the Adirondacks, where winter weather started as early as October, and snowstorms sometimes rolled through in May. Some locals claimed to have once seen snowflakes on July 4th.

The inmates caught up in the meat grinder referred to the place as the Siberia of the federal prison system.

As a medium-high facility, Black Bog Prison was just one step down from a penitentiary. Instead of solid walls, triple fences topped with razor wire prevented escape. Instead of guard towers, two perimeter patrols circled the mile-long road around the prison twenty-four/seven, armed with Smith & Wesson pistols, Remington shotguns, and M-4 carbines.

Behind the razor wire, the prison housed nearly eight hundred inmates, ranging from white-collar embezzlers to rabid rapists to black-hearted murderers. As in any prison, various gangs thrived. *Surenos*, Mexican Mafia, Bloods, Texas Syndicate, D.C. Blacks, Aryan Brotherhood...all had carved out their space inside. But regardless of affiliation, all paid tribute to a single man.

Nazareno Pedregon, a.k.a. "The Nazarene Dragon."

A drug lord affiliated with the Mexican cartels, Nazareno had earned his nickname by crucifying his enemies and then setting them on fire. While personally overseeing the orchestration of cocaine pipelines in Montreal, he had been arrested by the Royal Canadian Mounted Police, which to this day, made him seethe with embarrassment. No DEA task force takedown with black helicopters and submachine guns and snarling dogs. Instead, he had been captured by fucking *Mounties*.

In prison, he embraced a Jesus persona, wearing white robes and sandals. Instead of the long hair typically associated with artist renderings of Christ, he kept his head shaved and had tattooed a crown of thorns all the way around his scalp, complete with beads of blood. He had also tattooed disturbingly realistic nail holes on his wrists and feet.

His message, however, was anything but peace, love, and redemption—as the man now being dragged into the cell, which was meant to house six inmates but was utilized only by Nazareno, was about to find out.

The two enforcers, members of MS-13, the notoriously violent gang with a penchant for gruesome murders, dropped the terrified man at Nazareno's sandaled feet. A middle-aged Caucasian with no gang affiliation, Timothy Winkerson was the orderly who cleaned the warden's office.

As soon as the MS-13 goons released his arms, Winkerson crawled on his hands and knees to touch the tattooed nail holes on Nazareno's feet, just like a penitent sinner pleading for forgiveness back in the days of the incarnated Christ. "Please, Mr. Pedregon, I'm begging you."

Nazareno glared down at him. "Begging me for what?"

"To spare my life. I get out in eight months. I have a son and daughter waiting for me at home."

"Your family means nothing to me, you worthless dog," Nazareno growled. "In fact, when I am done with you, perhaps I will send word to have your family killed. I will have your son and daughter nailed to their bedroom walls."

"No! Please, I'm begging you."

"Yes, begging. I heard you the first time." Nazareno drew back his foot, then slammed it forward, kicking Winkerson in the face. The top of his foot, toughened from a lifetime of martial arts training, caught the man on the chin. Winkerson snapped upright in a kneeling position, head rolling dazedly on his shoulders. Nazareno kicked him again, this time in the chest, sending him sprawling on his back with a bruised sternum. Nazareno could have kicked him hard enough to crack the bone and puncture the lungs, had he so chosen, but he wanted Winkerson alive...for now.

Nazareno gestured to the two enforcers. They lifted the groaning Winkerson and dragged him over to the toilet, flopping him facedown over the bowl. One of them pulled out a six-inch-long hunting knife—no crude prison shanks for the Nazarene Dragon's enforcers, not when nearly every correctional officer had been bought off—and laid the honed edge against Winkerson's straining neck, like a butcher about to cut a hog's throat over a blood trough.

"Please!" Wilkerson screamed, voice muffled from having his head stuffed into the toilet. "Tell me what I've done! Tell me how to make it right!"

"You know what you've done," Nazareno snarled. "Warden Ghastin told me what you said to her while you were cleaning her office today."

"I didn't say anything! I swear!"

Nazareno walked over and kicked him in the ass. "Lie to me again, and I'll have your tongue cut out."

After a long pause, Winkerson said, "I'm sorry, Mr. Pedregon. It just slipped out."

"Tell me," Nazareno commanded. "I want to hear it from your own lips. Tell me what you said to her."

"I told her she had a beautiful chest."

"I do not believe those were your exact words."

"I...I said she had nice tits."

"At last, we come to the truth."

"I meant it as a compliment!"

"I'm sure you did. After all, they are indeed nice tits, right?"

Knowing there was no good answer to that question, Winkerson kept his mouth shut.

"I didn't ask you for silence," Nazareno warned. "I asked you a question."

"Yes," Winkerson whimpered. "They're nice."

"What are?"

"Her...you know."

"Say it."

"Please..."

"Say it!" Nazareno roared.

"Tits," Winkerson whispered, quivering in terror.

"Damn right, they're nice," the drug lord replied. "And you know what else they are? They're mine. Not yours, *mine*. Warden Ghastin is off limits to you. Consider her my personal property, and keep your filthy, fucking hands off her."

"I didn't touch her!" Wilkerson protested.

"You touched her with your eyes. You looked at her and imagined what it would be like to hold those breasts in your hands. You fucked her in your mind, and that pisses me off."

"I'm sorry!"

"You will be," Nazareno said ominously. "From now on, when you clean her office, you keep your eyes to yourself. Don't look at her, not even a passing glance. Am I clear?"

Winkerson, realizing that "from now on" meant he wasn't going to be killed, started to nod fervently, but was brought up short by the blade at his jugular. Instead, he said, "Yes, Mr. Pedregon, perfectly clear."

"Excellent. Now, I wish we could just take your word for it, but unfortunately, I need more assurance than that. I could have your eyes gouged out. God knows that would solve your problem."

"No," Wilkerson moaned. "Please don't. I'm begging you…"

"But then," Nazareno continued, ignoring the pleading convict, "you wouldn't be able to clean Warden Ghastin's office, and she tells me you do a good job… when you're not busy raping her with your eyes."

Wilkerson didn't even waste his breath protesting. He just remained bowed over the toilet, awaiting his fate.

"But your eyes are not really the problem," Nazareno said. "The problem is desire, lust, thinking with your balls, and being a slave to your dick." He paused for a moment, then nodded, pretending to reach a decision that, truthfully, he had made before Winkerson had even been dragged into his cell. "I believe amputation will solve your problem."

Winkerson immediately started struggling against the two enforcers, nearly cutting his own throat in the process. Which might have been preferable to what came next.

"NO!" the orderly screamed as they yanked him to his feet. Instead of slicing his neck wide open, the hunting knife cut away his gray prison-issue sweatpants, followed by his boxers.

Naked and exposed, Winkerson, still screaming even though he knew nobody, prison staff or inmates, would come to his rescue, was forced to sit down on the toilet as if taking a dump.

The knife went between his knees. It was sharp, but not *that* sharp; the enforcer had to saw back and forth to get the job done. Winkerson screamed in agony as blood splattered the porcelain and crimsoned the water.

Nazareno fired up a cigar until the end glowed red-hot. He approached Winkerson with a cruel smile carved on his swarthy face.

"Let's see about getting that wound cauterized, *amigo*."

The pain and smoke and gagging stench of burning flesh let Winkerson know you didn't always have to die to go to hell.

THREE

Vesper Lake

As the Wrangler's tires rumbled over the old railroad tracks and rolled into Vesper Lake, Kane reflected that while the mountain views might be awesome, the town wasn't much to look at.

It was situated around a small lake—Vesper Lake, he assumed—about three miles in circumference. A single two-lane road ringed the lake, with houses built along the water's edge and the town's limited businesses occupying space on the other side. Just about every house featured a dock—some in disrepair, others freshly-renovated—with either a fishing boat or a pontoon boat tied off.

Kane did a lap around the lake to familiarize himself with the area. The southern end featured a gas station, a bank, a hardware store, Baldy's Groceries, and a liquor emporium. Most of the eastern side of the lake was dotted with houses.

At the northern edge of town was the Cammeaux Logging Company. As he drove past, he saw rows of heavy machinery and logging trucks and wood-chippers. A cluster of men huddled together on a smoke break stared at him with the same unwelcoming gaze he'd received back at Wolf Pond. Kane shook his head. Seemed like these mountain men didn't take kindly to outsiders.

Just past the logging company was a rundown restaurant with its windows shuttered, and right next to it was an old car dealership, also closed up and dilapidated. Clearly, the town's economy wasn't booming. Kane was willing to bet that Vesper Lake was pretty much supported by the federal prison and the logging company, and if not for those two entities, this place would be a ghost town.

He passed a public boat launch and the post office, then came upon the bar Ernie Foxx had mentioned—Saws 'n' Suds—perched at the northwestern edge of the lake. There weren't too many cars in the parking lot.

The road curved around a bend and snaked along the western side of the lake, mostly occupied by larger houses with bigger boats, indicating this was the wealthier side of town. Clearly in Vesper Lake, saying "the other side of the lake" was the same as saying "the other side of the tracks" in a more urban setting.

The only non-residential building on the western edge of the water was the sheriff's station, a standard two-story brick building that had probably been built sometime in the 1950s. There were two squad cars parked out front, along with a Ford Bronco. Kane could see yellow lights glowing through the windows.

He circled back around to Baldy's and picked up enough supplies for a week. Business was slow; there were only two other shoppers in the store, and they pointedly ignored him. The cashier was a bored, blonde, bubblegum-popping girl who looked to be about sixteen with purple streaks in her crow-black hair and angry red acne peppering her cute-in-a-plain-way face.

The bored look disappeared when Kane approached with his basket of groceries. Her eyes ran up and down his tall, muscular form in a frank, borderline-rude appraisal.

"Well, howdy, stranger," she greeted him. "You're not from around here, are you?"

"What gave me away?"

The girl popped her gum between her teeth, then licked her lips with exaggerated lasciviousness. "I've screwed every guy in this town and the next two towns over," she said, "but I ain't screwed you. That's how I know you're not from around here." She winked. "So, what are you doing later?"

"Not you," Kane said, giving her a grin to take the harsh edge off the words. He looked at her nametag—J. Bait—and back at her face. "Your last name really Bait?"

She brushed the tag. "No, some of the guys gave this to me as a joke. They said the 'J' stands for Jail. You get it? Jail Bait?"

"Yeah, I get it," Kane said. "Guess if what you said is true, it pretty much fits."

"Oh, it's true," Jailbait assured him. "But up here in the mountains, you ain't considered jailbait once you reach thirteen."

"Charming," Kane replied, handing her some money. "Keep the change. Maybe I'll see you around."

"God, I hope so," the girl said, stripping him with her eyes again.

"Never gonna happen, Jailbait."

"That's what they all say, mister. Hey, you got a name?"

"Sure do." He gave her another grin as he walked out the door. At least he had finally found a friendly face in this town. Sure, it was mostly hyperactive teenage hormones rather than genuine friendliness, but it still counted.

He popped into the liquor store to buy a bottle of Jack Daniels to accompany the Coke he had purchased at Baldy's, then drove around the end of the lake to Saw 'n' Suds. There were a few more cars in the parking lot now, and as he exited the Jeep, he could hear music coming from the propped-open front door. It was country music, and it made him want to get back into the Wrangler and leave. He hated that crap, with all its nasal twang and steel guitars. He was a rock 'n' roll kind of guy, but for the sake of a cold beer, he decided to suck it up and suffer the ear pollution.

After stepping through the open door, Kane found himself in a simplistic small-town drinking joint. The bar ran down the right side of the room, with high-top tables and chairs pushed up against the left wall, leaving a path straight down the middle. Halfway back, a short set of stairs led up to a lounge of sorts, with a few booths tucked against one wall. Kane glimpsed a stage at the back of the elevated area—a four-man country-western band jamming away with bucketloads of enthusiasm but not a whole lot of talent. On the dance floor in front of the stage, two couples rollicked to the southern groove, while a pretty redhead gyrated solo as a couple of beer-swilling lumberjack types in jeans and flannel shirts ogled her from the sidelines. She ignored them both but gave Kane a quick smile that made her green eyes sparkle.

Kane smiled back, more out of politeness than anything, then bellied up to the bar. He had it to himself, save for a middle-aged man slumped on a stool at the far end who looked downright miserable. Kane couldn't blame him. That was what country music did to you. Of course, the half-dozen empty shot glasses lined up on the bar in front of him probably helped.

The bartender wandered over. He looked old enough to be God's great-grandfather, with thick white hair matched by an equally-white beard that cascaded all the way down to his big brass belt buckle. He moved sprightly, though, eyes bright with the kind of vitality usually reserved for much younger men.

"Howdy, stranger," the barkeep greeted him. "What can I get ya?"

"What's on tap?" Kane asked.

"A little something I call 'Sex in a Canoe.'"

"What is it?"

"Coors Light."

"Then why do you call it 'Sex in a Canoe?'"

The bartender winked. "Cause it's fuckin' near water."

Kane chuckled. "Got any Bud?"

"Long as you don't mind a bottle."

"Bottle's fine."

"Regular or light?"

"Regular."

Almost like magic, a brown bottle appeared on the bar in front of him. With a practiced flip of his wrist, the barkeep sent the cap sailing. It arced into the trash can with the aerial precision of prime-time Michael Jordon draining a foul shot. "He shoots, he scores," the barkeep announced with a grin that revealed tobacco-stained teeth.

"It's almost like you've done that a time or two," Kane remarked.

"Been around these parts since Moses was knee-high to a grasshopper, and I've been slinging booze and brewskies pretty much the entire time."

"I'm guessing you're Fred."

"You'd be guessing right. Old Fred, that's what they call me. Who let you in on the secret?"

"Ernie Foxx."

"Renting his cabin?"

"I am."

Fred nodded. "It's a good cabin. I remember when his father built it. Back in '52, I think it was. Or maybe it was '53." He shook his head as if to clear the memory fog. "Don't matter, I guess. So, what brings you up here to God's country?"

"Just looking for a little peace and quiet."

Fred jerked a thumb toward the stage, where the band was abusing their instruments while the lead singer yowled like a tomcat with a sore throat. "You came to the wrong place if you're looking for quiet."

"Tell me about it." Kane turned to look, and when he did, the redhead caught his eye and treated him to another smile. Then she spun back toward the stage and swayed her ass to the rhythm. Kane had to admit it was a really nice ass, and she swayed it damn well.

Fred grinned at him. "See something you like?"

"What's not to like?"

"She's a local girl," Fred said. "Name's Luna Myers."

"Married?"

Fred snorted. "That girl's as untamed as a wild filly. You think if she had a husband, he'd be letting her shake her tail up there like that?"

"Good point." Kane took a swig of beer. It went down

nice and cold, washing away the road dust. "Not that it matters. Like I said, I came here to get away from things for a while. Not looking for a hookup."

"No reason you can't do both," Fred said. "Few days up in that cabin, you might find yourself getting lonely."

"I hear I've got bears to keep me company."

The band moved into a godawful rendition of *Sweet Home Alabama* as Frank nodded. "There's a man-killer up in them woods," he warned. "Been a bit since Gasper got a hankering to munch on a human, but you can bet your backside he's still around."

"Gasper?"

"Gasper the Grizzly."

"Didn't think grizzlies lived in the Adirondacks."

"We used to have a wildlife exhibit about fifteen miles from here," Fred explained. "Guy who ran the place had trained Gasper to do some basic tricks. Sit, play dead, roll over...that sort of thing."

"So basically, he treated a grizzly bear like a dog."

Fred shrugged. "Guess so. Anyway, few years back, Gasper escaped. Owner went looking for him. They found his remains the next day, strewn all over a pine clearing. After that, Gasper seems to have gotten a taste for human flesh, so every once in a while he pops up, kills a hiker or hunter, and then disappears again."

Kane felt like his leg was being pulled. "You're telling me that they can't track him? Bring in some blood-hounds or something?"

"Been tried," Fred replied. "Dogs, helicopters, traps, you name it. That damn bear is like a ghost."

"Maybe they should call him Casper instead."

Fred smirked, then grew serious again. "I know it sounds like a tall tale, sonny. Hey, I didn't catch your name."

"Call me Kane."

"Well, Kane, like I was saying, I'm sure a story about a killer grizzly roaming the woods sounds like a campfire story, but I assure you it's true. You plan on wandering around the Black Bog woods, best be sure you're packing the kind of heat that'll stop a bear."

"Duly noted," Kane said. "Thanks for the advice."

The stool next to him was suddenly occupied by the pretty redhead. "What advice is old Fred giving you?" Luna asked.

Kane turned his head to look at her, and her green eyes gazed right back. She was even prettier up close, with a light smattering of freckles dusting her face, which was slightly flushed from the exertion of dancing.

She held his eyes, corner of her mouth tugged up in a little smile, as he replied, "He was warning me to watch out for bears in the woods and pretty girls in the bar."

The other corner of her mouth quirked up, giving him a full-wattage smile. "Well, one of those is good advice. I'll let you figure out which one." She turned to Fred. "Can I get a Corona, Fred?"

"Sure thing, Luna." He popped the cap right into the trash again and handed it to her.

"Thanks." She took a long, appreciative swig, let out a satisfied sigh, and slid off the stool. She looked at Kane. "Care to dance?"

Kane glanced up at the stage area, where the two lumberjack types were scowling down at him. "Not sure your boyfriends would take kindly to that."

She took another drink, then tilted her head as if studying him in a whole new light, the playful smile still fixed on her face. "You don't strike me as the type who much cares what other people think."

"Not caring what other people think and deliberately

pissing off a couple of local boys who are clearly spoiling for a fight are two different things."

She leaned close and said softly, "Maybe I'm worth fighting for, cowboy."

He could smell the delicate perfume on her sweat-laced skin. Combined with her closeness and natural sensuality, the effect was intoxicating. He had come here looking for peace and quiet, though, not a barroom brawl. "I'll bet you are," he replied. "But I don't dance."

She looked deep into his eyes for a long moment, and she must have seemed something that caught her off-guard. For just a flickering second, her smile faltered, but it jumped back into place almost immediately.

As she sauntered back toward the dance floor, she called over her shoulder, "You change your mind, cowboy, you know where to find me. It's just a dance. It won't kill you."

Judging from the murderous looks the two men flung his way, Kane wasn't so sure about that.

"Back in my day," Fred remarked, "turning down a lady for a dance was considered ungentlemanly."

"I wasn't kidding," Kane replied. "I really can't dance."

"Can you fight?"

"Why?"

"Because it looks like you're gonna have to."

Kane swiveled his head and saw the two men approaching. *Dammit,* he thought. *Just what I don't need.*

They braced him, one thumping down on the barstool at Kane's left, the one recently vacated by Luna. The other leaned an elbow on the bar to Kane's right, invading his personal space in an obvious attempt to intimidate. Up close, the family resemblance became clear; these two clowns were brothers. Both sported close-cropped dark hair, brown eyes, and faces that might have been considered ruggedly handsome if not for the malevolent glint in their gazes and the cruel set to their thin lips. Kane sized them up in three seconds flat and came to a swift conclusion.

These guys were assholes.

Kane cut to the chase. "Can I help you, boys?"

The one on his left said, "The name's Nick. The guy on the other side getting up in your business is my brother Paul."

"Brother Paul," the one on the left echoed.

"Thanks for telling me," Kane said. "But I didn't really need to know."

"Actually," Nick replied, "you do. I think it's very important that you know the names of the guys who are gonna kick your ass if you don't stay away from Luna."

"Yeah." Paul grunted. "Kick your ass."

Still facing Nick, Kane jerked a thumb over his shoulder at Paul. "Does he repeat everything you say?"

"It's sort of his shtick," Nick said. "Some kind of compulsive disorder. He can't help it. Now, are we clear on what happens if you mess with Luna again?"

"You two fine fellas from the Vesper Lake Welcoming Committee will stomp my ass," Kane said. "Yeah, I think I got it."

"You're quite the smartass," Nick said.

"Smartass," Paul echoed.

Kane injected some steel into his eyes as he rasped, "I'd rather be a smartass than an asshole."

"What the hell is that supposed to mean?" Nick snapped.

"What the hell?" Paul asked.

Kane sighed and decided to let it go. "Listen, guys, I'm not looking for trouble."

"Well, you damn well found it," Nick growled.

"Found it," Paul said.

"Well, I don't want it," Kane replied. "So how about I buy you both a beer, and we can go our separate ways without any asses getting kicked."

"Sounds to me like you're a pussy," Nick said.

"Pussy," Paul agreed.

"You're entitled to your opinion. Now, how about that beer?"

"I don't want your damn beer," Nick said. "Just stay away from Luna, got it?"

"Got it?" Paul chimed in.

Kane stated, "You couldn't make it any clearer."

Nick vacated the stood and headed back toward the dance floor, where Luna had resumed her solo gyrations, shoulders moving, hips swaying, feet tapping. He snapped his finger at his brother. "Let's go, Paul."

"Let's go." The two brothers made their way back toward the stage, presumably to keep careful tabs and lustful eyes on Luna.

Kane looked at Fred. "Nice guys. Regulars, I assume?"

The barkeep nodded. "Local boys, and they've got some pull around these parts, so nobody messes with them. They've been trying to get into Luna's pants for years, but she ain't having none of it."

"I like her better already."

"She's a good kid," Fred said. "But mess around with her, and Nick and Paul, otherwise known as Jackass and Dumbshit, will be looking to make your life miserable."

Glancing at the dance floor, where Luna moved with natural grace and sensuality, Kane thought she might just be worth the fight. But then he remembered why he was here and shook his head. "Think I'll just mind my own business."

Fred shrugged. "Your loss."

"Any other trouble I should know about so I can steer clear?"

Fred pondered the question for a few moments and then nodded. "Yeah, reckon you should probably know about Mad Mike." He pointed at Kane's Budweiser. "You gonna nurse that beer all night like a pansy, or were you planning on buying another one?"

"I'm just having the one. Gotta drive."

"Just because you buy another beer doesn't mean you have to drink it."

"How about I buy it, you drink it," Kane said, "and then you tell me about Mad Mike."

"Now, that sounds like a swell plan to me." Fred helped himself to a Labatt's Blue, flipped the cap into the trash, drained half the bottle in one long pull, and let out a contented sigh. "Man, that hits the spot. Much appreciated, pal."

"Mad Mike?" Kane prompted.

"Cannibal hermit," Fred said matter-of-factly.

"Say what?"

"You heard me. Mad Mike is a hermit and a cannibal. Least, that's what they say."

"You're pulling my leg, right?"

"Negative. Now, if you run into Mad Mike, *he* might pull your leg. Pull it right off, and eat it like a drumstick."

Kane shook his head and smiled ruefully. "Ernie was right, Fred. You sure got some wild stories."

"They're not stories." Fred looked offended. "There really is a bear named Gasper up in the woods, and there really is a cannibal hermit out there too."

"You've seen him?"

Fred shuffled his feet and waxed defensive. "Well, not *seen* him, per se. But other people have, and everyone 'round these parts knows he lives somewhere up in the woods."

"Probably shacking up with a sasquatch," Kane said.

Fred either missed the sarcasm or chose to ignore it. "You'll know it's him," he continued, "because he's got a giant wolf for a pet."

"Thought there weren't any wolves in the Adirondacks?"

"So they say," Fred replied. "But they're full of crap."

"So wolves and bear and cannibals." Kane grinned. "Oh, my."

"Kiss my ass," Fred retorted, but he delivered it with a good-natured smile.

The band stopped playing just in time for a woman's voice to cut through the bar: "Get your hands off me!"

Kane's head came around in time to see Luna yank her arm out of Nick's grasp. He reached out and grabbed it again. Even from where he sat, Kane could see the man's fingers sinking cruelly into her flesh.

She pulled away again, his fingermarks stark red on her skin. "Are you deaf, asshole? Don't touch me."

All eyes watched the drama. Kane glanced at the other patrons and deduced from their body language that nobody intended to intervene. He sighed inwardly. Unless he was mistaken, the forecast called for some busted knuckles and broken bones in the very near future. No way could he sit this one out if things got any rougher.

Speaking loud enough for the whole bar to hear, Nick took a step toward Luna and said, "I think you're forgetting who runs this town, girl."

Standing by like some dimwitted enforcer, Paul muttered, "Forgetting, girl."

"I don't give a crap who your daddy is," Luna retorted. "Doesn't mean I have to let you play grab-ass."

"You know what?" Nick said. "I think you're right. Time to stop playing grab-ass and start playing something a lot more fun." He slapped a hand on the seat of her jeans, jerked her close, and rubbed his crotch against her.

"Fun!" Paul nearly slobbered the words, mouth hanging open in an excited hangdog grin that revealed his teeth. He stepped behind Luna and began thrusting against her backside. Cackling like fiends, the two brothers dry-humped her right there on the dance floor, bouncing her back and forth between them like a human pinball.

Not a soul in the bar moved to help.

Kane couldn't believe it.

What the hell kind of town is this?

Moving with fluid speed and predatory grace, he pushed away from the bar and climbed the steps before anyone even registered that he was in motion.

He reached the trio just as Luna managed to free her hand and drag her nails across Nick's cheek, tearing strips of skin from the corner of his nose down to his jaw. The wounds glowed raw-pink for a second before blood filled the welts.

Nick recoiled, then snarled, "You bitch!" His right hand crossed his left shoulder, ready to give her a backhanded slap.

"Bitch!" Paul shouted.

Kane grabbed Nick's wrist and yanked on it as if starting a lawnmower, using the man's momentum to spin him away from Luna. As he stumbled around to face

Kane, the warrior's other hand rammed a heel-of-the-palm strike into his solar plexus, driving him backward. Jerked in one direction and shoved in the opposite direction, Nick tripped over his own feet and crashed to the floor.

Paul froze in place, not sure what to do without his brother to lead him. He just stood there looking like a dumb puppy whose master has dropped the leash.

Kane pointed a finger at Paul. "Touch her again, and I'll break your face," he warned. "Now, pick up your brother and get the hell out of here before I lose my temper."

Luna smiled at him. "Little white knight action?"

"No, I just changed my mind about that dance."

"If you're still alive three minutes from now, you can have that dance, cowboy."

Nick climbed to his feet and snarled a curse. "You're dead, you son of a bitch."

He charged. Kane let him get close before ducking the wild, badly telegraphed haymaker the man threw. Nick's fist whistled over his head as Kane fired a short, hard right hook into the guy's gut, doubling him over with a whooshing gasp as the air exploded from his lungs. Kane then powered upright and shot a knee-strike into Nick's exposed flank. Everyone in the bar heard the wet crack of a rib snapping. Nick hit the floor again, mewling in pain.

"Dammit, I said, don't touch me!"

Kane pivoted to see Paul bear-hugging Luna from behind, lifting her off her feet with her arms pinned to her side. He moved to help, but before he got there, she rammed her head back into his nose. Cartilage crackled and crunched as his smashed nostrils spewed blood and snot like strawberry jelly.

Paul didn't let go. He crushed her tighter, squeezing

so hard it looked like he might collapse her ribcage. She kicked up hard between his legs, her heel bashing into his scrotum and driving his balls into his pelvis.

On the stage, the steel guitarist let out a low groan and muttered, "Hot damn, that's gotta hurt like a sumbitch."

With a protracted moan that sounded like a dying humpback whale, Paul released Luna and clutched his battered manhood. He slowly sank to his knees, eyes squeezed shut in pain and misery.

Kane walked over and kneed him in the face, making sure his nose was good and broken. The impact flipped Paul over on his back, out cold. "Warned you," Kane growled.

Luna said, "Cowboy, look out!"

Kane turned to see Nick on his knees, bracing himself with his left hand. With his right, he pulled a snub-nosed .38 revolver from an inside-the-waistband holster. He swung the pistol toward Kane. Murder lit his cold eyes like a neon sign.

Kane closed the gap in two quick strides and kicked the gun out of Nick's hands, giving him a broken wrist to match his broken rib. The .38 skittered across the dance floor as its owner gritted his teeth in pain.

Kane grabbed Nick by the hair and yanked his head back. "Gonna shoot me in the back, you gutless prick?"

"You're a dead man," Nick hissed. "You hear me? You came to the wrong town and messed with the wrong people."

"I'm not the one on my knees," Kane reminded him.

"You're gonna be flat on your back on the coroner's table, you son of a—"

Kane brought his knee up and slammed it between

Nick's eyes, knocking him out. "Shut the hell up." He let go of Nick's hair, and the guy sprawled on the floor, unconscious.

Kane straightened and faced the rest of the bar's patrons, who had edged closer, clustering around the combat that had just taken place. Well, if you called that combat. More like a beat-down. In addition to the two couples who had been sharing the dance floor with Luna, there were two men who had been drinking in a booth that Kane hadn't been able to see from the bar. The middle-aged man who had been slumped at the bar had also roused himself and moved closer, all of them forming a circle around Kane and Luna.

Hell, even the no-talent country band was giving him the hairy eyeball.

Old Fred climbed the stairs to the upper level but hung back. He looked at Kane with respect, admiration... and sadness.

Kane scanned the small crowd circling him. Including the band—and not counting Fred—he now faced eleven potential brawlers. Unless some of them had hand-to-hand combat training, Kane could survive those odds. It just meant he would have to fight hard and dirty, with little room for mercy.

No problem.

But there was no way to take down all eleven unscathed. They would get their licks in, no doubt about it. He expected to be the last man standing, but not without some blood and bruises.

He thought about the Sig M17 tucked into a small-of-the-back holster, but he didn't want to resort to firepower to stop what was basically just going to be a good, old-fashioned bar brawl.

Damn it, he thought. *This is gonna hurt.*

Maybe he could talk them down. Sure as hell couldn't hurt to try.

"Really?" Kane looked each of them dead in the eye. "You're going to take up their fight?"

"They ain't really got much choice," Old Fred called from the back of the mob.

"There's always a choice," snapped Kane.

"Not when Sheriff Dunkirk runs this town, there ain't."

"What's that got to do with anything?" Kane asked.

"Those two boys lying on the floor, knocked the hell out, thanks to you? Nick and Paul?"

"Yeah," Kane said. "What about them?"

"They're Sheriff Dunkirk's sons."

Well, shit.

"Word gets back to the sheriff that some tourist put a beat-down on his boys and nobody did anything?" Fred continued. "Well, the sheriff will come down damn hard on these usually fine folks you now see gathered around you."

Kane rasped, "Anyone starts swinging, I'm gonna come down pretty damn hard myself."

Next to him, Luna said, "They ain't got much of a choice, cowboy. Dunkirk is king of this town, and nobody wants the king pissed at them."

Kane again considered shucking the Sig and stopping all this nonsense, but he again discarded the idea. Some things just needed to be done the hard way. He took a deep breath, exhaled it in a long, slow sigh, and said, "Looks like I'll be dancing after all."

"Thought you couldn't dance, cowboy?"

"This is one dance I know," Kane said. "Let's get it over with."

The nearest guy shrugged, muttered, "Sorry, man," and opened the fisticuff festivities with a wild, poorly-aimed haymaker.

Kane easily dodged the blow and exploded into a whirling, spinning, kicking, punching dervish of violence. He swept legs out from underneath bodies. Busted noses with brutal back-fists. Hip-tossed combatants into each other. Head-butted faces. Smashed knees. Punched guts. Kneed groins.

Adrenalin roared in his eardrums like thunder but not enough to drown out the grunts of pain, the crunch of collapsing cartilage, the wet spurts of blood, the tearing of ligaments, the sharp cracks of bone. The band stood on stage and watched the battle, their country-western crooning forgotten as the skull-banging music of mayhem took over the bar.

Seven men formed the initial wave of attack. Kane left them decimated on the floor in just under a minute. He took some licks here and there—a kick to the thigh, a left cross to the jaw, a shot to the ribs—but nothing he couldn't shake off with some ice, ibuprofen, and Jack Daniels. The men squirming on the floor would need casts, crutches, and plenty of stitches.

Kane shook blood off his punished—and punishing—knuckles and stared at the band. Other than him, Luna, and Fred, they were the only ones left standing in the room. The drummer exchanged glances with the steel guitarist, and they both looked at the bassist. Finally, all three turned to the lead singer—a bearded, beer-bellied, Stetson-wearing big boy who looked like a ZZ Top wannabe—as if waiting for him to make the first move.

The beefy singer sighed in resignation and looked at Kane. "Don't wanna fight ya, mister. But we ain't got no choice."

"Everyone keeps telling me that," Kane said, "but it's a lame-ass excuse. We all got choices."

"Easy for you to say. You don't live in this shitty town."

"For your sake, I hope the hospital isn't shitty. Because if you come down here to tango, you're going to the ER."

"Like I said," the singer repeated, "no choice."

"Hope you fight better than you play."

The big guy smiled, a bit sadly. "Not really."

That turned out to be the truth.

They came at him with their instruments. The drummer tried stabbing him with his drumsticks. Kane took them away and snapped them in half. In a real fight with an enemy, he would have jammed the splintered end into the man's throat, but these were just down-trodden civilians. They didn't deserve to die. Besides, he had come here to get away from killing, not engage in more of it. He punched the drummer in the temple, knocking him out.

He ducked as the guitarist swung his instrument like a Viking war axe, feeling the rush of displaced air as it whooshed over his head. He pivoted and fired a sidekick into the guy's gut, doubling him over.

He immediately dodged to the side as the bassist joined the battle, chopping down with his guitar. The instrument smashed into the floor and shattered, leaving the musician holding the neck.

"Shit!" the man groaned. "I was all about that bass."

Kane didn't know if it was meant to be a joke or not, nor did he care. He powered upright and crashed a hard right cross into the bassist's jaw, putting him down on the floor next to his busted guitar.

The steel guitarist was still doubled over, clutching his stomach, with strings of spit and vomit dangling from his gasping lips. Kane finished the job with a kick to the face that jerked the guy upright and then a wicked uppercut to the chin that toppled him like a felled tree. His head bounced off the floor with brain-rattling force. He wouldn't be waking up anytime soon.

"Look out!" Luna yelled, but the warning came too late.

Kane felt something hard hit him right between the shoulder blades. No real damage done, but it definitely hurt. He turned toward the ZZ Top reject of a singer and saw him twirling his microphone by its cord. That was what he had used to strike Kane; he'd swung the microphone like a whip with a metal club attached to the end.

Kane stared at him, and the big man shrugged almost apologetically.

"Put it down," Kane said. "Don't make me hurt you."

Another shrug. "Like I said," the singer replied, "I—"

"Yeah, yeah, I know," Kane growled. "You don't have a choice. Bunch of bullshit."

"Listen, mister," the singer said. "We both know you're gonna kick my ass seven ways from Sunday, and there's not a damn thing I can do about it. Just do me one favor, will ya? Don't hit me in the throat. I don't want to ruin my vocal cords."

Kane thought about telling him his voice couldn't get any worse but decided not to bother. He moved in quickly, easily evading the lumbering blows the singer launched his way, and put the guy on the ground with a couple of body strikes followed by a left-right combo to the face.

Shaking his bruised knuckles, Kane looked at Luna

and Fred with a crooked grin. "Not gonna lie, I've always wanted to knock out a country singer."

They both stared at him. "Who are you, cowboy?" Luna asked.

"Nobody. Just a guy."

"A guy that just scrapped with eleven other guys and won," Fred said. "I ain't never seen nothing like it."

"I got lucky."

Fred snorted. "Somehow, I seriously doubt that."

Kane headed down to the lower level, Luna and the old-timer following. He threw some bills on the bar and strode toward the open door, feeling the cool night breeze drafting in. "Thanks for the drink, Fred. Probably best I hit the road now."

"Reckon you're right," Fred said. "Less'n you want to end up in Double D's jail cell."

"Double D?"

"Sheriff Duncan Dunkirk," Fred explained. "We call him Double D. Just not to his face."

"Got it," Kane said. "You two have a nice night."

"Wait," Luna called. "I'm coming with you."

Kane immediately considered the possibilities, most of which involved the pretty redhead naked in his sleeping bag. He'd been celibate since his relationship with Cara had ended. Maybe it was time to enjoy female companionship again.

Then again…

"That might be a bad idea," he said, while the hot blood hammering through his veins called him seven kinds of a fool. "Seems like I've caused you enough trouble for one night."

"You didn't cause me trouble, you saved me from it," Luna replied. "And a bad idea would be me still being here when the sheriff shows up and finds out I'm the reason his boys got the crap kicked out of them."

"She's right," Fred said. "You need to get her outta here, Kane."

Luna put her hands on her hips, tilted her head, and gave him a wink and a smile. "Come on, cowboy. I don't bite."

Kane winked back. "Maybe I do."

"I'll take my chances."

"My Jeep's outside. You can ride shotgun."

Fred waved as they walked out the door. "You two kids have fun now."

They rolled out of town with moonlight sparkling on the calm waters of Vesper Lake. As the adrenalin overload ebbed from his system, Kane reflected on how he had come to a remote mountain town to get away from violence, only to find himself the subject of a violent brawl just a few hours after arriving. Sometimes he felt like a giant shit-magnet. But at least he hadn't killed anybody.

Yet, some cynical inner voice sneered.

Kane shut it down. There had to be more to life than violence and bloodshed. Sometimes you had to kill to live, but that didn't mean you had to live to kill. They might call him Reaper, but there had to be more to his life than just death and destruction.

He glanced at the woman sitting next to him. She caught his look and smiled at him, green eyes luminescent in the moonlight. She looked vibrant, alive, and carefree. Part of him knew he might be making a mistake taking her back to the cabin. But another part suggested that spending time with someone like her, someone so full of life, might be exactly what he needed right now.

As if sensing his pensive thoughts, Luna reached over

and lightly touched his shoulder. "You all right, cowboy?"

He looked into her sparkling eyes for another heartbeat, then turned his head to watch his headlights punching through the autumn darkness. In a quiet voice, he replied, "Still trying to figure that out."

FOUR

Black Bog Federal Prison

Kumi Ghastin was not the first woman to ever reach the rank of warden within the United States Federal Bureau of Prisons, but she was the first Japanese-American woman to do so. Once upon a time, that fact had filled her with pride and a great sense of accomplishment.

Before she'd sold her soul to evil incarnate.

Born to poor parents in the tiny town of Utashinai in Japan, her family had immigrated to the U.S. when Kumi was just three years old, seeking the proverbial better life. They found it in Harker Falls, a quiet farming town on the eastern border of upstate New York, just a stone's throw from Vermont. Her father had worked at one of the dairy farms, then the local hardware store, then apprenticed with a plumbing and heating company before opening his own plumbing business when Kumi was fourteen.

With more money came a bigger house and a better

school, where Kumi had blossomed into a straight-A student. She suffered racism, of course, but ignored it, refusing to give the brain-cell-deficient racists the satisfaction of seeing her bothered by their cheap, ignorant insults.

Not everyone exhibited racism. With her alabaster skin, long, black, silky hair, and curves in all the right places, she had attracted plenty of male attention in high-school. More than one would-be suitor who got too grabby found himself rejected with a swift karate chop or kick. Her body might have blossomed, but her sexuality remained dormant. She graduated with high honors but without a boyfriend.

That all changed in college. She picked up a Master's degree in Criminal Justice from John Jay College in midtown Manhattan, maintaining the high honors that had marked her entire scholastic career. Her hormones also kicked into overdrive, and she screwed her way through a series of steamy but short-lived romances. Her bed-hopping ways soon earned her undesirable nicknames that had nothing to do with her oriental heritage.

In an effort to repair her badly damaged reputation, she stopped dating altogether and went celibate for the entirety of her junior year. But when Luke Ghastin transferred in from the University of Rochester, that all changed. He sat next to her in a forensic evidence class, and not only was she struck by his good looks, but also by his intelligent manner of speaking. He possessed a depth that surpassed the men she had known in the past. He seemed to be truly interested in her mind, she thought, and not just her body.

Their pre- and post-class conversations soon became coffee-shop marathons, and eventually—because she took this relationship slow and steady rather than fast and hot—became regular dates. They were five official dates in before he made a physical move, and by then, she was more than ready to consummate their feelings. She didn't tell him until much later, but it was the best sex of her life. Not just because of the intensity of her orgasms, but because it was the first time she had made love to someone with whom she felt a true, deep connection.

Marriage came shortly after graduation, followed by the birth of a daughter. With her master's degree, she easily qualified for a position with the Federal Bureau of Prisons, and by the age of forty-one, she found herself Associate Warden of Programs at the Federal Correctional Institution in Tallahassee, Florida.

She got passed over for promotion to warden a half-dozen times, always to men far less qualified but who were part of the "good ol' boy" system. Feeling she had no choice, she played the EEO card, using her gender and race as leverage. The agency caved and promoted her to warden, but gave her a little "fuck you" by transferring her to one of the least desirable correctional institutions in the federal system.

Black Bog Federal Prison.

Knowing it was blatant retaliation but refusing to give them an ounce of satisfaction, Kumi accepted the promotion—and transfer—with a bright smile. Inside, she had cringed. Black Bog Federal Prison was a notoriously bleak place, as cold as hell most of the time, and rumored to be about as lawless as the Old West.

She had been stationed there less than three months when Nazareno "The Nazarene Dragon" Pedregon arrived.

His takeover had been swift, ruthless, and unstoppable. Nazareno possessed a cobra's charisma and enjoyed access to billions of cartel dollars, plus he exhibited a merciless willingness to brutally destroy those who opposed him. Through a combination of bribes and threats, he had rapidly corrupted the vast majority of the prison. Those who weren't outright corrupted were at least wise enough to remain silent. Those who tried to go the whistleblower route about the wickedness festering behind the walls of Black Bog Federal Prison were found rotting in ditches with their tongues cut out.

Kumi tried to have him transferred to a high-security penitentiary, but that request got shot down immediately, making her realize that Nazareno had high-ranking prison officials in his pocket. She called in federal inspectors, who showed up just long enough to emphatically tell her never to call them again and get with the program.

It was after those federal inspectors left that Nazareno had walked into her office unannounced, unshackled, and unescorted by any correctional officers—another sign that the entire prison had bowed to his will.

She didn't frighten easily, but her heart had hammered in her chest as he just stood there and studied her with his dead-eyed shark's stare. Droplets of sweat beaded his shaved scalp and make the inked blood on his crown of thorns tattoo gleam with faux realism.

Projecting outward calm even as her guts twisted into knots, Kumi had put down her pen, crossed her arms, and asked, "What are you doing here?"

Nazareno hadn't spoken a word. Just approached her desk, sandaled feet silent on the carpet, and placed two photographs in front of her.

The first was a picture of her daughter at her college campus, taken through a telescopic lens. The second was a photo of Luke, asleep in their bed at home, taken through their bedroom window.

The blood had frozen in her veins, and Kumi stared up at him in horror.

"You will do what I command when I command it," Nazareno had said. "Any refusal, even the slightest hesitation, and your family will die. I will have your husband flayed, and his flesh fed to dogs. I will have your daughter taken to an MS13 hellhole, where she will be gang-raped until she begs for death. Then I will have her scalped and holes drilled in her skull. Gasoline will be poured into these holes, and then I will have her brain set on fire."

Kumi had not hesitated to react. Nazareno clearly expected her to beg and grovel and promise to do whatever he wanted, but she chose a different option—one completely unexpected.

She had attacked.

Her radio featured an emergency alert system, but she knew pressing the red button would be a waste of time. Nobody would come to her aid. She might technically be the queen of the prison, but everyone knew Nazareno reigned as the undisputed king. Nobody would interfere with whatever happened next.

So she tried to kill him with her bare hands.

She had read Nazareno's file from cover to cover. She knew he was an expert in savate, judo, and aikido, but she also knew she just needed one good strike to the neck to take out the cartel kingpin. Her father had taught her that karate should never be used with lethal intent, but this situation called for a desperate exception.

"*Kiai!*" she had screamed, moving in for the kill.

Nazareno had effortlessly kicked her ass.

And then he did much worse.

Afterward, she had sprawled listlessly on the floor amidst her torn clothes, battered and bruised, Nazareno's power over her unequivocally asserted, his control of the prison complete. The beat-down and the violation had not broken her, but the threats against her family had. Since she had not been able to defeat the drug lord, she would be compliant. She had no doubt that Nazareno's horrific threats were anything but idle.

That had been nearly two years ago. Two years of hell. Two years of hiding the secret from Luke. Two years of knowing that vicious butchers kept a constant watch on her family.

Tonight she was working late to catch up on the endless cycle of paperwork pushing that constituted a warden's daily routine. Nazareno might be the top dog around here, but there were nearly eight hundred other inmates. Black Bog Federal Prison might be corrupt as hell, but it still had to function like a normal prison, at least from the outside looking in. The show must go on.

She signed her name on a form denying an inmate's claim against an officer who had allegedly stolen a candy bar and a can of Coke from the convict's locker. She knew she could only get away with that decision because the inmate belonged to the Aryan Brotherhood, one of the few gangs not directly under Nazareno's thumb.

As she tucked the claim form back into a manila envelope for routing and processing, Nazareno walked into the office. The fact that there were five locked doors inmates had to get through—two of them controlled by correctional officers—before reaching the warden's area proved just how deep the corruption ran at Black Bog Federal Prison.

Kumi laid down her pen. In her head, a scenario played out like a movie in which she jammed the pen into the drug lord's ear and impaled his brain or stabbed it into the hollow of his throat and watched with a satisfied smile as he choked to death on his own blood.

But of course, that was all just a vengeful fantasy. The reality of how this visit would go down would be far different.

"Nazareno," she greeted him. Her long black hair, pulled back in a ponytail, had slipped over her shoulder. She flipped it back, knowing it would probably be in Nazareno's fist pretty soon.

The drug lord's cold eyes locked on her like a viper staring at its prey. "When I take time out of my busy day to pay you a visit, the least you can do is smile when you see me."

For the sake of her endangered husband and daughter, she bit back the *"Kutabare"*—Japanese for "fuck you" —that rose to her tongue and instead plastered a bright, blatantly-faked smile on her lips. "Sorry," she said. "It's been a long day, and I'm ready to go home."

"Of course," Nazareno replied. "Home to where your beloved Luke is waiting." The perpetual threat to her husband remained unspoken but was implied behind the otherwise harmless words.

She nodded, acknowledging both his words and the tacit threat they contained.

"Don't worry," he said. "This won't take long."

Kumi steeled herself. When Nazareno said that, it usually meant he was about to take her hard and rough. It would be brutal, but it would be quick—usually just sixty seconds or so. Less, if she screamed. It helped him get his rocks off.

Instead, he walked over and handed her a slip of paper with two names on it: Yvonne Fariss and Bonnie Little. Kumi recognized both. They worked in Financial

Management, better known as the business office. Yvonne held a contract specialist position, and Bonnie was an accounting technician.

Kumi looked up with a frown. "What do you want with business office people? There's no way we can transfer government funds into your accounts without raising serious red flags at the Treasury Department."

Nazareno smiled—no warmth, just a crocodile-like baring of his teeth—and shook his head. "You misunderstand. It's not *dinero* I want. I have all the money I need. Hell, *Dios* comes to me for a loan sometimes." He chuckled at his sacrilegious wit.

"Then what are these names for?" Kumi asked.

"I want them killed."

Kumi blanched. "Why? For God's sake, Mrs. Fariss retires next year."

"Mrs. Fariss and Mrs. Little will both be permanently retired tomorrow."

"Nazareno, please! I'm begging you to reconsider."

"Would you prefer it to be your daughter instead? I'm told the victim actually lives long enough to feel their cerebral fluid boiling."

"No! No, of course, not."

"Then make it happen," the drug lord commanded. "Word on the compound is that those two *putas* are making noise about calling their congressman and reporting what is going on here at the prison."

Good for them, Kumi thought. But then she realized that actually, no, it wasn't good for them. Their refusal to be corrupted and their contemplation of taking action had earmarked them for early graves. "Couldn't you just pay off the congressman?" she suggested.

"Of course, I could," Nazareno said. "But why should

I? It's much cheaper to kill two bitches than it is to bribe a politician."

Kumi thought about telling him that Yvonne and Bonnie both had families, but decided not to waste her breath. You couldn't appeal to a man's sense of decency when he had none. Nazareno was the kind of person who would watch a toddler get dismembered with the same emotional detachment most people feel when looking at a dead fly.

Resigning herself to the inevitable, she asked, "How would you like it done?"

"Give the names to SORT," Nazareno instructed. "Goatsack and his boys will take care of the rest."

Kumi nodded. SORT stood for Special Operations Response Team, the prison's version of SWAT. While the other specialized operators in the prison—DCT, short for Disturbance Control Team—utilized batons, shields, and stun munitions, SORT was considered the lethal option when things went sideways. DCT might kick an inmate's teeth in; SORT would blow those teeth out the back of the inmate's head if necessary.

The SORT leader was Duff "Goatsack" Cantwell, a grizzled correctional officer just a year away from the Bureau of Prison's mandatory retirement age of fifty-seven. Duff only stood five foot ten, but every inch of it was hard-packed muscle, like slabs of granite attached to his skeleton. A fitness enthusiast—some might argue "extremist"—he hit the gym a minimum of three hours a day, and most of those hours were spent lifting weights. He chugged protein powder the way some people guzzled coffee and sported the linebacker shoulders, tree-trunk biceps, and bulging thigh muscles to prove it.

Kumi stared at the names on the paper. She would

give the information to Goatsack in the morning, and
before noon, the women would be dead. More scars on
her conscience, more wounds on her soul, more guilt to
bear. But if that was what it took to keep her husband and
daughter safe, she would suffer the emotional anguish.

She looked up and gave Nazareno a nod. "It will be
done."

"Good."

"Anything else? I really do need to get home."

"Just one last thing."

Kumi's heart sank. "No," she murmured. "Please…"

"Take off your clothes."

"Please," she repeated. "Not tonight."

His eyes narrowed with anger. "Defy me again, and
your husband will be in a hundred pieces before you
make it home. Now take off your clothes."

Blinking back tears, Kumi stood up and unbuttoned
her blouse, then pushed her slacks down over her hips so
they fell around her ankles.

Before she could even kick them away, Nazareno
pounced on her, growling like an animal as he slammed
her down on the desk. There was an element of lust in
his attack, but she knew it was mostly about power,
about reminding her who was in charge.

As she suffered his abuse, Kumi closed her eyes and
wondered if she would ever wake up from the hell her
life had become.

FIVE

Dribble Creek Camp

The fire roared and crackled, the flames leaping at least eight feet high. Orange sparks drifted into the cloudless, star-speckled night before winking out in the velvet darkness.

"Now *that's* a bonfire," Luna said appreciatively.

Kane tossed on another log, causing more sparks to billow like dozens of fireflies. The sudden rush of heat made them push their chairs a little farther back from the blaze. "Don't want to end up like Shadrach, Meshach, and Abednego," Kane joked, reaching for his half-finished Jack and Coke. He'd already downed one.

Luna wrinkled her brow. "Who?"

"The three Hebrew children," Kane explained. "King Nebuchadnezzar, the fiery furnace?"

"No clue what you're talking about, cowboy."

"It's a famous Bible story."

"I'm not much of a Bible reader."

"Neither am I, but I still know the story."

"So tell me."

"I don't think so."

"Why not?"

Kane lifted his Jack and Coke. "Because sitting around a fire drinking whiskey and telling Bible stories just doesn't seem right."

Luna laughed. "You may have a point there." She took a drink from her red plastic cup. She had skipped the Coke, drinking her Jack on the rocks. Of course, the bag of ice Kane had picked up at Baldy's had been half-melted by the time they got back to camp, so it was more like Jack on the pebbles.

She caught one between her teeth and crunched down on it. The noise was surprisingly loud in the quiet of the woods. "You a God-fearing man, cowboy?"

Kane shrugged. He had told her his name, including the "Reaper" tag, but she insisted on calling him "cowboy."

"A shrug?" she teased. "Really? That's the best you can do? Come on, it's an easy question to answer."

Kane said, "Been my experience that there aren't any easy answers when it comes to God."

Luna stared at him for several long moments, while off in the distance, perhaps gazing at the silver sickle of the moon, a coyote cut loose with a long, mournful howl. Then she looked down at her cup, shook it so the ice rattled against the sides, and said, "Whoa, that's some deep shit there, cowboy. I think you're ruining my buzz."

Kane knocked back the rest of his drink. "You asked, I answered."

"Okay," she said, "no more religious stuff. Let's try something lighter, something with fewer landmines to navigate."

"Fire away."

"What brings you all the way out here?"

That sobered Kane up pretty damn quick. *Yeah,* he thought. *Something lighter, with fewer landmines. Let's talk about shooting a fourteen-year-old kid in the chest.*

Instead, he replied, "Just looking for some peace and quiet."

Luna scooted her chair closer to his and leaned in. Not close enough to invade his personal space or be misconstrued as making a move, but close enough that he felt the electricity of her nearness. "Bullshit," she said, smiling to take off any harsh edges.

Kane looked at her. She'd been pretty under the lights of the bar, but the flickering firelight infused her with an otherworldly beauty, like a forest nymph emerged from the shadow realm to spend a few fleeting moments in the world of broken men.

"Bullshit, huh? What makes you say that?"

"Because that's what it is," she replied. "Peace and quiet, my ass, cowboy. When I look at you, I don't see a man looking for peace and quiet."

"Yeah? What do you see?"

"I see a man running from something."

Damn, Kane thought. This girl was pretty *and* perceptive. Aloud, he said, "It's not what you think."

"Here's the part where you tell me you're not an outlaw."

"I'm not an outlaw."

"Well, like I said, cowboy, it's pretty clear that you're running from *something*. It's all over your face." She paused for a moment and then shook her head. "No, not your face. Your eyes. They're haunted. They give you away."

Feeling self-conscious, Kane turned away from her, as

if to hide his secrets and sins. He stared into the fire, pensive and brooding.

She let him have his silence for a while, then lightly touched his shoulder. "Hey, cowboy, sorry if I made you uncomfortable."

Kane shook his head. "It's not you. It's..." His voice trailed off.

"The thing you're running from," Luna finished for him.

He sighed. "Yeah, I guess it is."

Her hand rose from his shoulder to his cheek, as gentle as the brush of an angel's wing. "Want to tell me about it?"

"I can't."

"Can't or won't?"

He turned and discovered she had moved even closer. The air grew hot with an energy that had nothing to do with the fire. "Shouldn't," he answered.

Her lips brushed his, not so much a kiss as a ghost of one. "Tell me anyway," she said softly. "Confess your sins, cowboy."

Kane stared into her eyes, the reflection of the firelight in her pupils intoxicating. "What happens after that?"

She kissed him then, deep, slow, and lingering. When they parted, she whispered, "Redemption."

Maybe it was the booze. Maybe it was his troubled spirit needing to unburden itself. Maybe it was the isolation. Maybe it was the carnality and desire burgeoning between them. Or maybe it was a combination of all those things that worked in tandem to batter down his defenses.

In the darkness, as the fire burned and the moon glowed and the coyotes howled, he told her everything.

He left out names and locations and national security protocols, but other than that, he held nothing back. The woods were his church, the fireside was his confessional, and Luna was the angelic priestess to whom he bared his soul.

She said nothing as he spoke, letting his words bleed into the night as if they were hallowed and sacred, when in fact, he knew them to be profane and cursed by the endless violence behind them. He expected her to flinch when he talked about his kills, the body count, the stacked corpses of his warrior life. But she remained still and quiet, listening, letting him talk, letting him lance the poison with no hint of judgment or condemnation.

He finished by telling her about the boy, about putting a bullet through the kid's chest. "Not sure I can kill again after that," he said. "Maybe it's time for me to hang up my guns."

She looked into his eyes as if peering into his soul, and he wondered what she would find there. Honor, sure, and a warrior's sense of right and wrong...but also so much darkness, so many scars.

She slowly uncoiled from her chair and stood in front of him, silhouetted against the bonfire behind her. Still staring deep into his eyes, she began unbuttoning her shirt.

Kane started to protest. "Luna..."

"Hush." She let the shirt slide off her shoulders and fall to the ground. The firelight caressed her skin and cast her breasts into pools of shadow.

She stepped out of her jeans and came to him, a naked angel offering salvation. Almost involuntarily, his hands reached for her as she straddled him in the chair. She slid her hand between their bodies, working his belt buckle and zipper to free his arousal.

"I'm not sure we should do this," Kane said, but the huskiness in his voice betrayed his desire.

"You need this, Kane." It was the first time Luna had called him by his name. "You've spent too long walking with Death."

"That's why they call me Reaper."

She leaned forward and kissed him with hunger and passion. "And they always will," she said when their lips parted. "But that doesn't mean you can't also live."

"It's not fair to you," Kane said. "Pretty soon, I'll ride out of town, and you'll never see me again."

"Let tomorrow worry about itself," she replied. "I'm not asking you to be with me forever. Just be with me right now. You need this, Kane. *We* need this."

He knew she was right. To hell with the Reaper. Tonight he just wanted to be John Kane.

He crushed her mouth in another hot, reckless kiss as he pulled her fully onto his lap. A groan vibrated in his throat as she lowered herself onto him, enveloping him in silken heat as their desire surged.

He surrendered fully to the moment, to the primal rhythm, as they moved together in synchronicity with the heartbeat of the night. The flames threw shadows over their entwined bodies as they abandoned all control.

Luna cried out as he made love to her with something close to desperation, reaching for the briefest fragment of life, of *living*, of snatching something good and alive and vibrant from the cold jaws of death. He had confessed his weaknesses to her, his sins and transgressions, and now her needs to her, his weaknesses, his transgressions, and now her trembling body granted him absolution.

Afterward, she laid with him in the chair, curled up in his arms.

Kane stroked her hair. "Thanks for that."

"It wasn't just a one-night stand, you know."

"No," he agreed. "It was more than that."

"You're surrounded by death, Kane, but that doesn't mean it has to define you. Your job might be to kill, but your life can be about more than just blood."

"I know. Thanks for reminding me."

She smiled. "It was my pleasure."

"Trust me, the pleasure wasn't all yours."

They stayed like that for a while, content to simply share the moment, to hold each other in the darkness while the fire popped and crackled.

Eventually, Luna said, "You know you have to go back, right, Kane? The world needs men like you."

"What do you mean, 'men like me?'"

"Good men."

"I told you what I've done, Luna. I'm not a good man."

"You're a good man who has to do bad things to protect innocent people."

"Maybe I don't want to do those bad things anymore." Kane mentally pictured the young boy going down with a bloody hole drilled in his chest. "Maybe I'll just stay here and never go back."

"Trust me, you don't want to stay here. Vesper Lake is an evil town."

"Evil?" Kane echoed. "You mean, like vampires and werewolves?"

"No, when I say evil, I'm talking about the manmade kind. Drugs and guns and corruption. You dig below the surface of this town, it's blacker than the devil's soul."

"Sounds like my kind of game. Maybe I should call in my team."

Luna clutched his arm. "No, you can't."

"Why not? That's what we do," Kane said. "My team

would roll into town, kick some ass, kill whoever needed killing"—*If you can actually pull the trigger again,* he silently added—"and set things right."

Luna shook her head. "Nazareno has kill squads planted in the town. At the first sign that he's been crossed, they'll go on the warpath, and it'll be a slaughter. They'll burn Vesper Lake to the ground."

"Who the hell is Nazareno?"

"The puppet master," Luna said. "The mastermind behind it all."

"The name sounds familiar for some reason."

"Nazareno Pedregon. The Nazarene Dragon, famous for crucifying his victims and burning them alive."

Kane nodded. "That's right. Cartel boss, caught up in Canada running narcotics over the border."

"That's him," Luna confirmed. She waved a hand in a westward direction. "He's down there in Black Bog Federal Prison, but he's got a crushing grip on this town."

"His operation is still running?"

"Meth and heroin, mostly, from what I hear. They cook the meth locally, but the H comes from a supplier in Quebec, supposedly with ties to the Rizzuto crime family."

"Mafia." Kane muttered the word with the same distaste he might have used if he was talking about dog shit. "I miss the days when the Mob didn't mess with drugs."

"Times change," Luna said.

"And not always for the better." The autumn air started to cool the sweat on Kane's skin. They would need to head inside soon or move closer to the fire, but for now, Luna seemed content to curl up against his chest, and he was content to let her stay there. "Any idea how they move the drugs across the border?" he asked.

"Logging trucks."

Kane recalled the logging company at the end of the lake. "Cammeaux Logging Company?"

Luna nodded. "They're based out of Ontario, and if you dig deep enough, you'll find that Nazareno owns them, although naturally there are several layers of separation. They transport the heroin in hollowed-out logs, crossing the border north of Plattsburgh and then picking up Route 3 to come down here, where they add the meth to the load before heading south. Not sure where it ends up after that, but Albany and New York City are the most likely destinations."

"Who runs the operation? Nazareno might pull the strings, but he's in prison, so he needs someone with boots on the ground to run things for him."

"Remember I told you Sheriff Dunkirk is the king of this town?"

"He works for Nazareno." Kane didn't phrase it as a question.

"Exactly. Dunkirk and his two dickhead sons oversee the pipeline. They've also branched out on their own, and have a side business running guns."

"Where do they get the guns?"

"They're military weapons. Fort Drum is about a hundred miles west of here. One of the soldiers on base cooks the books and hooks up the Dunkirks."

"Sounds like this town is one big shithole."

"The town is full of good people," Luna said. "They're just scared. When Nazareno's goon squads first rolled into town, they tortured and killed several people to make examples out of them, as a warning about what would happen if we stepped out of line."

"There are more of you than there are of them," Kane pointed out. "Sometimes, you just have to stand up to the bastards of the world."

"Sheep don't stand up to wolves," Luna said. "The folks in Vesper Lake are good people, but they're not fighters."

"Those who act like sheep will be slaughtered like sheep. That's the way of the world." Kane felt a chill run through him at the grimness of his words. Or maybe it was just the night air finally getting to him. Either way, it was time to retire to the cabin. "We should probably go inside."

She climbed off him and gathered up her clothes as he kicked dirt onto the fire. He hooked an arm around her naked shoulders as they walked back to the lodge. Inside, she put on her shirt but nothing more, and even that, she only closed with one button. Kane wondered if she knew how alluring it made her look.

He fired up the woodstove with a mix of pine logs and hardwood, and it chased away the chill in no time. He turned to Luna, who was sitting on the bunk with her bare legs tucked beneath her. "Want something to eat? I could rustle us up some sandwiches."

"What, no filet mignon and lobster tails?"

"Sorry, fresh out."

She faked a sigh of disappointment. "I guess a sandwich will have to suffice, then."

Kane whipped together some processed ham and provolone cheese on whole wheat. Before he sat down, he pulled the SIG M17 from the small of his back and set it on the table next to his paper plate.

As Luna climbed off the bunk and sat in the chair across from him, she gestured at the pistol and asked,

"Did you have that thing on while we were...you know..."

He nodded. "I always have a weapon within arm's reach."

She shook her head. "I know I said the world needs men like you, but that's kind of sad."

He shrugged. "It is what it is."

She took a bite of her sandwich, chewed thoughtfully, and asked, "Do you think you could clean up this town?"

His answer was simple, direct, and matter-of-fact. "Yes."

She set down her sandwich and reached across the table to lay a warm hand on his forearm. "Would you do it if I asked you to?"

He answered honestly. "I don't know." He locked eyes with her. She didn't look away. "Is that what you're asking me to do?"

"I don't want you to pull the trigger again because of me," she said. "But if you decide on your own that you're still going to fight the good fight against the evils of this miserable world, then maybe you could start right here."

"Thought you didn't want my team rolling into your town?"

"Not your team. Just you and me and any man or woman in Vesper Lake who is willing to fight alongside you."

"What you're suggesting will get good people killed."

"Good people are already *getting* killed," Luna countered. "Ten minutes ago, you said the people in town need to stand up to Nazareno and his goons."

"Stand up for themselves. Not have me do it for them."

"You want them to take the war to the bastards who control the town."

"Exactly."

She said, "Every army needs a general."

"You want me to teach the sheep how to fight?"

"Something like that."

Kane set aside his sandwich, no longer hungry, but craving another shot of whiskey. "I killed a kid last week," he said. "That fucked with my head, and I came up here to see if I can un-fuck it. I'm not sure the best way for me to make peace with what I did—"

"What you *had* to do," Luna interjected.

"Is to kill some more," Kane finished, ignoring her interjection, even while his brain acknowledged its truth.

He expected more pushback, but instead, she replied, "You're right, Kane, and I'm sorry for putting this pressure on you."

"I just hope you understand where I'm coming from."

"I do," she said, and he could hear the sincerity in her voice. "Let's leave it like this—you take the week to do all the reflecting and soul-searching you came up here to do. If you decide your guns are still in the game, all I ask is that you consider helping us. If you decide to lay down your guns for good, then..." She smiled. "Well, then maybe you'll think about staying up here longer than just a week."

"Fair enough."

Her hand had remained on his arm, and now her fingers moved, softly caressing his skin. "I've had enough talk about death and killing." She stood up, and the single button holding her shirt closed somehow came undone. It fell open, the warm light of the gas lamps spilling down the smooth slopes of her breasts. In a soft voice, she said, "Come to bed, and let's celebrate life."

She crawled onto the bunk, the shirt falling to the

floor along the way, allowing him to gaze upon all the passion—all the *life*—she had to offer.

He turned off the lights, plunging the cabin into darkness broken only by the orange glow seeping from the woodstove. By the time he slid into the bunk beside her, his clothes had joined her shirt on the floor. The Sig remained on the edge of the table, within arm's reach because Kane knew better than most that even in moments of living, death was never far away.

He soon forgot about the gun. Forgot about everything but the ecstasy of the moment as Luna opened herself to him. Not just physically, but spiritually, their souls entwining with the same intensity as their bodies.

As they moved together, giving and taking from each other exactly what they needed, they gasped out their release like hopeful prayers. Kane knew he would never forget these slivered heartbeats of passion, never forget her gentle touch. The preachers and prudes might call it simple lust, but Kane knew it was something more than that. Something deeper and more powerful.

Healing.

They made love long into the night, and as they fell asleep in each other's arms, Kane drifted into the most peaceful rest he had known since pulling the trigger five days ago. She was an angel in disguise, heaven wrapped in human flesh, and even if only for a few brief moments, she had brought some measure of peace to his troubled soul.

SIX

Black Bog Federal Prison

Some people accused Duff "Goatsack" Cantwell of being a needle jockey and ridiculed him for riding the steroid train to destination Muscle Mass. But Goatsack emphatically denied the allegations and had proof of sorts—oversized testicles. Ask anyone on the SORT team who boasted the biggest balls, and they would, down to the last man, say Goatsack. They not only meant it figuratively but literally as well.

It was common knowledge that juicing caused testicular atrophy, but Goatsack's balls were double the normal size. Not only did it prove his muscles were natural and not chemically enhanced, but the extra weight caused his scrotum to sag, earning him the nickname Goatsack twenty-five years ago when he took his first post-training shower after joining SORT. Somebody had pointed at the lathered-up rookie, cackled like a hyena, and announced, "Yo, Duff, looks like you got a goat's sack swinging there between your knees."

Every team member eventually earned a nickname. Duff had been christened with his on his very first day.

As the SORT team skulked in the woods that ringed their outdoor training area, waiting for their targets to show up, Goatsack mentally acknowledged that a quarter-century was a long time to be doing this kind of work. The endless strength training, endurance runs, obstacle courses, rappelling, low-crawling, and other hardcore shit he and his team were expected to master took their toll on his body.

Some said SORT was a young man's game, but he had defied the odds. However, his body—particularly his knees, which needed surgical replacement—had paid the price. He had turned fifty-six four months ago, meaning mandatory retirement was fast approaching. With thirty years of service, his pension would be nothing to scoff at. Factor in all the money Nazareno had stuffed into his coffers over the last few years, and post-prison life would be more than comfortable.

As much as his knees hurt and his muscles ached, as much as a sweeter life waited for him once he turned in his law enforcement credentials and rode off into the sunset, he loved the thrill of door-kicking too much to give it up just yet. He was a smasher, a shooter, an operator. It was in his blood.

Speaking of blood…

Warden Ghastin had summoned him to her office first thing this morning and supplied him with the names of two women Nazareno wanted dead. Goatsack thought the warden looked like crap as if she hadn't slept a wink, her almond-shaped eyes dull and ringed with black, despite the makeup she had slathered on to hide the flaws.

None of that meant jack-all to him. He had gone there to receive his kill-list, not ponder the pretty warden's problems. Besides, he had a damn good idea of what those problems were. It had become obvious over the years that Ghastin had been bent to Nazareno's will by threat of violence rather than by bribery. She didn't *want* to belong to the drug lord; she simply had no choice.

Goatsack and his team, on the other hand, had willingly embraced their role as Nazareno's personal hit squad. Before the cartel king had arrived, the SORT team had consisted of nineteen men and one woman, but those numbers had quickly been whittled down. A core of nine remained, the ones loyal to Nazareno—or rather, loyal to his cash—and who had a taste for blood. Goatsack and his boys had betrayed their oaths and broken their badges, turning into murderous mercenaries for more money than the United States government could ever dream of paying them.

He was perfectly okay with that.

Crouched at the base of a nearby pine tree, fallen logs and tangled brush screening him from the training field, Shawn "Breezy" Brindisi growled, "Where the hell are those two bitches?" The team had dubbed him Breezy because he was always passing wind. He'd been on SORT for just over eight years and was a skilled tactician. He'd been a lieutenant once but had gotten busted back to a senior officer after he'd caught his wife in bed with a coworker and punched the guy's lights outs.

"Steady," Goatsack said. "Simmer down. They'll be here. They never miss their morning walk."

The training area was shaped like an oval and ringed

by a quarter-mile running track. Every morning, shortly after the start of their shift, Yvonne Fariss and Bonnie Little came down and walked a mile on the track, getting in some exercise on the government's dime while they bitched and moaned and gossiped. Goatsack didn't know either of the women very well, but their reputation as busybodies was well-documented throughout the prison.

They would soon realize they should have kept their noses out of Nazareno's business. The drug lord did not suffer interlopers.

To Goatsack's left, the team sniper—Vernon "Yippy" Cayea—used his rifle scope to scan the top of the ridge where Yvonne and Bonnie would first appear, following the gravel pathway that led from the warehouse area down to the SORT field.

"Any sign of them yet, Yippy?"

"Negative," the sniper said, keeping his eye tight to the scope. "But they'll be here. Those two mouth-breathers never miss their walk unless it's raining."

"Yeah, 'cause witches don't like to get wet," Goatsack growled.

"I hear that." Yippy chuckled.

In position behind the sniper, Tom "Big Belly" Bartlemis asked, "We're taking these bitches off the count, right?" The team called him "Big Belly" because no matter how hard he worked out, the man could not get rid of his beer gut. It was an island of softness amidst a sea of solid muscle. Strange, because Big Belly rarely drank alcohol.

"Ten-four," Goatsack confirmed. "Nazareno wants them deep-sixed and tossed in the bog."

"Can we fuck 'em first?"

Goatsack stared at him. "The hell did you just ask me?"

"You heard me."

Goatsack shook his head in disgust. "No, you *can't* fuck them first. We might be killers, but we're not psychos."

Big Belly looked disappointed at the news, then abruptly brightened up. "Can we fuck 'em after?"

Goatsack heard Breezy mutter, "That big-bellied son of a bitch ain't right in the head, boss."

Before Goatsack could reply, Yippy said, "Heads up, boys. Here they come."

The SORT leader saw the two women crest the ridge and start down the hill to the track. Yvonne was short but in good shape, her black hair liberally streaked with gray. Bonnie was also short, but much rounder, with frizzy brown hair that tumbled to her shoulders. They both wore windbreakers to ward off the early-morning chill.

They hit the track and started walking at a brisk pace, voices carrying to the nine heavily-armed operators waiting for them in the trees on the other side.

"Can you believe they promoted that worthless idiot to business administrator?" Yvonne said. "Like, good Lord, what experience does he have that qualifies him for that position?"

"There were way better picks on the best-qualified list," Bonnie agreed. "You just know he must have lied on his resume. He doesn't know anything about accounting."

Goatsack keyed his mic and spoke in a low voice to his team. "Let them come around to this side of the track. When they're adjacent my position, me, Breezy, and Belly will move to intercept. Yippy, you stay back and provide overwatch. The rest of you, circle around and box them in. Make sure you take their radios. Last thing we need is them hitting their body alarms."

The two women rounded the far end of the track and started moving toward the team's position. Another hundred meters and the trap would be sprung.

"And I hear the union president is getting that promotion he's been bucking for," Yvonne griped. "Wonder how many grievances he had to shred in order to score that cushy management position?"

"I know most people like the guy," Bonnie replied, "but I think he's two-faced. I don't trust him one damn bit."

"Didn't you want to sleep with him at one point?"

"Let's just say if he had knocked on my door, I wouldn't have said no."

Yvonne laughed. "You're such a hussy."

Goatsack snapped, "Now!"

The team emerged from the woods, Heckler & Koch MP-5 submachine guns tight to their shoulders.

The SORT leader aimed his HK at the two women. "Don't move!" With his linebacker bulk wrapped in a ballistic vest festooned with flash-bangs, flex-cuffs, and extra magazines and his head covered with a tactical helmet, Goatsack knew he probably looked like a human tank rolling up on them.

Yvonne nearly jumped out of her skin. "Holy crap!" she exclaimed as the team formed a wall of black Kevlar around her and Bonnie. "You boys scared the hell out of me."

Bonnie proved to be a bit feistier. "What the hell do you think you're doing? Get those damn guns out of my face."

Behind her, a tall, lanky SORT member named Michael

"Goodbye" Goddeau stepped forward and nudged her roughly between the shoulder blades with the muzzle of his MP-5. "Shut up," he snarled. "Or I'll put a bullet in your spine right here, right now, and make you go bye-bye." That was why the team called him Goodbye—because he was the quickest on the trigger, always ready to kill at a moment's notice. But he never called it "killing." He always called it "going bye-bye," in some kind of psychological glitch that made him feel better about what they did.

Two other SORT boys—Ken "Duck" Dukette and Todd "Happy" Gladden—moved forward and relieved the women of their radios, taking away their ability to call for help. Then Pete "Sirius" Pelkey and Nicholas "Red Cent" Lincoln slapped flex-cuffs on them.

Yvonne looked worried. "Is this some kind of drill? A training exercise or something?" She wriggled her wrists within the plastic cuffs. "Damn, you think you put them on tight enough? They're cutting off my circulation."

Goodbye kicked the women in the backs of their knees, collapsing their legs out from under them. They both slumped into kneeling positions in the dirt.

"Asshole!" Bonnie snarled. "Who the hell do you think you are?"

Goatsack crouched in front of them. "I'll make this short and sweet. Well, not so sweet for you, sorry to say. No, this is not a training exercise. This is an execution. You two babbling bitches have been making noise about calling for a congressional inquiry, and that really pissed off Nazareno."

At the word "execution," Yvonne's face blanched ghost-white.

Bonnie proved to be made of sterner stuff. "Heard rumors you jerkoffs were working for that scumbag but didn't want to believe it."

"Oh, you can believe it."

"Then let's get this over with," she snapped. "What's the plan?"

"Simple," Goatsack said. "Drag you down to the firing range and pump you full of bullets, so it looks like you accidentally crossed a live-fire exercise." He shook his head in mock sadness. "Tragic, really. You two should have paid better attention to where you were walking."

Yvonne looked like she was about to faint. Her eyes turned glazed and glassy with the dull sheen of shock.

Bonnie spat, "You'll never get away with this."

Goatsack smiled without mirth. "The investigators have already been paid off, the coroner's report will say 'death by stupidity,' and the BOP bigwigs will sign off on that assessment before Nazareno's money even hits their offshore accounts." The smile vanished quicker than a sleight-of-hand magician making a card disappear. "Face it, sweetheart, you screwed with the wrong people."

"Kiss my ass."

"Funny." Goatsack smirked. "I think that's exactly what Big Belly over there wanted to do."

Big Belly grabbed his crotch and cut loose with some exaggerated pelvic thrusts. "Not too late, boss. She's gonna die anyway. Waste of good female flesh, you ask me."

"Yeah, well, nobody asked you, so keep it in your pants." Goatsack stood up and waved his finger in a circle, signaling the team. "Get 'em down to the range, boys."

They cut through the woods, walking along a game trail that clung to the bank above the brook that fed water into the brackish bog. Trout darted in the stream, and deer droppings peppered the path.

The prison's outdoor firing range had been

constructed on the southern edge of the bog, with a high sand berm serving as a backstop. The range was one hundred yards long, with mechanical targets at one end and covered shooting benches at the other. Farther back, nestled in the woods at one hundred and fifty yards, was a sniper's nest. Behind the benches loomed a small cabin where the team stowed some of their equipment. A generator shack squatted a little farther up the drive.

As the SORT team and their two prisoners emerged from the woods, Goatsack spotted two corpses sprawled at the edge of the bog. The foot of one of the corpses—a Hispanic male covered in demonic tattoos—actually rested in the black water that gave the bog its name. The other corpse—a black man with bargain-basement tats that identified him as a Blood—slumped face-down next to him, arm slung across the Hispanic's chest in a lover's embrace.

Goatsack gave the bodies a quick once-over. Looked like they had died last night and been dumped here this morning. The Hispanic had a horrific head injury, his skull split wide open from crown to bridge of his nose. The Blood was missing his eyes—just mushy, gore-soaked craters remained—and his neck was broken, twisted spinal bones bulging grotesquely beneath the death-mottled skin.

The SORT leader grunted, happy it was autumn and not summer. The summer meant flies, and with these kinds of wounds, the corpses would have been crawling with the things, hundreds of them, enough that the insectile buzzing would have been heard from twenty meters away. But the coolness of fall had killed off all the bugs.

Duck ambled over and took a look. As the team's secondary sniper, he lived for headshots, which he nailed with staggering consistency. The team said the only way to avoid being killed by Dukette was to duck, and that had become his moniker. "Losers from last night's Pit session?" he asked.

Goatsack nodded. "Looks like. That means the corpse detail will be along shortly. Let's get this over with."

"Ten-four." Duck began shoving the two women toward the target end of the range.

Goatsack stared at the butchered bodies for another moment. The Pit was what the inmates called the gladiator-style fights held in the prison's mothballed textile factory. They weren't a regular occurrence; they only took place when Nazareno called for them. The combatants battled to the death, often with various weapons. The bodies of the losers were dragged down here to be dunked in the bog, never to be seen again. The winners lived to fight—and die—another day.

The SORT leader turned away. The corpses weren't his problem. A couple of correctional officers would escort an inmate work detail down here at some point today and dispose of the deceased.

His job right now was to create two more bodies. It was a regular murder fest at Black Bog Federal Prison these days.

As he stepped over to the firing range, he saw Yvonne blubbering pathetically, face wrinkled with fear, streamers of snot oozing from her quivering nostrils. "Please," she begged. "I have a granddaughter. She's only five years old."

Goatsack ignored the pleas. His blackened, calloused heart had long ago immunized itself against such pathetic, desperate attempts to appeal to his humanity. He accepted blood money from a savage drug lord and slaughtered in his name. His humanity had disappeared in the rearview mirror years ago.

Bonnie stayed defiant in her final moments. Flex-cuffed, on her knees in front of the targets, she stared daggers at Goatsack. "I'll see you in Hell, you son of a bitch."

The SORT leader gave her a slight nod as the team lined up, weapons at the ready. "You can bet on it, sister." Then he raised his HK and flicked the selector switch to full-auto mode.

His team waited, fingers on triggers, for his command.

He didn't drag out the moment.

"Light 'em up!"

Nine submachine guns rattled to life in near synchronicity, hurling 9mm death downrange at 1,300 feet per second. Yvonne died screaming her granddaughter's name—"Charlene!"—while Bonnie stayed hard as nails to the bitter end, screaming obscenities—"Fuck you, assholes!"—as the bullets ripped the life from her.

The merciless salvos chopped them open and shredded their vitals. They shuddered and jerked and twisted beneath the high-velocity impacts. The hammering force smashed them over onto their sides, dead and blank-eyed as rivers of blood soaked into the dirt.

When the guns stopped their lethal chatter, silence swept in like death's cold wind to take its place.

It didn't last long.

"Rest in peace, miserable bitches," Happy intoned as he performed a tactical magazine exchange.

Red Cent chuckled. "More like rest in pieces. Hot damn, we shot the hell outta them."

Goodbye called, "Hey, Big Belly, you still wanna have a go at 'em?"

"They're still warm, ain't they?"

"You're a sick, sick man, Belly."

Goatsack stepped away from the post-execution chatter and radioed the warden on her private, secure channel.

A moment later, her digitized voice came through his earpiece. "Go for Ghastin."

"It's done," he said.

A pause, then, "I'll let him know."

"Ten-four. Goatsack out."

He switched back to his regular radio channel and watched his team as they cracked jokes and pretty much acted the opposite of how normal people would react after gunning down two innocent women.

Goatsack knew there wasn't something wrong with just Big Belly, there was something wrong with all of them.

He just didn't give a damn.

SEVEN

Dribble Creek Camp

Sated by the intense lovemaking and emotional salvation Luna had provided, Kane slept in longer than usual. By the time he rousted himself out of bed, careful not to wake his pretty companion, the sun was well on its way to peeking over the mountains. Looking out the window, he saw the morning light accentuating the bright foliage and high clouds scattered across the azure canvas of the sky.

Movement caught his eye. A red squirrel scampered in one of the pine trees that surrounded the cabin, hauling some kind of nut in its mouth. The bushy-tailed varmint startled a blue jay, which flapped itself into flight with a piercing screech, losing a few feathers in the process. They floated toward the ground, drifting on the morning breeze.

Kane felt the pull toward nature, the need to be outside, breathing fresh air, seeking the peace and solitude that can only be found in the wilds. He yearned to feel the wind on his face, to look up and see nothing but infinity. He wanted to walk where the wolf walked and be alone with his thoughts.

He regretted nothing with Luna. Last night's confession as the coyotes howled, as well as the physical aftermath, had been something he had not even known he needed. But right now, he craved aloneness.

He dressed quietly, then filled his backpack with a water bottle, beef jerky, apples, and granola bars. Then it was time to select his weapons.

He saw no need for two different handguns, so he decided to leave the Sig M17 behind. The Desert Eagle would be enough. He planned on heading deep into the woods, so he doubted he would run into Sheriff Dunkirk, his sons, or any of the cartel's kill squads. But if he did, the semi-auto .44 Magnum hand cannon would provide plenty of man-stopping power. If it was good enough for grizzlies, it was good enough for scumbags.

He considered the shotgun. The Beretta was a badass beast, all right, but did he really need to lug around its extra weight? If he was expecting trouble, then yeah, sure, sling that bad boy and be ready to blast. But this was an introspective walk in the woods, not a tactical strike where his survival hinged on having the most firepower. Again, for what he might encounter—namely, wild animals—the Desert Eagle sufficed. The shotgun would be overkill for this outing.

He strapped the handgun to his right hip using a custom-designed leather holster to support the semi-auto's metallic bulk. An extra-wide heavy-duty leather belt prevented the handgun from dragging his pants down. He counterbalanced the weight on the left side with two spare magazines, fully loaded, and his Ka-Bar knife.

He donned a light jacket and shrugged into the backpack as Luna stirred. She rolled onto her back and stretched like a cat, which caused the covers to slip down and leave her chest exposed. The sight made Kane want to ditch his gear and crawl back into bed with her.

She caught his eye and smiled. "Going somewhere, cowboy?"

"A walk."

"Want some company?"

"Actually, I think I need to do this alone."

She nodded, and her eyes let him know that she understood. "If you want, I can leave while you're gone," she said. "No awkward goodbyes that way." The question was there but unspoken. *Do you want me to leave?*

He quickly put her mind at ease. "I'm not ready to say goodbye."

She smiled happily. "Then I'll be waiting for you when you get back."

Kane cinched the backpack tight on his shoulders, gave her a kiss, and then closed the door behind him as he left the cabin.

Outside, the coolness invigorated him and blew off the last dregs of sleep better than mainlining caffeine. He followed the footpath that meandered away from the cabin in a westerly direction, threading between two giant, moss-covered boulders before skirting a depression full of fallen trees tangled together like nature's version of pick-up sticks.

The well-defined path was easy to follow, but when it curved south to drop down into a cedar-filled hollow, Kane turned northwest and struck out through unmarked woods, climbing a steep, rock-strewn slope that plateaued on a pine-covered ridge. The ridge ran north-south, and he opted to head north. South would take him to lower ground and, eventually, bring him out to the trailhead by Ernie Foxx's house.

He was looking to get farther away from people, not closer, so north was the way to go. Earlier this week, he had studied maps of the area and discovered that there was at least twenty miles of wild forest to the north and east. For a man looking to get lost—figuratively or literally—those were the directions to head.

It was not easy going. Off the beaten path, the ground was rough, with rocks and fallen logs often hidden beneath decades of undergrowth, ready to trip him and turn an ankle. At times, the trees were so thick that the canopy blocked out the sun, and the intertwined branches clutched at him like skeletal fingers, seeking to impede his forward momentum and drag him into claustrophobic closeness.

He bulled forward, unfazed. He had slogged through jungle vegetation so dense that it made this look like wet tissue paper, had dragged his boots through waist-high mud while snakes slithered around him and leeches latched onto his flesh. Sure, the Adirondacks featured some formidable terrain, but nothing compared to the green hells of Southeast Asia or South America. Damn, just *thinking* about Colombia set his teeth on edge. He hated that place.

By noon, he estimated he had pushed at least three miles into the backwoods. He found a sundrenched ledge and perched himself on one of the flat-topped rocks to rest and eat. The cool water felt damn good going down. He savored an apple and followed it up with some jerky.

As he chewed on the dehydrated beef, he allowed the beauty of the mountains to wash over him. The fall foliage could only be called spectacular, brilliant reds, oranges, purples, and yellows setting the forest on fire. The air back home in Texas smelled good, but it couldn't hold a candle to the fresh mountain breezes wafting over the rock ledge.

Growing up, Kane had hunted with an uncle—Uncle Rocky—who had a favorite saying: "The woods are my church, the deer stand is my pew, birdsong is my choir, and God is everywhere." For his uncle, being out in nature had been a truly religious experience; he had no need for stained glass windows or whitewashed steeples. "You want to feel the Creator's presence," Rocky used to say, "then your butt needs to spend some time in creation. Anything else is just plain ol' horseshit."

Kane smiled at the memory. A lot of the prim-and-proper churchgoers hadn't cared much for Uncle Rocky's brand of rough-and-tumble faith, but Kane had never doubted the man walked closer to God than most.

Sitting here on the rocks, surrounded by trees painted with colors so brilliant they could only come from nature, with the sun and breeze hitting his face, Kane could almost feel what Uncle Rocky had been talking about. Kane was not religious—a life of killing, of seeing the evils men do, had hardened his soul, but he did believe there was something out there. Something bigger than mortal men and their foolish, often wicked plans.

Here on this mountain, Kane felt closer to that "something" than any other time in his life. Not in a "the heavens opened and the angels shouted 'Hallelujah!'" sense, but far more subtle. A slight shift in his internal darkness, a sliver of light piercing the shadows, a half-step retreat from the demons inside.

Kane leaned back and stared up at the cloud-speckled sky as a sunlit hawk circled high on the thermals. A bird of prey, a hunter. Kane felt another shift deep down where guts and balls met brass and bone and recognized the moment for what it was.

Not a revelation, but a resurrection.

On top of this mountain, under the piercing eyes of the hawk and God or fate or destiny or whatever you chose to call it, Kane felt the warrior within him reborn. Looking back, he knew the rebirth had started with Luna, with his confession, his baring of his internal wounds, and her subsequent surrender of herself so he could begin to heal. The cauterization of his inner torment that had begun last night in the dark was now complete, in the cold light of day.

The hawk abruptly tucked its wings and dived, voicing a primal scream as it streaked toward the ground like a feathered missile. While he knew it had to be a trick of the wind, Kane could have sworn he heard a message in the raptor's wild cry.

You are a warrior, and warriors do not walk away from the fight.

Trick or not, the words hit home.

He was born to walk through hell. Destined to face the flames and make sure wickedness did not win the day.

That was who he was. That was who he would always be.

The hawk's scream was replaced by a wolf's howl.

But not the eerie, haunting, mournful tenor of a typical wolf's song. No, this howl was full of pain and hurt. There was still savagery in the sound, but it was tempered with fear. It dropped off sharply at the end, devolving into a sudden, snapping snarl.

Kane climbed to his feet. The howl had originated in the valley at the base of the ledge, close enough to prickle the hair on the back of his neck. He shrugged into his backpack as the wolf let out another howl that climaxed in another angry, hurting snarl. Listening intently, Kane swore he heard the faint sound of clinking metal.

He picked his way down the ledge, dropping from rock to rock, careful not to twist his ankle or put his full weight on any loose boulders. Be stupid to survive cutthroat wars with the cartels, only to die in a back-country avalanche of his own making. Carefully but steadily, he descended to the valley floor.

Beneath the forest canopy again, away from the direct rays of the sun, the air was cool and still. The breeze of the higher ground did not reach down here. The pungent scents of moist earth, rotting wood, and crisp foliage filled his olfactory senses.

But he wasn't focused on smells. He was focused on sounds.

One sound in particular.

He stood still, head cocked, listening, waiting for it.

Seconds later, the wolf obliged.

The predator's anguished cry echoed through the woods. Even infused with pain, the howl was sonically powerful, reverberating through the trees to fill the forest with one of the most haunting, soul-stirring sounds in nature's musical repertoire. The wolf's primal song pulled at Kane like a magnet.

He found a game trail that snaked through the trees and followed it, hunching to keep from getting ensnared in the tangled branches interlocked above the narrow path. He saw deer tracks, raccoon tracks, rabbit tracks... and wolf tracks.

A moment later, he saw the wolf.

The trap had been set at the crossing where two game

trails intersected. One ran parallel to the ledges that formed the valley's southern perimeter, the other made its way up from a small brook about fifty meters away. The wolf had placed its right front paw in the trap, and the steel jaws had clamped shut, holding it fast.

As Kane approached, he saw blood streaming down the animal's leg and caught a glimpse of white amidst the red-matted fur. In its struggle to escape, the wolf had pulled so hard that the teeth of the trap had dug all the way down to the bone.

Even injured, it was a majestic creature, with a thick, charcoal-gray coat and a white underbelly. Despite being trapped, the wolf radiated raw, primal power. It bared its fangs in a warning snarl as Kane moved closer, making soothing sounds that might have worked on a domesticated dog but were probably useless on a wolf. Still, he didn't know what else to try, and he wanted to help the animal.

"Easy, boy," he said softly. "I'm not gonna hurt you."

The wolf pasted its ears flat against its skull and snarled again, making it clear that if Kane came any closer, he did so at his own peril.

Kane didn't blame the wolf for its hostility. That was just the way of the world, man versus beast. He crouched just out of range of the wolf's teeth, slipped off his backpack, and took out some jerky.

The wolf ignored him, thrashing around like a beached fish as it struggled to free itself from the trap. The chain rattled like crazy, but the animal only managed to shred even more skin from its leg. The wolf slumped over on its side, ribs heaving, exhausted.

Kane neither retreated nor advanced. He just stayed crouched and watched the tortured animal rest. The wolf's eyelids slowly drooped closed, like blinds being lowered on a window. The foam-flecked jaws hung open, tongue lolling out to anoint the ground with hot drool, sharp teeth exposed in black-and-pink gums.

Kane wasn't sure how long they remained like that, but eventually, the wolf's chest stopped heaving, and it seemed calmer despite the trap still attached to its bleeding leg. The animal's eyes gradually opened and when it regained full cognizance, it locked gazes with the human who still crouched by its side.

Kane felt something pass between them, a shifting of the dynamic, a lowering of the primal shields that made wolf and man enemies. Maybe the creature realized that Kane could have killed it while it rested but had kept watch instead. The wolf's dark eyes remained bestial, but they brimmed with abnormal intelligence, as if trying to convey to Kane that the animal understood he was friend, not foe. Or perhaps it was the kinship between two warriors, which needs no vocabulary, no articulation.

Whatever it was—and Kane made no attempt to define it, content to let the mystery of the moment simply exist—he knew that the wolf would not harm him now.

He offered a piece of jerky to the wolf and the beast accepted it gratefully, swallowing it whole. Next, Kane scooped a small hollow in the earth near the animal's muzzle and filled it with water from his bottle, which the wolf quickly lapped up.

"All right, boy. Let's see about getting you out of this thing."

Kane gently ran his hands through the thick fur around the wolf's neck, then glided down over the firm shoulder muscles, letting the animal acclimate to his touch. The wolf turned its head and let out a low whine, but that was it.

Kane's hands moved down the leg, careful not to touch the wound, until they reached the cold metal of the trap. He wasted no time in prying open the jaws, and the wolf pulled its leg free. It scrambled to its feet but made no effort to pull away from Kane. It just stood there and watched him, the hurt limb just barely touching the ground, unable to bear any weight.

Kane knew the next part would really test just how much the wolf trusted him. The wound needed to be bandaged, and there was no way to do that without causing the animal pain. Would the wolf recognize the healing in the hurt? Or would it sink its fangs into Kane's neck?

Only one way to find out.

He reached into his backpack and took out a handkerchief that he had packed in case he needed a tourniquet. "Easy, fella," he said as he reached for the wolf's leg again. As he wrapped the kerchief around the torn flesh, the wolf flinched, but other than that, it held still.

Kane tied off the makeshift bandage, making sure the wound was fully covered, then reached up and ruffled the fur on top of the wolf's head. "Good boy," he said. He rose to his feet, muscles aching from holding a crouched position for so long.

The wolf's ears abruptly snapped forward, alerting Kane that someone or something was behind him. A second later, a deep voice growled, "You mind telling me what the hell you're doing with my dog?"

Dog?

Keeping his movements slow and unthreatening, Kane turned around and saw a tall, thin, scarecrow of a man dressed in fringed buckskins and wearing a raccoon hat, complete with a striped tail that hung down between the man's shoulder blades. Save for his gaunt build, the guy looked like he had stepped off the cover of some mountain man novel.

Of course, the mountain men of yesteryear didn't have AR-15 rifles like the one currently aimed at Kane's midsection. Even in the shadows of the woods, it was clear that the muzzle didn't waver much. Clearly, this mountain man—and Kane had a good idea who he was looking at—had no problem threatening someone with lethal force.

Kane kept his hands out to his sides. Even if he had wanted to engage in a gunfight with the stranger, the Desert Eagle was holstered beneath his jacket. No way in hell would he be able to draw and shoot before the AR-15 plugged him with a half-dozen holes.

"Asked you a question," the man said. "What are you doing to my dog? Won't ask you a third time."

No, you'll just shoot me in the head and slap me on a plate, Kane thought. Aloud he replied, "You're Mike, right?"

"So you've been to town and heard the stories about ol' Mad Mike," the man grunted. "Good for you. They tell you I'm a cannibal?"

"Yeah, they mentioned it."

"Good. So unless you start answering questions instead of asking them, you know what I'm gonna put in my soup tonight."

Kane glanced down at the wolf, which was still bearing all its weight on just three legs, then back up at Mike. "Came across your wolf caught in a trap and—"

"Dog."

Kane paused. "What?"

"That's my dog, not a wolf."

Kane looked down again, then back up. "Okay. Your dog got a name?"

"Sure does. I call him Wolf."

Kane stared at him. "You're fucking with me, right?"

Mike broke out in a grin. "Yeah, actually, I am." He slung the AR-15 over his shoulder and started walking toward Kane. "Been watching you the whole time. Heard Beta howling, so I came looking. You got here first. I almost killed you, truth be told, but then I saw what you were doing. Wouldn't have believed it if I hadn't seen it with my own two eyes. Beta doesn't let anyone touch him but me, but looks like he took to you just fine."

"Why do you call him Beta?" Kane asked.

"Because I'm the alpha, and that mutt damn well knows it."

Mike pulled up about two arm-lengths away. Beta hobbled over and rested his head against the mountain man's thigh, earning himself a scratch behind the ears. "So," Mike said, "did you make yourself a new friend?"

"Well," Kane replied, "I couldn't just leave him—"

"Wasn't asking you." Mike cut him off. "Asking the mutt."

"Oh." Kane held up his hands in a *sorry* gesture. "My bad."

Beta looked up at his master. Mike looked down at the wolf and jerked his head toward Kane. "Friend?" he asked again, making sure his tone turned the world into a question.

Beta limped back over to Kane and sat down on his haunches beside him.

Mike shook his head. "Well, I'll be damned. Never thought I'd see the day." He grinned at Kane, who was taken aback to see that some of the mountain man's teeth were filed down to points. "So I guess you're in the friend category. If my mutt trusts you, then I trust you."

"What happens if Beta doesn't trust someone?" Kane asked.

"He rips their leg off, and we watch them bleed out."

"Then what?"

"Kibbles 'n' Bits."

"You turn them into dog food?"

"Something like that." He pointed a finger at Kane. "I know what you're thinking about asking." He shook his head. "Do me a favor and don't. I know what people in that crappy little town say about me, and they're free to form whatever opinions they care to. But it seems like every damn person I come across out here asks me the same damn question, and frankly, it's a bit rude, don't you think?"

"Hadn't given it much thought," Kane replied.

"Listen, all you need to know is that my mutt likes you, so I'm definitely not going to eat you."

"Glad to hear it."

Mike moved past him, heading down the trail that paralleled the rock ledge. Beta hobbled along behind him, moving pretty well for only having three good legs. "Anyway," Mike said, "I owe you for what you done for Beta, so unless you got somewhere to be right this second, why don't you come back to my place and have a cup of tea?"

"Thanks," Kane replied. "But I'm more of a whiskey guy."

Over his shoulder, Mike said, "Come on, now, don't be rude. Rude people leave a sour taste in my mouth."

Kane mulled it over for a minute. Then he shrugged, muttered, "What the hell?" and followed Mad Mike deeper into the woods. He promised himself that if the hermit even looked at him the way most red-blooded American men look at a juicy T-bone steak, he was pulling his .44 and blowing the man's pointy teeth out the back of his head.

A quarter-mile up, the game trail widened into a proper footpath. The trees thinned out, hardwoods now mixing with the ubiquitous pines. Another quarter-mile and they arrived at Mike's cabin, which was constructed of rough-hewn logs and significantly larger than Kane had expected.

"You build this yourself?" he asked.

"You think many people want to hike four miles back in the woods with a man they suspect of being a cannibal to help him build a cabin?" Mad Mike answered rhetorically.

Beta bounded into the bushes and emerged a moment later with a bone in his mouth. He carried it over and laid it at Kane's feet, practically beaming with pride.

"He must really like you," Mike said. "That's his favorite bone."

"It looks like a human femur."

"Could be. Lots of people die back in these woods."

"Die? Or get killed?"

"Both."

Kane knew better than most that monsters sometimes come in human packages. He wondered if he would be doing the world a favor to put a bullet in the back of Mike's head and call it a day. Easy enough to do, since the hermit led the way inside, putting his back to Kane. But then Beta would probably try to avenge his master, and Kane would be forced to put the wolf down. He decided to let this play out a little longer.

The interior of the cabin was nicer than Kane had anticipated. The roof rose at a sharp pitch to shed snow during the long Adirondack winters, and the exposed support beams wove a wooden web overhead. To Kane's right, a set of stairs led up to a small loft. Along the cabin's south side were a stove, countertops, and cabinets. At the west end, opposite the front door, was the kind of natural stone fireplace that rich people paid tens of thousands of dollars to replicate in modern multi-million dollar mansions.

An oak table so thick and heavy that it looked like it belonged in a medieval castle dominated the center of the cabin. Birch tree stumps served as the table's legs. The surface was roughed up with knife scars, scratches, and gouges. The wood was stained dark.

In the center of the table perched a human skull, the occipital crest cracked open in a splintered gash. Looked like it had been done with an edged weapon like an axe or hatchet. A wax candle jutted through the cavity.

Beta curled up under the table as Kane pointed at the skull. "Is that real?"

Mike went to the cupboard and took out two mason jars. "Sure is." He grabbed a jug from the counter and came over to the table, setting one of the glasses down in front of Kane.

"Did you kill him?" Kane asked frankly.

"Me? Hell, no." Mike uncorked the jug and poured some clear liquid into each Mason jar. "Whoever that poor sucker was, the Indians killed him."

Kane lifted his glass and sniffed. Smelled like gasoline mixed with blackberries. "Indians, huh?"

Mike grabbed his own glass and knocked back a third of the contents in one hit, followed by a belch that would have made a barbarian proud. "Yep, Indians," he replied. "Don't tell me you're one of those idiots who thinks Indians only lived out west. Everyone knows about the Apaches and the Comanche and the Sioux, but they forgot about the eastern Iroquois tribes." He pointed at the cracked open skull. "I reckon a Mohawk did that."

"What makes you say that?"

"The stone blade from the tomahawk was still buried in the bastard's head when I found it. Looked Mohawk to me." He took another swig and then shrugged. "But I ain't no Injun expert." He pointed at the Mason jar in Kane's hand. "You gonna drink that or what?"

"This sure as hell ain't tea."

"Don't tell me you were really expecting tea." Mike snorted. "I know better than to judge a book by its cover, but you don't look like a stupid man."

"I'm not, usually." *Of course, you did voluntarily come to a cabin in the woods with a man suspected of cannibalism.* "What is it, anyway?"

"Blackberry moonshine," Mike replied. "Got a still out back."

"Here goes nothing." Kane took a swig.

It felt like fucking battery acid scorching his throat.

He managed to save himself from a full-fledged sputtering fit, but couldn't hold back a cough as the bootleg liquor burned his gullet with napalm heat.

Mike grinned. "Not bad for an amateur. That stuff will put so much hair on your chest that if you run around naked in the woods, people will mistake you for a Sasquatch."

"Holy hell," Kane said. "That stuff should be illegal."

"It is."

"Figure of speech."

"We don't worry much about legalities 'round these parts," Mike said. "Sheriff Dunkirk is too busy running guns and drugs, and any state or federal law that might stick its nose in where it's not welcome has been paid off. Believe me, ain't nobody coming back here to bust me for moonshine. Even if they tried, Beta would just rip their throats out."

"He's attacked-trained?"

"Sure is. Got a book about how the police train their K-9 units and used those methods to teach Beta."

"The police don't train their dogs to rip out throats."

Mike shrugged. "I made some modifications."

"Beta ever kill anyone?"

"Only when we're hungry."

The mountain man's face was deadpan, making it impossible to decipher the truth behind the stone-faced mask.

Kane shook his head. "You're a character, Mike. Hard to know if you're telling the truth or pulling my leg."

"According to the nitwits in town," Mike said, "I wouldn't pull your leg, I'd chop it off and eat it like a damn drumstick."

"Speaking of town," Kane said. "For a hermit, you seem to know an awful lot about what's going on down there."

"That's because the crap going on in that worthless town has poked its ugly head into my woods."

"How so?"

"Sheriff Double D Dumbass and his boys put up a shack about a half-mile from here. It's where they keep the guns in between shipments. Got a guard posted and everything. They carved a trail down the backside of the mountain to an old logging head off the main road between Black Bog and Vesper Lake. The logging truck pulls in, picks up the guns, and moseys on down the highway, lickity-split."

Kane knew he should just leave it alone, but the warrior within couldn't just let it lie. "Can you show me where the shack is?"

Mike eyeballed him. "Why? You some kind of hero or something?"

"Just curious."

"You know what curiosity did to the cat, right?"

"Do I look like a cat to you?"

The corner of Mike's lip quirked up in a grin. "Oh, you look like one cool cat, all right." He pointed at the mostly-full glass in Kane's hand. "Tell you what, cool cat. You finish the rest of that without stopping, I'll draw you a map to the shack."

A drinking challenge? Kane thought. *What are we, frat boys?* But he said, "Deal," raised the Mason jar to his lips, and drained the blackberry moonshine in three huge gulps.

This time he didn't give up even a single cough.

Mike looked suitably impressed. "Dang, boy. Chugged that like a champ."

Kane shrugged. "What can I say? I'm a fast learner. Now, about that map."

The hermit waved his hand dismissively. "No map necessary. Just follow the trail back to where you found Beta in the trap, then take the game trail down to the creek. Pick up the trail on the other side, and it'll take you up to a clearing on a knoll. You'll see the shack there."

"Obliged." Kane pushed his chair back from the table. "I'm gonna go take a look at that gun shack, then try to make it back to my cabin by dark."

Mike cocked his head to the side like a quizzical dog —or in his case, a quizzical wolf—and said, "You really *aren't* gonna ask me, are you?"

"You told me not to," Kane replied. "And I believe in respecting a man's wishes." *Unless they're a cartel scumbag wishing not to die when I've got them in my sights.* "I reckon your business is just that—your business. If the rumors aren't true, then I'm sorry as hell you got saddled with that kind of reputation."

"What if the rumors *are* true?"

Kane grinned. "Then thanks for not having me for supper."

Mike sized him up like a chef checking out a Thanksgiving turkey. "Too tough," he said, his tone yet again making it impossible to tell if he was serious. "Nothing but lean meat and hard gristle on your bones. Need more fat."

"Right," Kane said. "Everyone knows the best steaks have marbling."

"Spoken like a true carnivore."

Outside, Kane crouched and Beta hobbled over to say goodbye, even reaching up to give his face a quick lick as he ruffled the wolf's ears. "Yeah, you're a good boy," Kane said, giving him the rest of the jerky. As the wolf gobbled it down, Kane stroked the fur on the back of his neck and asked Mike, "Where the hell did you get a wolf, anyway?"

"Stole him from a family of Sasquatches."

Kane grinned. "Fair enough, Mike." He shrugged into his backpack and tightened the straps. "Nice meeting you."

"Happy hunting. Say, if you're really planning on taking a peek at those guns, you're gonna need a weapon. You can borrow one of mine if you like."

Kane reached beneath his jacket and pulled out the Desert Eagle. "Thanks, but I brought my own."

Mike smirked. "Had that this whole time, did ya?"

"Sure did."

Mike shook his head. "Like I said, fella...you're one cool cat."

"Call me Kane."

With a farewell wave, he headed back down the path and picked up the pace. The sun had started its afternoon descent, and while he wasn't afraid of the dark, he had no desire to be stuck in the deep woods after sunset.

He took a left at the intersection, following a crooked game trail that meandered through mossy rocks and spruce saplings on its way down to a small stream that was maybe a meter wide. The burble of the water made a pleasant sound, joining with birdsong and the rustling of leaves to create nature's symphony, but Kane did not pause to enjoy the primordial music. He moved with purpose, a man on a mission.

He hopped the creek and pulled himself up the opposite bank, picking up the game trail again. Looking up the slope, he could just see the top of the knoll, the trees thinning out as the trail threaded upward. It was lighter up there, the sun not blocked by the thicker woods below.

Kane went into stealth mode without really thinking about it, a nearly subconscious act as he ghosted up the hill. Mad Mike had warned him the place was guarded, and Kane had no intention of advertising his presence.

He walked carefully, mindful not to crunch the fallen leaves or crack any branches under his boots. He took his time making the ascent, reaching forward to use saplings and vines as handholds to pull himself up.

As he climbed, Kane again felt the resurrection of his warrior spirit. He still mourned the death of the kid in Mexico. Hell, he would mourn that kid for the rest of his days. But the grief and regret and doubt were now eclipsed by his deep-rooted drive to fight the forces of darkness. To battle the bastards who preyed upon the innocent, to wage war against the evil savages who trafficked in death and misery.

Luna had practically begged him to clean up her town like he was some kind of old-fashioned Wild West lawman—Wyatt Earp with a Desert Eagle instead of a Colt Peacemaker. Despite the resurgence of the warrior within, there was a part of him that knew he should just stay the hell out of this fight.

But he also knew he couldn't just walk away.

As he climbed the knoll, knowing he would soon engage in violence against someone who deserved it, he felt the pre-combat rush of adrenalin start its hot surge through his bloodstream. He had heard others describe the sensation as narcotic, but it never cranked that far for him, never turned him into a carnage junkie.

He did not lust for the kill. Pulling the trigger, putting bullets downrange, sending evildoers to their deaths... that was a necessity, not an addictive need. He had seen his fair share of thrill-killers during his time in international hell-zones, and he vowed to never cross that line.

The exception was when he killed in the name of vengeance. When someone made it personal, when someone brought harm or death to the ones he cared for, Kane felt no remorse at the visceral satisfaction he experienced when he struck them down.

Just a few meters short of the top, the game trail abruptly cut ninety degrees to the left to run parallel to the crest of the knoll. The animals that used the trail obviously did not want to cross the clearing and expose themselves to predators.

Kane had no such concerns. In fact, he was hunting predators, and as far as he was concerned, it was open season.

The clearing stretched approximately sixty meters in diameter, covered with wild grass and blueberry bushes. At the nine o'clock position to Kane's left, the shack that allegedly held the illicit guns squatted in the afternoon sun. It looked surprisingly well-made and had a green metal roof perched on walls that measured roughly twenty-five feet by fifteen feet. Kane had expected to see some rundown shed that looked like a white-trash meth cookhouse, but Sheriff Duncan and his boys apparently took their gunrunning enterprise seriously.

The front door was slightly ajar, an open padlock dangling from the hasp. No sign of the sentry, so Kane figured he was inside.

He drew the Desert Eagle, double-checking to make sure there was a round in the chamber, then moved up over the top of the knoll and slid across the clearing quickly but quietly, the grass and blueberry plants hushing his footsteps. No way would the sentry inside be able to hear him coming.

He reached the door without incident. He paused to listen but heard nothing inside the shack. Maybe the guard was sleeping. Or maybe Mad Mike had been wrong, and there wasn't even a sentry posted.

Only one way to find out.

He leveled the Magnum, ready to sweep for targets once he breached, and kicked the door all the way open. He started to rush forward but caught himself at the last possible second.

Just before stepping on the huge bear trap lying on the floor just inside the shed.

The sixteen-inch-wide steel jaws gaped open like a shark's maw, jagged teeth ready to cleave through flesh and dig into bone. Designed to withstand the frenzied thrashing of a panicked bear, Kane knew that if he had stepped on the paddle in the middle of the trap, those metal jaws would have damn near severed his leg. As a defensive measure to protect the apparently unmanned shack, it was simple but effective.

After verifying the shack was devoid of human presence, Kane grabbed the chain and dragged the trap off to the side, nudging it carefully into the cobwebbed corner. Then he turned his attention to the stacked wooden crates.

Kane had expected an arsenal, but there were only twelve crates in the shack, stacked two-high along the western wall. All of them were marked U.S. Army.

He holstered his .44 and took out his Ka-Bar, using the heavy blade to pry open one of the lids. As suspected, it was packed with M4A1 carbines, chambered for 5.56 X 45mm NATO, and capable of full-auto firing. He opened another crate and found more of the carbines, these equipped with M203 grenade launchers.

Once this was over, he would notify Fort Drum that one of their soldiers was doctoring the inventory and making money on the side selling military hardware to the bad guys. Straight to the brig, and see you in fifteen years.

He was setting the lids back in place when someone snarled, "Who the hell are you?"

Kane still had the knife in his fist, but he kept his hands well out to the side in a surrender stance as he slowly turned around. "Listen," he said. "I'm not stealing anything."

"Didn't ask you if you're stealing shit," the man retorted. "Asked who the hell you are."

Now facing the guard, Kane saw a man of average size and build, hair hidden beneath a battered Boston Red Sox baseball cap. An unkempt beard that looked rough enough to burnish copper shrouded his vaguely vulpine features. His brown eyes narrowed to suspicious slits as he glared at Kane. In his hands, he held an M-4 carbine, no doubt obtained from one of the crates. Kane didn't see any ammunition lying around, but it was still a safe bet the rifle was loaded.

It was also pointed right at him.

Kane's mind raced through his options at turbocharged speed. It took him less than two seconds to decide to bluff his way out of this.

He injected cold authority into his voice as he rasped, "They call me Reaper. I work for Nazareno." He hoped dropping the kingpin's name would buy him some play. "You want to tell me why you weren't watching the guns? Give me a good explanation, and maybe I won't have your eyeballs burned out of your skull with a blowtorch."

The mention of Nazareno clearly struck a chord with the sentry. He swallowed hard but didn't lower the rifle. "I was taking a shit," he said defensively. Then his voice hardened. "And speaking of shit, I think you're full of it."

"Yeah? What makes you say that?"

"Nazareno doesn't know about these guns."

Kane's lips peeled back from his teeth in a wolfish grin. "He does now. That's why I'm here. Dunkirk is cutting Nazareno in on the deal, and my boss sent me here to check things out."

The sentry seemed unsure. Kane knew the story had a whiff of bullshit, but the sentry no doubt knew that if it turned out to *not* be bullshit and he actually shot one of Nazareno's enforcers, he would suffer an agonizing death that might very well include swallowing his own burnt intestines.

"How do I know you're telling the truth?" the sentry asked.

Kane sighed as if dealing with a dimwitted child. "How do you think I knew about the bear trap inside the door?"

"Could be you just got lucky."

"Or maybe Dunkirk told me about it so I wouldn't step on the damn thing."

"Maybe," the sentry allowed. But he still kept the M-4 leveled.

Kane cursed silently. The bluff had been worth a shot, but it clearly wasn't working. Time to try something else.

There was no way to draw the Desert Eagle before the sentry drilled holes in him. That left the knife. The infamous Twenty-one Foot Rule theorized that an attacker wielding a blade could cross twenty-one feet of ground before a gunman could draw and fire their weapon. Kane estimated that he and the sentry were just about that far apart. Problem was, the sentry didn't need to draw a gun. He already had one out, ready to rock. No way could Kane close the gap before the M-4 started popping off rounds.

But maybe the knife could...

He immediately turned the thought into violent action.

Exploding into motion, he whipped his arm forward. The blade sailed across the shack in a tumbling blur of metal.

The millisecond he felt the knife leave his hand, he threw himself to the side.

The sentry got off a single shot that sizzled through the space Kane had just vacated and punched a hole in the wall. Then he started yowling in pain.

Kane was not an expert blade thrower. He practiced enough to be proficient but not enough to be precise, and the Ka-Bar was not designed to be a throwing knife. He had aimed for the sentry's throat, hoping to split his Adam's apple.

Instead, the knifepoint struck the man high on his

cheek, cutting through the skin to skid off the facial bone beneath. Deflected, the blade sliced open the sentry's ear, cleaving through the cartilage. He didn't drop the M-4, but he let go of it with his left hand so he could slap a palm over the bloody injury.

Having dodged a literal bullet, Kane reached for his Desert Eagle, but the holster hung beneath his jacket, making a fast draw impossible. The sentry recovered from the shock of his wound quicker than anticipated and swung the M4 toward him with one hand.

Kane abandoned his hope of getting the Desert Eagle out in time and instead rushed forward. He had covered half the distance when he saw the sentry's finger tighten on the trigger. One-handed, it would be a wild shot, but at a distance of only a dozen feet, Kane wasn't taking any chances.

He launched himself into a power-slide that carried him beneath the muzzle of the rifle as it spat flame. He sensed rather than felt the superheated air above his back as the bullet scorched past.

Then he crashed into the sentry's knees like a defensive lineman sacking a hesitant quarterback. The man tumbled down and the carbine clattered from his grasp, but as he fell, the sentry managed to slam an elbow directly into Kane's spine.

Pain flared through his system, not permanently crippling, but momentarily debilitating. Seizing his advantage, the sentry brought up his knee and gave Kane a shot in the ribs. Nothing cracked, but his pain levels spiked even higher.

Growling like a wounded, angry animal, Kane reached over his shoulder. His hand knocked off the man's baseball cap and grabbed a fistful of greasy hair. Heaving like a bucking bronco and pulling the sentry's hair at the same time, he managed to throw him off. The sentry crash-landed just outside the door.

Both men scrambled to their feet. At six-foot-four, Kane towered over the sentry by several inches, and he saw the fear in the man's eyes as he realized he was woefully outclassed.

Still, that didn't stop him from swinging as Kane stalked forward. The warrior batted aside the blows and grabbed the sentry's jacket with his left hand. As he pulled him close, dragging him back inside the shack, he slammed a brutal punch into the sentry's midsection. He followed up with a thundering strike to the jaw that sent the man tumbling sideways.

Kane let go of the jacket as the sentry tripped over the fallen M4 carbine. He tried to regain his balance, but it was no use. At the last possible second, the man saw what was about to happen and let out a strangled *"NOOOO!"* that cut off abruptly as he fell face-first into the bear trap.

His nose flattened against the paddle and triggered the powerful spring. The metal jaws snapped shut. The serrated steel teeth chopped through his skull just behind the ears, shearing off the back of his head like a machete taking off the top of a coconut.

Kane picked up the M4 as the sentry twitched spastically, but there was no need for a mercy shot. The body still shuddered as bioelectrical impulses short-circuited, but with half the man's head missing, there was no doubt he was dead.

Kane retrieved his knife. There wasn't much blood on the blade since the ear isn't the juiciest appendage, but what little there was, he wiped off on the dead man's jacket before sliding it back into its sheath.

He slung the M4 across his back, then bent over to

free the sentry's corpse from the trap. He dragged it out into the sunlight, not really caring whether he left any DNA evidence on the body. This was a lawless town, and he seriously doubted there would be an investigation into the man's death.

Out of the shadows of the shack and in the full light of day, the lethal wound was even more gruesome. Not that Kane cared; he had seen enough gore to last a lifetime.

He turned away from the body to study the shed. He wanted to burn the damn thing down, but he didn't want to risk a forest fire. He would come back after he had taken down Sheriff Dunkirk and freed Vesper Lake from the crushing vice grip of the cartel.

Yeah, he decided, after he brought blood and thunder to the cartel presence in town and cleaned out the corruption rooted there, then he would worry about destroying the guns.

He closed the door and secured the padlock.

Something growled behind him.

It was a low, rumbling sound, and Kane felt some primal alarm awaken deep in his bones. The combat adrenalin, not yet fully evaporated from his blood, was now replaced by adrenalized fear. It chilled his veins like arctic ice.

The urge for flight was strong, but Kane's willpower was stronger. He leashed his natural instincts and instead turned to face the threat.

A huge grizzly bear stood less than twenty yards away.

On all fours, the grizzly measured at least five feet at the shoulder, and Kane put its weight somewhere north of 1,200 pounds. The huge head was lowered, now near the ground and angled forward aggressively. The bear's mouth hung open, its menacing growls flowing over teeth that were at least two and a half inches long. Drool slobbered from the muzzle as the black nose twitched, scenting the air, filling its nostrils with the scent of fresh-spilled human blood. Strings of saliva stretched toward the ground like thick spiderwebs as the bear's salivary glands kicked into overdrive.

Kane swallowed hard, knowing he was face to face with Gasper, the man-eating grizzly.

The bear huffed, then reared up on his hind legs as if to display his dominance over the human he now faced. Even with his heart pounding, Kane noted the majesty of the beast, which easily towered ten feet high.

The grizzly raised its snout toward the sky and let out a challenging roar, clacking its jaws together in a warning. The right paw swiped at the air like boxer feinting a jab. He glimpsed the wicked, curved, four-inch claws that would shred him to confetti and rip out his spine in seconds flat if the bear decided to attack.

Kane's hand crept toward the Desert Eagle. No way in hell would he get it out in time to stop Gasper's charge if that was what the grizzly decided to do, but maybe he would be able to bring it into play as the beast took him to the ground. Better to die fighting than just lie there and get ripped apart.

The bear dropped back down on all fours and shuffled forward a few steps, growling ominously once again. It stared at Kane with the hard eyes of a predator, challenging, threatening, and domineering. It projected brute strength in that killer's gaze.

Kane knew the conventional wisdom about not looking a wild beast in the eye, but with his back to the wall and nowhere to run, he had no other play.

He locked stares with the grizzly, showing no fear and

letting the man-eater know that *this* man would not be backing down. Then, well aware there was a razor-thin line between balls and stupidity, he did the exact opposite of what the bear would expect him to do.

He walked right at the beast.

Gasper lifted his head and let out a challenging roar but made no move to charge. The violence in the grizzly's black eyes was now joined by curiosity as he stared at the human moving toward him when he should have been running away.

With slow, deliberate movements, eyes deadlocked with the bear's, Kane stepped to the sentry's corpse. He crouched, never breaking the stare-down, and slid his hands beneath the body. Next he stood up, levering with his arms, and rolled the dead man toward Gasper. Then he stepped back to signal to the grizzly that the body was an offering. *This was mine*, the gesture was intended to say. *But now I give it to you.*

Kane halted when he felt his back once again pressed against the wall of the shed. His hand delved beneath his jacket to grip the Desert Eagle, but he fervently hoped he wouldn't need it. If it came down to that, he was pretty much screwed. With a whole lot of luck, he might be able to kill the bear, but not before Gasper extracted his pound—or several pounds—of flesh with those giant claws.

Kane kept the desperation and fear that were slithering through his guts on a short leash, doing his damnedest to make sure the grizzly couldn't smell them.

The bear, his head low and swinging from side to side like an executioner's pendulum while he made snort-snuffle noises with his nose, stepped forward with cautious but purposeful strides, flattening the blueberry bushes beneath his massive paws. The dark eyes switched from Kane to the corpse and back again as his brain, less than a third of the size of a human's, tried to decipher the man's intentions.

The grizzly took his time crossing the clearing, plenty long enough for Kane to intimately familiarize himself with the pounding rhythm of his heart slamming inside his chest. Every instinct screamed at him to run, but he gritted his teeth and stood his ground.

Gasper nudged the corpse as if to confirm the man was dead, then looked at Kane again.

Kane stuck to his plan of staring the beast square in the eye. Wasn't like he could do anything else anyway. Only ten feet separated him and the grizzly now. If Gasper lunged, Kane wouldn't have time to get his gun out before the bear ripped his face off.

The grizzly gave the corpse a sniff, then looked at Kane again.

"Go on," the warrior muttered under his breath. "Just take it."

The bear's head snapped up at the sound of Kane's voice, and he gave the man another long, hard, black-eyed stare.

Kane knew enough about wild animal behavior to guess that the grizzly was probably trying to decide whether he needed to kill the human. Gasper had clearly identified that this was Kane's kill, and in the wild, if you wanted to take another alpha predator's prey away from him, you typically had to kill him. The fact that Kane was voluntarily offering him this kill probably confused the bear.

After what seemed like an eternity but was probably only a minute or so, the grizzly decided it didn't need to tangle with Kane in order to get a meal. He lowered its head, opened his jaws wide, and sank his teeth into the back of the dead man's neck. He gave Kane one warning growl as if to say, *"Don't mess with me right now, man,"* then shook the body fiercely, whipping it back and forth, snapping the vertebrae to make sure the sentry was really dead.

Satisfied the sentry wasn't just playing possum, the bear dragged the body into the woods. The corpse would be dinner, but Gasper clearly preferred a private meal.

Relief flooded through his hyper-adrenalized system as Kane watched the grizzly go. A little smile touched his lips as the beast vanished into the woods with his prize. *"Bon appetit*, buddy."

He waited ten minutes before he slipped off the knoll and circled wide to begin the journey back the way he had come.

Back to the cabin.

Back to Luna.

EIGHT

Dribble Creek Camp

Luna didn't get out of bed until noon. The combination of staying up late, the passionate sex, and the overall feeling of peace and comfort she felt in Kane's presence despite his clearly troubled spirit worked to lull her back into a deep sleep after he left. Outside, the leaves rustled and the birds sang the squirrels chattered, but inside the cabin, there was only the gentle breathing of a contented soul at rest. If she had helped Kane exorcise some of his demons last night, he had returned the favor, and he didn't even know it.

Hunger finally pulled her out from under the covers. She got dressed and then, stomach rumbling, she scrounged for breakfast—or was it lunch?—and found some eggs in a cooler, along with a package of sliced ham.

A loaf of bread sealed the deal, and one hot cast iron skillet later, she had whipped herself up a breakfast sandwich. She would have liked to melt some cheese over the top, but it looked like Kane hadn't bothered picking any up at Baldy's. Maybe she could go back into town later and remedy that. She would just have to dodge the sheriff's boys. Better yet, maybe Kane would accompany her, and if Nick or Paul showed up, he could kick the crap out of them all over again.

She took the sandwich outside and ate on the deck, washing it down with a Coke. It was a little cool despite the sun, but it helped wake her up. Plus, she found the earthy aromas of the forest soothing.

She stared at the mountains and chewed slowly, her thoughts turning inward and plunging below the surface into a deeper—and at times darker—place than the shallow comfort zone where most people chose to live out their lives. She considered herself a wild and free spirit, but she also fancied herself something of a philosopher. Not the structured theories of Freud or Jung or Nietzsche, but a philosophy of her own creation. When it came to deep thinking, as in all aspects of her life, she played by her own rules.

For example, most people dismissed love at first sight as nothing more than lust, but she believed—*knew*—you could fall in love with a total stranger. That was why she had approached Kane last night at the bar. She had taken just one look at him and felt something deep inside her stir, something that went beyond physical attraction. At that moment, perhaps sensing his emotional wounds, she had felt something for him and had acted on it.

For most people, sex was little more than animalistic coupling. They called it passion or lovemaking or intimacy, but in reality, it was rarely more than the pursuit of carnal satisfaction. Climax was the goal, orgasm the destination, physical release the desired outcome. Luna knew there was nothing wrong with that, but she also knew it paled in comparison to the mating of two souls.

She had believed that all of her adult life, but never experienced it...until last night. Kane had bared his soul to her. Let her glimpse his wounds, his scars, his doubts and darkness and demons. Her soul had responded by letting down its guard. As their bodies joined, so did their broken spirits, and in the consummation, they each found healing.

Lost in his own brokenness, Kane probably didn't know that he had healed her every bit as much as she had healed him. Maybe when he got back, she would tell him about her past, about the abuse, about the horrors of her childhood that had taught her to stand up to men with fire and defiance. Maybe she would tell him she had killed her father with a ceremonial tomahawk when she was seventeen because she refused to suffer even one more violation at his sick, perverted hands. Maybe she would even tell him about burying her father's body in these very woods.

Or maybe she would just thank him for giving her love that was not dark and twisted and full of thorns.

She was no fool. She knew this love could not, would not last, nor was it meant to. Even in the midst of their passion last night, even as their flesh and souls merged, she'd sensed that Kane's heart belonged to another. She had felt him holding back some sliver of himself, some piece of his heart that had been compartmentalized. Something he could not give her because it belonged to someone else.

As Kane slept last night, he had dreamed, and as he dreamed, he'd murmured a name: Cara. The way he'd said her name made it clear, even in the darkest, drowsiest hours of the night, that she was the one who held the missing piece, the one who could put his broken self back together once and for all.

With the sun kissing her face and the soft breeze ruffling her hair, Luna smiled. Being a self-honest person, she admitted she felt a twinge of jealousy toward the unknown woman, but that was all it was—a little twinge. She thanked God or destiny or whatever whimsical name you wanted to call it for however long she had with Kane. She might shed a tear when he rode off into the proverbial sunset, but it would not be a tear of regret.

Neither of them had known until the moment it happened, but Kane had needed her, and she had needed him. Not forever, just for a time.

It was enough.

A chipmunk scrambled up on to the picnic table, pulling her from her thoughts. Tail flicking, the cute little rodent darted closer, nose and whiskers twitching, checking to see if she had any food for him.

"Sorry, little guy," she said. "All I've got is one last bite of ham and egg sandwich, and I'm guessing that's not what you're looking for."

The chipmunk chittered at her, then dashed to the edge of the table. As Luna popped the last morsel of sandwich in her mouth, the chipmunk suddenly stood up on its back legs and looked toward the trail, clearly on high alert.

"What is it, fella?"

A few seconds later, Luna heard it.

The sound of an engine approaching.

The rumble of a heavy-duty motor disturbed the stillness and serenity of the woods. With a loud squeak of alarm, the chipmunk leaped off the table and vanished into a woodpile. A jay perched in a nearby pine tree took flight in a flash of blue, screeching out a warning.

Luna felt a cold knot of tension coil in the pit of her stomach. She wasn't sure why—this could be nothing more than Ernie coming up to check on Kane—but she had learned to trust her instincts.

She darted back inside the cabin and grabbed the SIG M17 off the table. She was no gun expert—the only way she knew the make and model of the pistol was because it was stamped on the weapon—but she knew how to disengage the safety and pull the trigger.

She tucked the handgun into the waistband of her jeans at the small of her back, covered by the tail of her untucked flannel shirt. The hard metal felt cold against her skin. She made sure the Sig was loose enough to be drawn quickly if necessary.

Stepping back outside, she heard the sound of the engine shift as the vehicle started up the incline to the cabin. Her tension worsened as she recognized the sound of the motor. Knowing who was about to pay her a visit, she was damn glad she had armed herself.

The 1996 Ford Bronco crested the hillock, the chrome brush guard coming into view first like the blunt snout of some lumbering prehistoric beast. The rest of the truck followed, the oversized tires easily devouring the trail. A light bar was centered on the roof just above the wind-shield, the official red and blue sandwiched between two non-regulation spot-lamps. The truck was painted white, with the Vesper Lake Sheriff's Department logo painted on the side.

Behind the wheel sat Sheriff Duncan "Double D" Dunkirk.

Below his mirrored aviator sunglasses that looked like they belonged to a rogue cop in a 1986 action movie, the lawman's mouth curled into a cruel smile when he saw Luna standing outside the cabin. Nick rode shotgun, and she could see Paul wedged in the back.

The Ford halted next to Kane's Jeep. Dunkirk killed the engine, and all three men exited the vehicle. They moved slow and steady, no rush, acting like they were completely in charge.

The sheriff was in full uniform, including a .40 caliber Glock 22 pistol holstered on his right hip and magazine pouches on the left. A cowboy hat perched on his head, a gold sheriff's star embroidered on the front. The hat violated the department's uniform policy, but nobody in town, including the mayor, dared tell the crooked lawman he couldn't wear it.

Nick wore jeans and a light jacket. The ruts where Luna had clawed him the night before had scabbed over, leaving dark stripes on his face. He moved carefully, no doubt favoring the cracked rib Kane had given him. Peeking out from beneath the cuff of his jacket was the cast for his broken wrist. Even from twenty-five yards away, Luna could clearly see the hate in his eyes. It was almost as cold as the metal of the sawed-off pump-action shotgun he held in his left hand.

Deep down inside, she began to steel herself to the fact that if she wanted to survive this confrontation, she would probably have to kill for the second time in her life. The gun nestled at the small of her back felt like both a blessing and a curse.

Paul, wearing a duck hunter's vest and some kind of urban tactical pants that seemed stupidly out of place here in the forest, stood slightly behind his brother. Somebody had fixed his broken nose, but it still looked red and swollen. It would make a dandy target if—or more likely, *when*—shooting time came. He didn't appear to be armed, but Paul had always been more of a hand-to-hand brawler anyway. Still, she couldn't rule out that he had a pistol or blade concealed somewhere.

The Dunkirks lined up and walked toward her like a trio of outlaws strolling toward a high-noon showdown in some old western. Her adrenalin spiked and she struggled to control the shakes, just barely managing to keep them at bay. These three assholes knew they had her outnumbered and outgunned. They expected her to show fear. She'd be damned if she was going to give them the satisfaction of seeing her tremble. Besides, the secret Sig put her on a far more equal footing than the sheriff and his sons believed.

She would do her best to talk her way out of this one, but if violence turned out to be the only language they would listen to? Well, then she would shoot first and ask questions later. Better to be judged by twelve than carried by six, as the saying went.

The Dunkirks halted about fifteen feet in front of her, Nick on the sheriff's left, Paul on the right. Nick canted the shotgun over his shoulder in a casual manner, as if he didn't have a care in the world.

Sheriff Dunkirk reached up and touched the brim of his hat in a gentlemanly gesture that was as fake as a four-dollar bill. "Afternoon, Luna. Wondered where you'd run off to. We've been looking for you."

"Looking for you," Paul echoed.

"Well, you found me," Luna said. "So why don't you tell me what the hell you want so we can get this over with, and I can get back to my peace and quiet?"

Nick tapped the shotgun against his shoulder. "Peace and quiet ain't on the menu today, Luna."

"Ain't on the menu," Paul agreed.

"Where's your friend?" the sheriff asked. "I'd like to have a chat with him."

Luna didn't even try to play coy. "Out hiking," she replied.

"Who is he, Luna?"

"Calls himself Kane."

"You screw him?"

"Can't see how that's any of your business."

"Normally, I would agree with you," the sheriff said. "But this ain't a normal day."

"Ain't a normal day," Paul repeated.

Luna replied, "Looks like a normal day to me."

"That's where you're wrong," Sheriff Dunkirk said. "Because on a normal day, you wouldn't be hiding out with some two-bit stranger who rode into my town and proceeded to not only kick my boys' asses, but the whole damn bar's."

"Whole damn bar," Paul affirmed.

"Kane was minding his own business until these two assholes"—she pointed at Nick and Paul—"decided to damn near rape me right there on the dance floor."

"That a fact?" The sheriff smiled. "Way I heard it, you were shaking your stuff all over Saws 'n' Suds, pretty much begging for it."

"Begging for it," Paul said.

"So now dancing in a bar is justification for your two meatheads to have their way with a girl?"

The lawman's smile evaporated in the blink of an eye like a drop of dew hit by a blowtorch. "This is my town, bitch, and my boys will have any goddamned thing they please."

Luna knew the situation had just taken a serious downturn, transitioning from mock-pleasantries and fake chitchat to cold malevolence and angry threats. Her muscles tensed, ready to make her move when they reached the point of no return. Which, short of a miracle, wouldn't be long now.

She didn't raise her voice, but she injected steel into her tone when she said, "I don't care who you are, sheriff. I'm not a plaything for your boys."

"So, my sons aren't good enough for ya, but you'll spread your legs for a drifter."

"I'm sticking to my guns on this topic," Luna said, cognizant of the irony in the statement as she felt the pistol lying cool against her skin. "None of your business who I sleep with."

The sheriff shook his head. "You messed up last night, girl. Not only did you hurt one of my boys, but you stood by and let a fucking stranger hurt them even more. And then you added insult to injury by shacking up with that stranger." He hooked his thumbs behind his belt buckle. "I can't let that kind of behavior go unpunished, Luna. I let you get away with that shit, folks in town will start thinking they don't have to do what I tell them, and I can't have that."

Luna took one last shot at talking it out, knowing that if she failed, the next shot would come from the barrel of a gun. "Listen, sheriff, just walk away, and I'll make Kane leave town as soon as he gets back. Just get back in the truck and drive away, and I'll fix this."

The lawman shook his head again. "We've gone beyond that now, Luna. The time for walking away—for you and this Kane bastard—was last night. Since you didn't walk away then, we can't walk away now."

Luna's eyes narrowed as her heart started hammering. "What exactly do you want, sheriff?"

"Kane's life and your ass."

"Your ass." Paul sounded downright giddy at the prospect.

"You want Kane's life, take it up with him," Luna said. "You want my ass, you'll have to take it over my dead body."

"Don't make this hard, girl," the sheriff warned.

"Hard!" Paul hooted, and the growing bulge at the front of his pants testified that he was telling the truth.

"You heard me, sheriff," Luna said. "Those two sons of bitches who call you daddy try to put their hands on me, I swear to God I'll kill 'em."

"Enough of this crap." Nick started to bring the shotgun down from his shoulder. "I'll just kneecap the whore and bend her crippled ass over that table."

Now! Luna's mind screamed at her. *You've gotta move NOW!*

She reached behind her, fingers wrapping around the Sig. Just before the shotgun muzzle dropped down low enough to blast her, she whipped out the pistol and pointed it one-handed at Nick's face. Before anyone could react to her sudden move, she pulled the trigger.

The bullet plowed into Nick's right eye.

The shotgun fell unfired from his suddenly-spasming hands, and his head jerked to the side as a large chunk of his skull flew off in a spray of blood and brains. He corkscrewed to the ground, dead before his shocked face bounced off the dirt.

Snarling a curse, Sheriff Dunkirk reached for his Glock.

Luna darted sideways and took cover behind the massive stone fireplace as she heard the lawman roar, "You fucking *bitch!*" He punctuated the profanity with two quick shots, both of which ricocheted off the rocks.

Luna responded by blindly reaching around the corner and capping off a couple of rounds. She didn't expect to hit anything but hoped it would be enough to keep them at bay.

She clearly missed the sheriff because as soon as the sound of the gunshots stopped reverberating through the trees, he bellowed, "You fucking whore! You killed Nick! You're gonna die hard, Luna!"

"Die hard!" Paul cried out, and she could hear the grief in his voice. Apparently, even dumbasses loved their big brothers.

Following those outbursts, everything went silent.

Luna wanted to peek around the corner and see what the two men were up to, but she didn't want to risk catching a round in her eye socket like Nick.

She took advantage of the lull to examine her options.

The fireplace was built near the edge of the hillock, meaning the ground dropped off sharply just a few feet behind her. Not quite a cliff, but close, with swampy ground, rotting stumps, and tangled deadfalls at the bottom. Throwing herself over the edge would be better than the rape-murder fate the Dunkirks had in store for her, but it was a last resort, a desperation option. A suicide play, really, because the leap would most likely kill her.

Problem was, to her left and right loomed nothing but open space. If she tried to run in either direction, she would be exposed and vulnerable, and the sheriff would pick her off easily.

The best thing she could do was wait it out. They might try to come at her from the right and left at the same time—flanking, she thought it was called—but if they did, she could at least get off some shots and maybe get lucky.

She heard footsteps walking away from her, followed

by the sound of a truck door opening. A moment later, the door slammed shut, and the footsteps came back.

"Hey, Luna," Sheriff Dunkirk called. "I've got some bad news for you."

"Bad news," Paul echoed, his psychological compulsion still ticking despite his grief.

She almost remained silent, but then changed her mind. As long as they kept talking, it meant the bastards weren't actively trying to kill her at that particular moment. Given her pinned-down position, chatting was better than shooting.

"Yeah?" she said. "What's that?"

"I've got a grenade launcher, Luna, and I'm going to blow that fireplace to rubble if you don't get your murdering ass out here."

A grenade launcher? What the hell?

She risked a quick glance around the corner, keeping low and only exposing her right eye for a few seconds. She saw the sheriff holding an assault rifle that sort of looked like an M-16, only shorter. There was some kind of black tube beneath the barrel that she assumed was the grenade launcher.

She slid back behind cover, mind racing, sifting through her limited options. She could charge the Dunkirks with gun blasting, going out in a blaze of glory. Or she could take the suicide leap over the edge.

Either way, it looked like she was about to die.

No time to make peace with her Maker. She would just have to hope God was in a good mood when she knocked on Heaven's door.

Dunkirk snarled, "Have it your way, bitch. This is for Nick."

"For Nick," Paul said.

Luna heard a *whump* and instinctively knew there was a grenade whistling her way.

Time for this angel to fly.

She threw herself over the edge into space.

The world exploded around her.

The blast smashed her in midair like a giant's invisible fist, hurling her even farther out over the edge. Stone shrapnel slashed all around her, peppering her body like buckshot. As she started her descent toward the trees and boulders below, something crashed into the back of her head. She fell the rest of the way in blackness.

When she hit the earth, body breaking as it bounced off unyielding rock and wood, she didn't feel a thing.

* * *

Kane was two miles northwest of Dribble Creek Camp when he thought he heard gunshots. He paused and listened intently. Sound could travel a long way up here in the mountains, but sometimes the thick forest acted as a natural noise barrier, making it difficult to decipher the source of the sound and where it was originating from.

It sounded like a single shot from a handgun, followed by a couple more shots from a different handgun, followed by two more shots from the first one. But he couldn't be sure.

He had just started walking again when he heard the explosion. This time the sound was easier to pinpoint. It had definitely come from the vicinity of the cabin.

Kane felt something curdle deep down in his guts. These woods made running impossible, but he picked up the pace, moving toward the cabin—and Luna—as swiftly as the rugged terrain allowed.

He steeled himself against what he might find when he got there.

* * *

Luna woke up in a world of horrific pain and wondered if she had gone to Hell when she died.

Everything hurt. Thorns were twisted and tangled in her hair, and she could feel lacerations all over her scalp. Her left eye was swollen shut, and her right cheek was ripped open so badly that she could feel the breeze on her exposed teeth. Her nose was flattened and askew, caked with blackened blood.

She tried to move her arms and nearly passed out from the sharp agony. They were both broken. More pain seared through her sides, and it was hard to breathe. From somewhere deep inside her battered brain came the knowledge that she must have snapped some ribs and punctured a lung.

Turning her head and using her one good eye, she discovered that she was lying on the picnic table, the planks rough against her back since her shirt was nothing but shredded rags. She tried moving her legs and they responded, so they weren't broken, and neither was her spine. But her knees felt like someone had hammered on them with a meat tenderizer, and her right shin was gashed to the bone.

Through the nauseating waves of pain, it all came back to her. Killing Nick. Taking cover behind the fireplace. The grenade. The explosion. Flying through the air.

Blackness.

Clearly, the fall had not killed her, although, given the agony racking her battered body, death might have been the more preferable outcome. But that didn't explain how she had ended up back here.

As if on cue, Sheriff Dunkirk stepped out of the cabin, followed Paul, and proceeded to supply an explanation.

"Gotta tell ya, Luna," the lawman said. "It was a real bitch hauling your busted ass back up here."

"Busted ass," Paul muttered. He had removed his vest, revealing a shirt soaked with sweat. Twigs and brambles clung to his pants. The sheriff might be claiming credit for dragging her back up the hillock, but it looked like Paul had done the actual work.

"Whuh...why?" Luna struggled to form the word. It hurt like hell to talk. The movement of her jaw caused the flap of skin from her torn to cheek to move as well, sending fiery pain blazing through her face. She truly didn't understand why they had carried her back up here. They could have just killed her at the bottom of the hillock.

"Two reasons," Sheriff Dunkirk replied. "One, I want your boyfriend to see what we did to you when he gets back. Two, since you didn't do yourself a favor and die when you jumped off that fucking cliff, I figured we might as well have a little more fun with you."

"Fun with you," Paul repeated.

The sheriff walked over and stood directly behind her. Tilting her head back, she saw him pull a large folding knife from his pocket and flick open the blade. The shiny steel glinted in the afternoon sunlight.

Suffering from pain behind anything she had ever experienced, Luna inwardly raged against the injustice of it all. If only she had just died in the explosion. Or if only the fall had killed her. Then she wouldn't have to endure whatever torments the Dunkirks had in store for her.

Oblivion would be a mercy at this point because life had become a living nightmare.

"Just...kill...me," she moaned. "Please..."

"It's coming, girl. Right after Paul does."

Through her haze of pain, she didn't grasp what the sheriff's words meant, but when she felt Paul tear away the shredded remnants of her jeans, she became sickeningly aware that her hell on earth was about to become a whole lot worse.

She tried to fight, but half-blind, with broken arms and a punctured lung, it was impossible to fend him off. She managed a few feeble kicks that he easily swatted aside. Then Paul began to brutally punish her stricken body, grunting like an angry gorilla as he took out his rage on her.

She just laid there, unmoving, waiting for the inevitable end. She didn't even feel the sheriff take his turn. She stared up at the sky as a hawk rode the thermals far above her, perhaps waiting for her soul to join it in the heavens.

She watched the hawk circle for an unknown number of heartbeats, then slowly closed her eyes. She heard the sheriff say something but couldn't make out the words. Whatever it was, it no longer mattered.

The last thing she felt was the razor-sharp blade cutting her throat.

NINE

Dribble Creek Camp

Kane approached the cabin from the west, using the trail that snaked through the giant boulders just beyond the outhouse. Patches of sweat stained his clothes, and he was breathing a little hard from the exertion of double-timing it over two miles of rough terrain, but the Desert Eagle XIX L6 was rock-steady in his hand.

He pulled up behind one of the boulders to recon the scene. Parked next to his Jeep Wrangler was a kitted-out Ford Bronco with the sheriff's department emblem painted on the door. Clearly, the law—or the abomination that passed for law in this town—had paid the cabin a visit. Given the thrashing he had dished out to the sheriff's sons last night, Kane highly doubted the man had come up here to protect and serve.

The outdoor fireplace was a pile of rubble, scorch marks on the rocks indicating it had been blown apart by some kind of bomb or grenade. Kane couldn't figure out why someone would do that, but he didn't have all the puzzle pieces yet. Hard to put together the big picture with limited scraps of information.

His eyes moved to the picnic table. Dark stains covered the surface. He recognized coagulated blood when he saw it. Had this been a few months earlier in the hot summer months, the puddle of sticky gore would have been buzzing with black, bloated blowflies.

Something dark and cold crawled through his veins. It was impossible for whoever had spilled that much blood to still be alive. That much blood meant no survivor. Somebody had died here today.

Kane gritted his teeth. If that somebody turned out to be Luna, he vowed there would be more bodies on this mountain before the sun set.

But he was jumping the gun. No point in swearing revenge until he knew for sure whether or not she was dead. Maybe the blood belonged to someone else.

A man could hope.

He moved out from behind the boulder with the Desert Eagle leading the way. Coming in from the west, no windows faced his direction, so nobody could snipe him from inside the cabin.

He darted across the top of the hillock and took up position to the right of the door. He pressed his ear against the wall and listened.

Nothing.

He couldn't hear any movement or voices in the cabin. Not the creak of a floorboard, not the scrape of a chair, not a murmured conversation. Nothing.

Then, abruptly breaking the silence, came a growled voice from inside.

"Time to gut this bitch."

Kane knew he couldn't wait any longer.

He kicked in the door and charged through, muzzle-first.

It took him two seconds to realize he'd been fooled.

In the first second, his eyes took in Luna's dead, naked body, swinging from a hangman's noose in the doorway between the mudroom and the main room. He didn't have time to catalog her various wounds, but the image of her deep-slashed throat seared into his retinas like a tattoo needle.

In the next second, he realized someone lurked behind him. He started to turn and caught a glimpse of Paul Dunkirk as the sheriff's son hit him with what felt like a million volts from the stun gun in his hand.

The Desert Eagle fell to the floor as the electricity in Kane's body began to misfire. Another heartbeat and his muscles started to seize and spasm. Dizziness swarmed his brain. Another crackling second, and his sense of balance went bye-bye. He dropped to his knees, inca-pacitated.

Through all the shaking and shuddering, Kane saw a man wearing a sheriff's badge—Sheriff Duncan Dunkirk, he presumed—step into the room, pushing aside Luna's body to come through the doorway. Behind him, her corpse swung grotesquely.

"Nice to meet you, Kane," the sheriff said. "Can't believe you fell for that trick." He reached behind him and patted Luna's naked thigh. "Then again, love makes fools of us all."

"Fucker," Kane spat as his teeth chattered and his jaw muscles twitched.

"Yeah, yeah. Sticks and stones and all that shit." The sheriff stepped forward and lifted his foot. "Lights out, tough guy."

"Lights out," Paul echoed.

The heavy sole of the lawman's boot crashed into Kane's face hard enough to leave a tread-print on his forehead. He flipped backward, powerless to do anything as his electrical circuits continued to misfire. He crashed down on his side, reeling but not quite knocked out.

The sheriff's follow-up kick banged into his temple, and Kane plunged into unconsciousness.

When he regained consciousness, the first thing he saw was Luna's smile above him. It took him a few seconds to remember where he was and realize it wasn't her smile, it was the red slash carved in the pale, white flesh of her throat. He silently cursed himself for getting involved with her, for driving into this rotten town and getting her killed. He knew she wouldn't have wanted him to blame himself for her death, but he couldn't shake the feeling of guilt. He had come here looking for some kind of redemption, and she had paid the price.

"Well, well, look who's returned to the land of the living?"

Sheriff Dunkirk sat at the table in the main room, while Kane was stretched out on the floor, turned on his side due to his hands being cuffed behind his back. His head throbbed from the vicious kicks. He hoped he didn't have a concussion. His ankles were bound together with duct tape. Must be the small-town sheriff didn't carry leg shackles with him.

Kane didn't know how long he'd been knocked out, but it was long enough for his muscles to stop seizing. They still ached like hell, but he was used to pushing past pain and would do so again if the Dunkirks gave him a chance to settle the score.

Of course, with his hands cuffed behind him and his legs wrapped in enough duct tape to immobilize a pissed-off honey badger, getting that chance seemed like a real long shot at this point.

Paul stood over him. No sign of the stun gun. "Land of the living," he repeated.

Kane looked up at him. "You're a goddamned idiot. You know that, right?"

Paul kicked him in the stomach so hard that Kane thought he might have ruptured his spleen.

The sheriff chuckled. "Some folks might say an idiot is someone who spouts insults while they're trussed up like a hog on Fourth of July."

"Fourth of July," Paul echoed.

Kane turned his head and spat. No blood. That was a good sign. Didn't change the fact that when it came his turn to do the kicking, he intended to rupture Paul's internal organs until he puked red by the gallon. They had killed Luna. There would be no forgiveness.

Sheriff Dunkirk caught his mood. "You got killing in your eyes, boy."

"Take these cuffs off, and you'll find out there's plenty of killing in my bare hands."

"Not gonna happen," the lawman replied. "You've got skills, that much is obvious. You took on a whole stinking bar last night and walked away with barely a scratch."

"Barely a scratch," Paul repeated.

"Only a pussy kicks a man when he's on the ground."

"Nice try, boy, but I know what you're trying to do, and I ain't falling for it. Only a fool gives up the upper hand once he's got it. Now, care to tell me your name?"

"Why? You planning to put it on my gravestone?"

"I'm not going to kill you."

"Any reason why I should believe that?"

The sheriff smirked. "Because what I've got in mind for you is a fate worse than death."

"Worse than death," Paul agreed.

"So let's hear it," Kane said.

"Tell me your name—hell, make one up for all I care —and I'll give you all the gory details about what's going to happen to your miserable ass."

"Call me Kane."

"Real name or bullshit?"

"It's real enough." Kane flexed his wrists, testing to see if there was any give, any way to slide out of the handcuffs. No such luck.

"Well, Kane," Sheriff Dunkirk said, "you're not going to die. At least, not by my hand. But you *are* going to hell."

"Going to hell," Paul confirmed.

"Never cared much for riddles," Kane said. "Do me a favor and tell it plain."

"Let's see if this is plain enough for you," the sheriff replied. "You're going to prison."

"Prison!" Paul sounded like an excited eight-year-old screeching about Disney World.

Kane immediately understood his fate and felt cold despair slither through his guts like an unholy snake.

Sheriff Dunkirk confirmed it a second later. "I'm throwing your ass into Black Bog Federal Prison. There's more to you than meets the eye, Kane, and Nazareno will dig it out of you, or just dig out your eyes." He leaned forward in his chair as if wanting to whisper a conspiratorial secret. "And even if Nazareno decides to let you live, when word gets out that you raped and killed a pretty young girl like Luna? Well, let's just say the Black Bog inmates ain't no choirboys, and jailhouse justice is a real thing."

"Real thing," Paul said.

Up until that moment, Kane had not wanted to consider that Luna had been sexually assaulted, despite her body being naked. But the sheriff's words confirmed that particular horror, and now he had to live with it. The desire—no, the *need*—to avenge the atrocities committed against her burned through his veins like molten lava and set his brain on fire.

His cold, angry eyes locked onto the lawman's weather-worn face. "I've just got one question."

"So, ask."

"Which one of you raped her?"

Without hesitation, the sheriff replied, "We both took a turn."

Paul beamed proudly. "I went first," he said. "She liked it."

"And then I took a turn," Sheriff Dunkirk said. "Then I cut her throat."

Through gritted teeth, Kane stared at Paul and rasped, "You get to die first, you son of a bitch." His eyes shifted to the sheriff, dark, icy holes of hate and rage. "But you'll die harder."

The lawman appeared unfazed. "Tough words from a man who'll be dead by dawn." He stood up and gestured to Paul. "Get him in the truck."

The sheriff cut down Luna's body as Paul hauled Kane to his feet. Kane made the snap decision that if they cut the duct tape off his ankles so he could walk, he was going to try to take them out using just his feet. Kick their knees, bring them down, and then stomp them into unconsciousness or break their goddamned necks.

That notion went out the window a moment later when Paul slung him over his shoulder like a bag of concrete mix, grunting from the effort—at six-foot-four and packed with hard muscle, Kane was not a feather-weight—and carried him outside. Whether deliberately or by accident, he banged Kane's head off doorjambs and walls a bunch of times on the way out. Kane cursed every blow because right now, that was all he could do.

His last image of Luna was Sheriff Dunkirk dragging her naked, bloody body into the corner. The evil smile on the lawman's face made Kane want to blow his teeth out the back of his head. He again vowed that Luna's murder would not go unavenged. He would either make the sick bastards pay for what they had done or die trying.

Right now, the latter seemed more likely.

Paul shoved him into the back of the Bronco, which had been retrofitted with a prisoner cage, bouncing his head off the side of the truck in the process.

"Oops," Paul said with mouth-breather sarcasm. "Sorry."

"Don't sweat it," Kane replied with a wolfish smile. "Someday, I'll return the favor and crack your skull."

Circling around the front of the Ford, Sheriff Dunkirk said, "I admire your fighting spirit, Kane, I really do. But your grasp on reality is a little lacking."

Turning his head, Kane saw Nick Dunkirk's body stuffed into the cargo box behind him, the back of his head blown open. He hoped like hell Luna had done it, that she had managed to kill the bastard before she died. It would be just like her to go down fighting.

As he opened the driver's side door, Sheriff Dunkirk caught Kane looking at the corpse and confirmed what Kane had suspected. "That bitch killed my son," he growled. "Everything we did to her, she had it coming."

Kane stared straight ahead and stoked the fires of hate burning deep down inside. He would need all that hate, all the fury and sorrow and thirst for vengeance, to survive what came next. His will to live would be fueled by those dark emotions. He was about to be thrown into a wicked, violent hellhole. If he wanted to have any chance of coming out the other side alive, he would need to tap into his primal instincts.

As the sheriff settled into the driver's seat, Paul riding shotgun, Kane asked, "What are you going to do with Luna's body?"

"She'll be cremated," the lawman replied, turning to give him one of his trademark *I'm-an-evil-shmuck* grins.

"Cremated," Paul said, laughing like it was the best joke ever told.

A moment later, Kane saw what they were grinning and laughing about.

Smoke started rolling out the cabin's open windows and he saw flames flickering inside, like catching glimpses of hell through a thick, black fog.

"You're a real bastard, Kane." The sheriff smirked. "Brought poor Luna all the way up here, raped her, cut her throat, and then burned the place to the ground." He shook his head in mock disbelief. "Yup, you're a bad, bad man."

Yeah, I'm a bad man, all right, Kane thought. *And you two assholes are on my shit list.*

Some people just didn't know when they'd fucked with the wrong person.

The Ford Bronco easily handled the rough trail as they drove away from Dribble Creek. Two miles later, as they crossed the grassy field by Ernie Foxx's house, Kane saw Foxx standing outside, Doofus beside him. As they got closer, Kane saw that Foxx was staring off into the distance, back the way they had come. No doubt, smoke from the burning cabin had billowed high enough to be spotted.

The Ford pulled up next to Foxx, and Sheriff Dunkirk cranked down the window. "Afternoon, Ernie. Sorry to tell you that I've got some bad news."

"Bad news," Paul said.

Foxx looked at Kane for a second—was that sympathy in his eyes?—then at the sheriff. "Bad news, huh? Worse than the fact that my camp seems to be on fire?"

The lawman nodded. "Dunkirk nodded. "Afraid so, Ernie. You see, this son of a bitch—" he jerked a thumb over his shoulder at Kane, "raped and murdered Luna up at your cabin, then set it on fire." He shook his head. "Hope you got insurance. You really ought to be more careful about who you rent your place to."

Foxx seemed taken aback by the news. "My God. Luna's dead?"

"Yep. This goddamned drifter cut her throat from ear to ear."

"Ear to ear," Paul echoed.

Foxx looked at Kane again. He clearly didn't believe a word of the bullshit the sheriff was feeding him, which was nice, but didn't help him much. Foxx was one of the sheep he and Luna had talked about last night. A good man, but unwilling to fight the evil strangling the town. As a gun enthusiast, Foxx no doubt had an arsenal in his house, but they would remain weapons of leisure, not weapons of war. Especially a war against law enforcement, no matter how corrupt.

Some people saw a tin star pinned on a man's chest and believed the man wearing it was untouchable.

In Sheriff Dunkirk's case, Kane considered the tarnished star a target and would happily put a bullet through it.

"Can't abide rapists and murderers," Foxx said. "So if he did it, I hope he gets what he's got coming to him."

Sheriff Dunkirk's tone changed abruptly, oozing menace. "What do you mean, 'if he did it?' You calling me a liar, Ernie? That what you're doing?"

Foxx held up his hands. "No, sir. Not me. If you say John did it, then he did it."

"Oh, so it's 'John,' is it? Didn't realize you and him were on a first-name basis."

"C'mon, sheriff." A pleading tone crept into Foxx's voice as he realized he had gotten on the lawman's bad side. "I know his first name because I rented him the cabin."

"Sounds like you two are downright good and goddamned friendly. He just told me to call him Kane. Didn't offer a first name."

Kane snarled, "That's because I don't give out my first name to assholes like you." He was trying to deflect the sheriff's rising anger back onto him.

The lawman ignored him and continued to speak to Foxx. "Gotta tell ya, Ernie, I find this completely unacceptable. You believing a stranger over your own sheriff, I mean."

"It was a slip of the tongue, sheriff. Just a poor choice of words. If you say he did it, then that's what happened."

Sheriff Dunkirk opened the Bronco's door and climbed out of the vehicle. Kane clenched his teeth in frustration. This was going to end badly, and there was nothing he could do but sit in this damn cage and fume.

"Problem is," the sheriff said, clipping his syllables to signify his displeasure, "I don't fucking believe you, Ernie."

"Sheriff, I swear—"

"Shut up."

Still sitting inside the Bronco, Paul echoed, "Shut up."

Ernie obeyed.

The sheriff drew his Glock 19.

"Hey," Ernie protested. "What the hell?"

"I said, shut up."

"Shut up," Paul repeated.

Ernie obeyed again but kept a wary eye on the drawn pistol.

Kane brought his duct-taped feet up and kicked the steel mesh barrier in frustration. "Dunkirk!" he roared, doing his damnedest to reclaim the sheriff's attention. "Dunkirk, you motherfucker!"

Paul turned around in the passenger seat and pointed a finger at him like a schoolmarm scolding an unruly child. "Shut up, asshole, or I'll cut your tongue out."

Sheriff Dunkirk ignored the hostilities going on inside the truck, focused on the hostility taking place outside it. The Glock stayed down by his side, but he took a step toward Foxx. "I can't allow this to stand, Ernie," he said. "I let you start questioning me, pretty soon word'll get out, and the whole damn town will be questioning me. That's how rebellions start, and I'll not be having any rebellions on my watch."

The door to the house opened, and a woman stepped out onto the porch in what looked like some kind of purple-dyed buckskin housedress. Calling her obese would have been a mild exaggeration, but she definitely edged in that direction. The bag of Cool Ranch Doritos in her doughy hands wasn't doing anything to change that. Despite it being mid-afternoon, she wore pink and green curlers in her hair.

"Sheriff, what in the blue blazes is the meaning of this?"

Judging a book by its cover, Kane had expected her voice to be shrill. It was actually soft and pleasant, although more than a little annoyed.

With a stricken look on his face, Foxx tried to wave the woman away. "Go back inside, Franny. Have another doughnut, and let us men finish our chat."

"I don't know who you think you're talking to," Franny snapped, "but it better not be me."

"Just a little misunderstanding, Franny," Sheriff Dunkirk called out. "Might be best if you do like Ernie says and go back inside until we get things straightened out."

"Yeah? And it might be best if you kiss my ass. How about that? And if it's just a little misunderstanding, why is your gun out?"

The sheriff stepped closer to Foxx. He kept his voice low enough to not be heard by Franny, but his words floated back through the open Bronco door to Kane. "Cat or wife, Ernie?"

Foxx blanched. "What do you mean?" The look on his face made it clear he knew exactly what the sheriff meant.

The lawman spelled it out anyway. "Best way to stop a rebellion is to crush it right in its tracks before it can even get started. I could just put a bullet in you and be done with the whole thing, but I ain't gonna do that. But you are gonna pay a price. So, cat or wife?"

"For the love of God, don't do this!"

"Don't go bringing God into the devil's work," Sheriff Dunkirk growled. "Last chance, Ernie. If you don't pick one, I'll kill 'em both."

"Kill 'em both," Paul repeated.

Foxx said, "I can't..."

"Fine, have it your way." The Glock started to swing up.

Foxx yelled, "Franny, RUN!"

The panic in his voice let his wife know something was terribly wrong. She dropped the bag of Doritos and tried to run back into the house.

Foxx lunged for the gun, but the sheriff was too quick. The Glock's sharp *bang!* sent a .40 caliber bullet ripping through the air.

The projectile smashed into the back of Franny's head just as she made it to the doorway. Dead on her feet, the lethal impact flung her lifeless body forward and into the house. Even from inside the Bronco, Kane heard the heavy crash of her corpse hitting the floor.

Foxx managed to grab Dunkirk's wrist, but the old man proved no match for the sheriff. The lawman jerked his arm away and lashed the barrel of the Glock across Foxx's face, splitting the flesh over his cheek down to the bone. Foxx stumbled to the side, tripped over Doofus, and went down in the dirt.

The cat crouched and hissed.

The Glock blasted again.

With a single, pained yowl, Doofus died.

"No!" Foxx sobbed, clutching at the Maine Coon's bloody fur.

Kane kicked at the steel mesh again, knowing it wouldn't accomplish anything but venting his rage and frustration. "Dunkirk!" he snarled. "You goddamned son of a bitch!" Given the chance, he would have torn the sheriff's head off his shoulders with his bare hands.

Paul slapped the barrier with the palm of his hand. "Shut up!"

Sheriff Dunkirk crouched next to the fallen man and

his feline companion. "Don't ever cross me again, Ernie. Or next time, I won't be so nice."

Foxx stared up at him with weeping eyes. Kane knew a broken man when he saw one.

"We clear?" the sheriff asked, low and threatening.

Foxx nodded and choked on another sob.

"Think of all this as a chance to start fresh, Ernie. New camp, new cat, new wife. It's like you're being born again. Now that I think about it, you should probably thank me for what I've done here today."

Foxx bowed his head, tears dripping into the dirt.

Sheriff Dunkirk reached out, put the Glock's muzzle under the old man's chin, and forced his head back up. "Go on," the lawman hissed. "Say thank you."

Kane couldn't remember the last time he had wanted to kill someone so badly. "C'mon, Dunkirk!" he roared. "What more do you want from him?"

The sheriff turned his head toward Kane and smiled cruelly. "I want him to say thank you."

Kane knew if that if it was him down there in the dirt, the only thing he would tell Dunkirk would be to go fuck himself, even if that meant eating a bullet. He also knew that Foxx wasn't built that way. Some men find the grit and steel inside themselves when they are bullied and backed into a corner; others just crack.

Foxx cracked.

"Thank you," he croaked hoarsely.

Sheriff Dunkirk pulled the pistol out from under his chin, and Foxx's head immediately slumped again. The lawman patted him on the cheek. "You're quite welcome." He stood up and holstered the Glock. "My condolences on your losses today."

Still chuckling, the sheriff climbed back behind the wheel of the Bronco.

"You're a real piece of shit, you know that?" Kane rasped.

"His wife was fat bitch, and his cat was dumb as a box of rocks," the lawman replied. "I did old Ernie a favor, putting them out of his misery."

"Out of his misery," Paul repeated.

"Just so we're clear," Kane said. "I'm going to kill you."

"You're gonna have to break out of Hell to do it," Dunkirk said, shifting the Bronco into drive. "Next stop, Black Bog Federal Prison."

TEN

Black Bog Federal Prison

It took them less than ten minutes to reach the prison. A right-hand turn off Wolf Pond Road onto Route 73, then a quick left-hand turn onto an unmarked side road that ran along the base of a mountain before meandering through pine woods and stagnant wetlands. With the driver's side window rolled partway down, Kane could smell the dead water.

Coming around a bend, he spotted the bog for which the prison was named. The body of black water stretched for nearly a quarter-mile and looked to be at least two hundred meters across. All the trees around it were dead, and the whole area looked bleak and blighted.

As they swung into the prison's entrance, the Bronco's tires rumbled over a set of old railroad tracks that ran east-west along the northern edge of the marsh. Glancing in both directions, Kane saw that the crossties were rotted, and weeds had choked the gravel bed into submission. Clearly, no train had been through here in a long time.

"Where do those tracks go?" he asked.

Sheriff Dunkirk glanced at him in the rearview mirror. "Why the hell do you care?"

"Just curious."

"Some jackass city slicker with more money than sense tried to build a scenic railroad between Vesper Lake and Lake Placid," the sheriff said. "Laid about ten miles of tracks through the woods before calling it quits."

They drove through the parking lot and pulled right up to the front entrance. Inside the officer's station, Kane saw a prison guard talking into his radio. No doubt announcing his arrival and putting preparations in place.

Paul opened the door as Sheriff Dunkirk said, "You can behave yourself and come out on your own two feet, or I can have Paul drag you out by the ankles. Your choice."

"Your choice," Paul repeated.

Kane knew there was no point in resisting. Not right now, anyway. Better to save his strength for the battles to come. Once he was locked behind the razor wire, his life would become one big battle for survival.

"I'll walk," he said.

Paul nodded, pulled out a pocketknife, and leaned inside the prisoner cage to cut the duct tape.

As soon as he did, Kane brought his knee up sharply, smacking it into Paul's swollen nose. Fresh blood spurted.

Paul howled in pain and scrambled backward out of the Bronco, banging his head against the roof in the process. "You bastard!" he yelled.

Kane slid out of the truck and smiled thinly. "And then some."

Sheriff Dunkirk came around and took hold of Kane's handcuffs. "Cheap shot, Kane. I expected better from you."

"Being around you assholes brings out the worst in me."

Dunkirk marched him inside. The correctional officer behind the elevated desk nodded as they walked in. "Afternoon, Sheriff. What do you have for us today?"

"Off-the-books deposit."

"He got a name?"

"Calls himself John Kane."

"What'd he do?"

"Raped and killed a local girl."

The guard glared at Kane with disgust. "Should've just put a bullet in his head and dumped him in the woods."

"Figured Nazareno might like to use him in the Pit."

"He *is* a beefy slab of badass, ain't he?" The guard's eyes studied Kane's powerful frame.

"See something you like?" Kane asked.

"Shut up, convict, or I'll make you gargle pepper spray."

"Careful with this one," Sheriff Dunkirk warned. "He took on a whole bar last night and walked away with nothing more than bruised knuckles, so he's clearly got some hand-to-hand combat experience."

"Oh, yeah?" The guard nodded. "He'll be perfect for the Pit, then. As luck would have it, there's a match tomorrow night."

Through the barred window behind the officer's station, Kane saw a wide-shouldered man decked out in tactical gear lumbering down the walkway that seemed to lead to some sort of main building. An unseen control center, presumably monitoring the proceedings on CCTV surveillance cameras, buzzed him through two interlocking doors, and a few moments later, he stood in front of Kane.

"What do we have here?" the man asked, sizing Kane up. The guy was average height, maybe five-eight or five-nine, but bulked with muscle. The Velcro name tag on his Kevlar vest said GOATSACK.

Kane replied, "Just an innocent man that you're about to fuck with."

"Innocent?" Goatsack chuckled. "Well, hot damn, fella, you're gonna fit right in." He jerked a thumb over his shoulder. "Every last homeboy in there is innocent. Just ask 'em. Nothing but priests, choirboys, and Jesus-lovers, right down to the last swinging dick."

"No doubt," Kane said sarcastically.

Goatsack continued, "Thing is, buddy, I don't give a shit about your guilt or innocence. All I care about is that, for whatever reason, you're behind the razor wire, and that means your ass is mine."

"We'll see."

Goatsack's eyebrows shot up. "What did you just say?"

"Fancies himself a tough guy," Sheriff Dunkirk remarked. "Got a bit of the ol' badass in him."

"Does he, now?" Without warning, Goatsack swung a short, chopping uppercut into Kane's groin.

The fingerless leather tactical gloves the man wore did little to cushion the blow. Kane stumbled backward, biting back a groan, and fought the rising wave of nausea spiraling up from the pit of his stomach.

"How about now?" Goatsack asked. "Still feeling like a badass, boy?"

Kane ignored the pain, straightened his shoulders, gave the bully a tight-lipped smile, and said, "Feels like my balls just got tickled."

Sheriff Dunkirk let out a little chuckle. "Like I said, a badass."

"Badass," Paul agreed.

Goatsack grabbed Kane's arm and steered him toward the interlocking doors that would take him inside the prison. "My boys will cure him of that right quick."

The control center buzzed them in. Right before the door closed behind him, Kane heard the sheriff call, "Enjoy your stay."

Kane turned his head, fixed him with a grim stare, and mouthed the words, *"See you soon."*

For half a heartbeat, he saw a flicker of doubt in Dunkirk's eyes.

Then the second door popped open, and Goatsack hauled him toward a building with the words Receiving & Discharge painted in yellow on a large wooden placard.

"Welcome to R&D," Goatsack growled, shoving him down a narrow concrete corridor. "Usually, this is where we process all the paperwork and get you entered into the system. But since you're an off-the-books guest of Black Bog Federal Prison, none of that bureaucratic red-tape bullshit will be necessary."

A left-hand turn took them down another hallway, which ended in a large holding area with two cells, a body-scanner machine, a digital fingerprinting device, and stacks of brown boxes marked Inmate Property, with various names and registration numbers written on them in black marker.

Nine men, all decked out in the same tactical gear as

Goatsack, stood in the middle of the room. The welcoming party.

"Howdy, boys," Goatsack said. "Meet John Kane."

"Big fucker, ain't he?" one of the men muttered. "Guy's been eating his Wheaties."

Goatsack pointed at the speaker and said to Kane, "That there is Red Cent." He proceeded to point at the others, naming them as he went down the line. "Breezy, Yippy, Big Belly, Goodbye, Duck, Happy, and Sirius."

"Why the hell are you telling me their names?" Kane asked.

"Because I want you to know the names of the men who are going to stomp the shit out of you shortly." He shoved Kane toward the group. Big Belly grabbed one arm while Sirius grabbed the other. "Strip and hit, boys."

Knowing what was about to go down, Kane gritted his teeth as the team forced him into a small room off to the side that had the words Visual Search, which was just prison jargon for a strip search, stenciled above the door.

The room was only big enough to fit seven grown men, so Goatsack, Red Cent, and Duck stayed outside.

"Fine," Red Cent said when Goatsack ordered him to hang back. "Not like I wanted to see his dick anyway."

Inside the strip room, Kane was forced against the far wall. Breezy stepped forward with a handcuff key while the others drew their riot batons. "I'm going to take your cuffs off," Breezy said. "You so much as twitch toward me, these boys are going to beat you until at least seventy-five percent of the bones in your body are broken. We clear, big guy?"

"Yeah, I got it," Kane replied, knowing they were going to beat him anyway.

The shackles sprang loose, and Breezy stepped back. "All right, you know the drill. Strip."

Kane complied. Not like he had a choice, and besides, his time as a Marine had immunized him to the indignity of being naked in front of other men.

He tossed his clothes onto a table in the corner and faced the team, arms down by his side, but fists clenched to let them know that when the beat-down started, he wasn't going down without a fight.

They looked behind his ears. They shined a flashlight into his mouth, ordering him to lift his tongue. They made him lift his feet and wiggle his toes. They even checked his scrotum, all in the name of proving he wasn't smuggling any contraband. Kane endured it all stoically, knowing it was standard operating procedure for inmate intake.

"Turn around and face the wall," Breezy ordered.

Kane's jaw clenched as he slowly followed the instruction. He knew what came next. Time to make his stand.

Breezy gave the expected command. "Okay, convict. Bend over and spread those cheeks."

"Not gonna happen."

"Have it your way." Breezy tucked the cuffs into a pouch on his belt and drew his baton. "Crush him, boys."

Kane pushed off the wall as the team lunged forward, riot batons swinging.

He plowed a fist into Breezy's gut just below the Kevlar vest. The man grunted and slammed his club into Kane's upper left arm. Pain ricocheted down the appendage. He lowered his shoulder and slammed it into Breezy's chest, driving him backward into the others.

The rest of the team reached around and jabbed with

the rounded ends of their batons, thumping Kane on the shoulders. The blows hurt but didn't incapacitate, and he continued using his size and weight advantage to push Breezy backward.

But then Breezy managed to swing his baton down low and crack it against the side of Kane's knee. He lurched, leg buckling, and stumbled like a hamstrung deer.

It was all the opening they needed.

They were trained operators. Not at Kane's level, but they didn't need to be. They had the advantage of numbers, and once he hit the floor, they quickly overwhelmed him. The batons rained down one vicious blow after another. Naked and weaponless, the best Kane could do was curl up and try to protect his most vulnerable parts.

He brought his knees up to protect his groin, tucked his chin against his chest to make his face a difficult target, and covered his head with his hands. The batons beat brutal rhythms on his ribs, arms, thighs, and back.

The beat-down seemed to go on for hours, but Kane knew that was just an illusion. In real-time, it probably lasted less than a minute. Nothing was broken or busted as far as he could tell, but he would be a patchwork of black-and-blue bruises come tomorrow morning.

At least he was alive.

For now.

The team finally stepped back, breathing a little heavy from exertion—pounding the crap out of an innocent man was probably a great cardio workout—and brushing sweat from their brows. The windowless strip room was stifling, and full tactical gear was not conducive to cooling.

"Damn," Yippy said. "I need some water."

"You mean a beer," Happy corrected. "First round's on me."

Breezy gave Kane one last good kick in the ribs. "You take a beating good, I'll give you that. Didn't even get a yelp out of ya."

Kane slowly climbed to his feet, body protesting the pain and punishment it had just suffered. "You want yelps," he said, "buy a Chihuahua."

"Nah," Breezy replied. "Why would I buy a little rat-dog to kick? I can just come to work every day and kick ratfucks like you." He pulled some prison clothes off a shelf and tossed them on the floor at Kane's feet. "Get dressed, and get ready to meet your cellmates." He chuckled. "You're about to go from an ass-beating to an ass-reaming."

As Kane pulled on the white boxers, white t-shirt, brown socks, khaki pants, khaki shirt, and black composite-toe boots that served as the inmate uniform, he mulled his best course of action moving forward. Tonight's only mission was to stay alive and avoid getting gang-raped, but by tomorrow morning, he would need to make a play.

His best option was to somehow get to a phone. With one call to Team Reaper headquarters, he could reach all the way to the President. Less than an hour later, there would be all sorts of heavily-armed warriors on their way to pull him out of here and burn Black Blog Federal Prison to the ground—figuratively, and quite possibly, literally.

The backup option was to pull off an escape. He was sure it could be done, but he didn't know how yet. He needed more intel, and he wouldn't get it until he got inside. The question would be, could he stay alive long enough to gather the information, formulate a plan, and execute it? He could fend off multiple attackers if that was what it came down to, but he was still human. If some gang wanted him dead, they could make it happen through sheer force of numbers—overwhelm him, take him down, and stick him full of shanks. He would take some of them to the grave with him, but that wouldn't make him any less dead.

He exited the strip room, and Goatsack tossed him a mesh bag containing extra clothes, towels, and toiletries. "There's your welcome package, Kane. Time to see your new home. Follow me."

He unlocked a door and took Kane down yet another corridor. There was a heavy steel door at the end. Goatsack stopped and keyed his radio. "R&D to Compound, releasing one to D-Unit."

"Ten-four," came the reply in that digitized tone common to all radio traffic. "Send him."

Goatsack opened the door and Kane stepped onto the compound, getting his first look at the main part of the prison.

Walkways ran in all directions, crisscrossing at times, blacktopped paths leading to various buildings. To his left appeared to be some sort of administrative building, followed by the dining hall and the lieutenant's office, clearly marked by signs above their portals. Scanning left to right, he saw Laundry, Facilities, Education, Commissary, and Chapel.

Directly in front of him was a guard shack made from brick and heavily-barred glass. A pair of correctional officers, presumably the compound officers Goatsack had radioed moments before, stood on the concrete landing outside the building, thumbs hooked in their duty belts as they eyeballed the latest convict unlucky enough to get thrown into Black Bog Federal Prison.

Kane's eyes moved past them. To his right, the ground sloped uphill, and seven horseshoe-shaped housing units, each two stories high, were spread out across the crest. They each displayed a big letter painted on the brickwork above the entrance.

Goatsack pointed to the one marked D. "That's where you're going. Delta Unit. It's pretty much a gladiator school, so get ready to rumble. I'll be shocked if somebody doesn't try to put you through the paces before lockdown."

"What time's lockdown?" Kane figured he might as well glean whatever information he could.

"Twenty-two hundred hours," Goatsack replied. "Hope you understand military time, 'cause that's all we use around here."

Kane turned his head and looked at him. "I was a Marine."

"For real? I served in the Navy, so I gave you Marine dogs a few rides in my time. What'd you do in the Corps?"

"Recon."

Goatsack seemed genuinely surprised. "No shit?"

"No shit."

"No wonder you tore that bar apart with your bare hands." Goatsack gave him a look that was almost—but not quite—respectful. "How the hell did you end up in this sewer, Marine?"

Kane stared at him hard. "Dunkirk killed that girl and framed me for it. But I think you already know that."

Goatsack nodded. "Yeah, that sucks. The good news for me is that it only sucks for you."

"I'll make you a deal. Get me out of here, and I won't kill you when the time comes."

Goatsack's eyes narrowed to glittering slits, like

moonlight on a switchblade. "Just who the hell do you think you're talking to, Marine?"

"If you had any idea who the hell *you're* talking to," Kane replied, "you'd take that deal."

"Yeah? Why don't you enlighten me on who I'm talking to, tough guy?"

"Let's just say I'm not somebody you want to fuck with."

Goatsack laughed. "Buddy, by tomorrow morning, you're gonna be down at medical with both your arms broken, your kneecaps smashed, and your ass looking like a subway tunnel. We'll see if you're still talking tough-guy shit then." He pointed up the hill. "Delta Unit. Get moving."

As Kane moved past the man, he said, "Remember, I gave you a chance to do the right thing."

"I stopped giving a crap about the right thing a long time ago." Goatsack fired off a mocking little salute. "See you around, Marine." He went back into R&D and locked the door behind him.

As Kane made his way across the compound, he felt unseen eyes watching him, probably from the narrow, steel-barred windows in the housing units. He was the new fish on the yard, and the other prisoners would study him, eyeball him, watch to see what he was made of. Any sign of weakness, any sign of fear, and they would pounce on him like wolves taking down vulnerable prey.

He entered the guard shack, and the two compound officers motioned for him to go through a metal detector. He came out the other side without setting off the alarm.

One of the officers waved him over and made a spinning motion with his finger. "Turn around, convict. I'm gonna pat you down."

"Why? I cleared the metal detector."

"Because I goddamn said so," the officer snapped. "You'll get your admission and orientation speech tomorrow, but one thing you should know right now—you can be pat-searched by any staff member at any time. Refuse, and we'll drag your sorry ass into the Hole."

Kane didn't ask what "the Hole" was. Figured he already had a pretty good idea.

He turned around, put his hands on the wall, and let the officer pat him down, basically the prison version of a frisk. He knew this was just the correctional officers asserting their dominance, letting him know the pecking order. He thought about telling them that he already knew they weren't the alphas around here, that Nazareno ruled the prison, not them.

In the end, that would only piss them off, so he just held his tongue and let the officer pat down nearly every square inch of his body. Any more thorough, and he would have been giving Kane a hand job.

When he was done, the officer gave him a little shove —another classic dominance-asserting move—and pointed at the exit. "Out that door and straight up the hill to your unit. Check in with the officer when you get there."

Kane nodded. "Thanks for the massage."

"Careful, convict. A smart-ass mouth will get you all kinds of unwelcome attention around here."

"Duly noted."

"Get moving."

As he trudged up the hill, Kane again felt unseen stares prickling the hair on the back of his neck. He heard a few muffled shouts, mostly various prison-approved greetings.

"Eat dick, new fish!"

"You ain't in fucking Kansas anymore, Dorothy!"

"Goddamn, you a goliath!"

"Merry fucking Christmas, bitch!"

More disturbing were the catcalls, wolf-whistles, and bunk-share invitations.

He ignored them all, but the volume cranked up to ear-bleed decibels when he entered the unit. Over a hundred inmates milled about in the common area, sat at the tables bolted to the floor, or draped themselves over the railings on the upper tiers, and it seemed like every damn one of them started shouting at him the second he walked through the door.

It was a cacophony of human noise, an aural assault on the ears. Kane figured this must be what the dormitories of Hell sounded like.

A portly prison guard stepped out of an office to Kane's right and shouted, "SHUT UP!" at the top of his lungs.

The bedlam didn't disappear completely, but the decibels dropped to a more acceptable level.

The guard turned to Kane. His name tag read D. Simpson. "Who the hell are you?"

"John Kane."

"Don't care about your first name, Kane, because we ain't gonna get that familiar."

Kane shrugged. "Fair enough. What do I call you?"

"Sir or Officer will do just fine."

"Got a cell for me?"

Simpson pointed at a cell marked "101" in the left-hand corner of the unit. "Got an open bunk in one-oh-one over there. It's a four-man cell, so you'll be sleeping with three other guys." He sniggered. "In more ways than one, most likely."

"Not gonna happen."

"Yeah, that's what they all say." Simpson waved him toward the cell. "Good luck, and welcome to Black Bog."

"Pillow and blanket?"

"They're supposed to be on the bunk, but I'm sure one of your cellies has helped himself to them by now." Simpson shrugged. "Work it out amongst yourselves."

"I'm not sure you want me to do that."

Simpson let out an exasperated sigh. "Kane, this is Delta Unit, a.k.a. gladiator school. If there's only one fight per day in here, we call that a slow day. You need to throw down to get yourself some bedding, ain't nobody gonna bat an eye, and that includes me." He waved dismissively. "Now piss off, and may the best man win."

Cell 101 was vacant when Kane walked in. Simple enough setup: Two bunks, upper and lower, to his left, two more straight in front of him. A tiny desk attached to the wall beneath a bulletin board. Four lockers wedged between the bunks. A stainless steel toilet and a porcelain sink. The cinderblock walls were decorated with an eclectic assortment of Catholic iconography, family photos, and pornographic pictures.

Home sweet home, Kane thought grimly.

The upper bunk to his left was empty. No pillow, no blanket, not even a mattress. Just a vacant slab of metal with graffiti etched in the paint, mostly gang symbols. He sighed and slung his bag onto the bunk.

The cell door opened, and three men crowded in. One remained in the doorway while the other two bracketed Kane. They were all Hispanic and well-muscled. The pair bracing Kane sported tattoos identifying them as members of the violent MS-13 gang. Kane couldn't see any weapons, but he had no doubt all three carried some sort of blade.

The guy to Kane's left wore a red headband around

his clean-shaven skull. "Would you look at this *mierda*?" he growled. "They put a white boy in our cell."

"Yeah," his comrade replied. "Big *bastardo*, too." Three tattooed teardrops decorated the skin next to his eye. Kane knew that symbolized he had killed three people. Probably planning on getting a fourth tattoo tomorrow.

Too bad Kane had other plans.

"Yeah, he's too *grande*," Headband said. His hand moved fast, reaching behind him to produce a survival knife, point honed to wicked sharpness, with a serrated spine. It was not the kind of blade usually found in prison, further proof of just how lawless Black Bog had become under Nazareno's rule. Tattoo followed suit, lifting his shirt to pull a similar-looking knife from his waistband.

"I say we cut a few inches off him so he'll fit on the bunk better," Headband continued, staring into Kane's eyes with a hard, predatory look that probably scared the hell out of the average new fish. "What do you say, *cabron*?"

Kane felt the pre-combat adrenalin surge through his system but kept it masked. No point in letting these boys know he was ready for a fight. Play it cool, lull them into thinking they had him outmatched, and only go hardcore at the last possible second, if —or more likely *when*—it became necessary.

Kane said, "I've got no beef with you boys. Just hook me up with a mattress, pillow, and blanket, and I'll be good."

"Not the way it works around here, cocksucker."

"Name's Kane, not 'cocksucker.'"

"Your name is gonna be dog shit, *puta*, if you don't shut the hell up and listen."

"I'm listening," Kane said. "But so far, you aren't saying much worth hearing."

Headband snarled, "Fuck you, *cabron*. Time to cut you down to size."

They rushed forward in tandem, stabbing in synchronicity, expecting an easy target.

Kane was anything but easy.

And these boys were pure amateur hour.

He spun to the left. Headband's strike missed badly, leaving his arm overextended. Kane grabbed the inmate's wrist with his right hand and pulled him even further off balance. He then slammed the heel of his palm against Headband's elbow, snapping the arm with a grotesque crunch.

Headband had just started to howl in pain when Kane stomped down on the side of the Mexican's knee. Another sickening snap as bone broke, and Headband sank to the floor. Kane let go of his wrist as he fell and sledgehammered an uppercut into the man's falling chin, shattering his lower jaw. Headband flopped on the floor, knocked clean out. After he woke up, he would be drinking from a straw for weeks to come.

Due to the close confines of the cell, Tattoo had difficulty reaching Kane with his knife while the warrior disassembled his shanking partner. After Headband went down in a broken-boned sprawl, Tattoo hurdled his unconscious body, survival knife slashing toward Kane's neck.

Kane dodged, and the blade scraped the cement wall behind him. He chopped a punch into Tattoo's exposed ribs, which sent the man spinning sideways. The inmate stumbled over the toilet but caught himself quickly.

Kane glanced at the guy in the doorway. He just stood there with his arms crossed, watching the fight.

If the big bastard wanted to sit this one out, Kane wasn't going to complain.

He reached down and snatched up the knife that had fallen from Headband's limp hand.

Tattoo crouched, tossing his blade from hand to hand. That might look cool in the movies, but it was absolutely stupid in an actual knife fight.

"Time for you to bleed," Tattoo growled.

"Walk away before I stick this knife through your balls," Kane said.

"That's my *amigo* you just fucked up, *puta*. You need to pay for that."

"Come on over here, and you can get fucked up too. We'll call it a two-for-one deal."

Tattoo danced forward with the blade gripped in his right hand. He moved cautiously, but still possessed the aura of a man accustomed to having the upper hand. A man who killed at will. Too much time near the top of the prison's pecking order had made him arrogant.

Without warning, Kane exploded into motion, lunging forward. He used his left hand to knock Tattoo's knife to the side, pinning it against the wall. With his right, he slashed his own blade toward Tattoo's face, going for the eyes. This was a prison brawl, not a gentlemen's duel.

Tattoo jerked his head back just in time. The blow meant to blind him instead caught the corner of his mouth, sliced between his lips, and ripped out the opposite corner, leaving both his lower cheek flaps dangling like fallen curtains. Blood ran down the sides of his neck.

Kane seized his advantage. Now was not the time for mercy. He immediately back-slashed and caught Tattoo's right eye with the tip of the knife. It popped in a squishy burst. The blade skidded across the bridge of the man's nose and narrowly missed taking out the other eye as well.

Pivoting, Kane raked the edge of the blade across Tattoo's pinned right wrist, severing the tendons in one swift, bone-scraping cut. The inmate's knife tumbled from fingers that suddenly no longer worked.

Kane brought his blade back around and buried it in Tattoo's midsection a few inches below the ribcage. He felt the hard muscle give way to something much softer as the knife punctured deep.

He reached up with his free hand, grabbed the back of Tattoo's neck, and yanked him close enough to smell the stench of peppers on his breath. He kept the knife stuck in the man's belly.

"Listen to me and listen good," Kane rasped, voice low and menacing but loud enough to carry to the third Mexican standing watch in the doorway. "Right now, all you've got is a perforated intestine. With a few stitches, you'll survive that just fine. But feel that blade in you?" He gave it a little twist, eliciting a hiss of pain from the shish-kabobbed convict. "If I jerk that blade sideways, you'll be standing knee-deep in your own goddamned guts. And believe me, bucko, there ain't no coming back from that. You reading me?"

Tattoo nodded, his face a mask of blood, and his teeth —visible due to the dangling cheeks—clenched in pain.

"Good," Kane said. "Because believe it or not, I have no real desire to kill you. Unless you act the fool when I pull this knife out, you get to walk away with nothing more than some scars, one less eye, a crippled hand, and a hole in your guts." Kane paused. "Problem is, you're gonna want to act like a fool because your brain is all messed up, thinking I did this to you." He pulled Tattoo even closer. "But I *didn't* do this to you. You did this to yourself when you decided to fuck with the wrong person."

Kane glanced at the door. The guy standing there hadn't moved, but he was clearly paying attention.

"So you get to live," Kane told Tattoo. "The price for your life is for you to tell everyone in this shithole to leave me the fuck alone. Got it?"

Without waiting for a response, Kane pulled the shank out. It popped free with a wet sucking sound. Blood drooled from the hole to soak into the waistband of Tattoo's gray sweat pants.

"Go on," Kane said. "Get outta here."

The man in the doorway moved aside as Tattoo stumbled away, then resumed his doorway-blocking position.

Still holding the bloody survival knife, Kane looked him in the eye. "You and I have a problem?"

The guy stepped into the cell, grabbed Headband by the ankle, and dragged the unconscious inmate out. When he came back in, he pointed at the beds at the back of the cell.

"Bottom bunk's yours, *amigo*."

"Do I need to sleep with my ass to the wall?"

"I'm not interested in that sort of thing, and if I change my mind, there's a sweet little thing over in Bravo Unit who will do it for two cans of mackerel and a candy bar, so no reason for me to get myself killed trying to take you for a ride."

"I wake up and you're trying to share a bunk, I'll rip your throat out," Kane warned.

"Name's Pedro, and you've really got *nada* to worry about from me."

"Not looking for a little payback for what I just did to your homeboys?"

"They weren't my homeboys," Pedro replied as he

flopped down on the other bottom bunk. "I just happen to be assigned to their cell."

Officer Simpson barged into the room. "Good Lord, Kane, what the hell did you do to those guys?"

"You told me to get a pillow." Kane gestured at his bunk. "I got a pillow."

"You damn near killed one of them."

"'Damn near' and 'did' aren't the same thing."

"You can bet your butt that Nazareno isn't going to care about the difference."

"I won't tell him if you won't."

Simpson shook his head. "Trust me on this, he already knows."

Over on his bunk, Pedro nodded in agreement.

"You working for Nazareno?" Kane asked, fixing a challenging stare on the correctional officer. "Word on the street is that all you hacks are on the take."

Simpson pointed a warning finger at him. "I don't answer questions from a two-bit convict who rapes and murders women." He spun on the heel of his polished black duty boot and exited the cell.

Pedro grinned, revealing a gold tooth. "Damn, *hombre*, you fight like a pissed-off honey badger, and you don't mince your words. You gonna be real popular around here."

"I don't want to be popular. Just want to be left alone." *So I can figure out how the hell to get out of here.*

Pedro chuckled. "Too late for that, *amigo*. You just crippled and stabbed two of Nazareno's best enforcers."

"Those were his best?" Kane scoffed. "They were nothing but a couple of bitches who thought a blade made them badasses."

"Gonna be a hundred blades coming for you tomorrow," Pedro cautioned. "You're good, *amigo*, but if Nazareno wants you *muerto*, you gonna be dead."

"Guess I better get some sleep, then," Kane said. "Sounds like tomorrow is going to be a busy day."

Pedro chuckled again. "I like your style, Kane. I really do." He swung his legs over the side of his bunk and rummaged around in one of the lockers. He came up with a Snickers that he tossed to Kane. "Here. You missed chow, and I'm guessing they didn't give you a bag lunch in R&D before they kicked you up the hill."

"Thanks." Kane tore open the wrapper and devoured the candy bar. It seemed like weeks since he had sat on the rock ledges eating lunch and watching the hawk, and despite all that had happened since then—Beta, Mad Mike, the gun shack, the grizzly bear, Luna's murder, and his incarceration—he still found himself famished. Plus, he knew he would need all the strength he could find to survive whatever tomorrow would throw at him.

"Don't thank me," Pedro said. "I might have just served you your last meal."

"Don't bet on it."

Pedro hesitated, then asked, "You really rape and murder women?"

Kane kept his answer simple. "No."

"An innocent man." Pedro laughed. "That's what they all say. Just ask around."

"No doubt," Kane said. "But I'm telling the truth."

Pedro cocked his head. "You know what, *amigo*?" he said solemnly. "I believe you."

"Glad to hear it."

"You ain't got the look," Pedro explained. "Don't get me wrong, you look like a killer, but not a murderer. That make any sense?"

"More than you know."

"And rape? I just don't see it in you." Pedro waved a hand. "You look more like the type who would tear a rapist's head off his shoulders."

"You missed your calling," Kane said. "You should be a shrink, not a convict. What are you locked up for, anyway?"

Pedro's eyes shifted into dark pools of sorrow. "No offense, but not sure I want to tell you that."

Kane nodded. "Your business. Just tell me one thing."

"What's that?"

"Do I need to tear your head off your shoulders?"

Pedro hurriedly shook his head. "No, no, nothing like that." He sighed, then muttered, "Oh, what the hell," and said, "I killed a man."

"Did he have it coming?"

"Heard a priest once say we all have it coming."

"Not what I meant, and you know it."

"Yeah, I know what you meant." Pedro paused for a moment, then plunged ahead. "The man I killed was a coyote. You know what that means?"

Kane nodded.

"I paid him a lot of money to smuggle me and my daughter across the border."

"He didn't do it?"

"Oh, he did it," Pedro replied. "But as soon as we were in Texas, he pulled out a *pistola* and shot me." He pulled down his sweatshirt to reveal the puckered scar tissue of an old bullet wound just above his left collarbone. "I passed out from the pain, and when I came back around, the *hijo de puta* was raping my twelve-year-old daughter."

Kane said, "I hope you killed the son of a bitch."

"I picked up a rock and smashed him in the back of the head, knocking him off my daughter. He rolled onto his back and tried to pull his gun again, but I hit him in the face with the rock, and then I kept hitting him over and over again. I'm not sure how long I pounded him with that rock, but when I came back to my senses, there were ICE agents dragging me off the coyote, and his head looked like red oatmeal."

"Good for you."

"That's not how the courts saw it," Pedro said. "They cut me enough slack to avoid the needle or a life sentence, but I'm still locked up for twenty years."

"When's the last time you saw your daughter?"

Pedro turned away, but not before Kane caught the glimmer of tears that suddenly silvered his eyes. The convict swallowed hard, and around the lump in his throat, he managed to say, "That night. Five years ago. The ICE agents took her away. I never saw her again."

"Any idea where she is?"

Pedro shook his head.

Kane wanted to believe him, but he was no fool, and prisons brimmed with con men. A tragic story told with a slick tongue and crocodile tears were the main components of a duping game. "That's messed up," Kane said. "But how do I know you're not just bullshitting me?"

Pedro's head whipped around so fast that centrifugal force flung the teardrops right off his cheeks. Sparks of anger joined the sadness in his eyes. "What the hell is that crap, *cabron*? You say you're innocent and I take you at your word, but you ask me if I'm playing games?"

"I have my reasons," Kane said. "If you're telling me the truth, I might be able to help you."

"You want me to swear on my *madre's* grave or something *stupido* like that?"

"Is your mother dead?"

"No."

Kane stared at him for a minute, then let out a laugh. "You're something else, Pedro."

"I could swear on a stack of Bibles if that'll make you feel better."

Kane shook his head. "No, I believe you." Something in his gut told him Pedro's tragic backstory was the truth, and Kane had long ago learned to trust his gut.

"Good," Pedro said with a crooked smile. "Because I'm an atheist."

The men enjoyed a hearty laugh at that, each aware that laughter was a rare commodity in this godforsaken place. Deep down, Kane felt a twinge of guilt that he could even muster a laugh mere hours after finding Luna dead, but he knew that sometimes laughter was the only thing that kept the madness at bay.

They soon buckled back down to serious conversation. "I need to talk to the warden," Kane said. "How do I pull that off?"

"Easy," Pedro replied. "Just go down to chow line in the morning. Warden Ghastin stands outside the chow hall entrance at breakfast so the inmates can ask her questions. I think she's required to by policy."

"So, just walk up to her and start talking?"

"Yup. But if you're thinking she can help you, think again."

"I've got a card to play."

"I don't care if you've got a deck full of aces," Pedro said. "Warden Ghastin is Nazareno's bitch in every way it is possible to be somebody's bitch."

"She a willing bitch, or is there a blade to her throat?"

"Oh, there's a blade, all right," Pedro said. "A big fucking blade. Word on the compound is that if Ghastin doesn't play ball, her husband and daughter are dead meat, and it won't be nice and clean if you catch my drift."

"Sounds like somebody should turn Nazareno into maggot food," Kane growled.

Pedro looked alarmed. "Watch what you say, *amigo*. The walls might be listening."

"If I have my way, these damn walls are coming down."

"Hey, from your lips to God's ears."

Kane grinned. "Thought you were an atheist?"

Pedro shrugged. "Can't fucking hurt, right?"

ELEVEN

Black Bog Federal Prison

Despite Pedro's repeated assurances that nobody would mess with him that night, Kane still slept with his back to the wall and one eye open. In fact, *sleep* wasn't the right word for it. He would doze for no more than five or six minutes at a time, never fully relaxing. Officer Simpson made the rounds and secured the cell door at 2200 hours, but Kane knew that didn't make him safe. With the vast majority of the guards on Nazareno's payroll, it would be easy for one of them to crack open the door and let some assassins in to avenge Headband and Tattoo.

But it didn't happen, and eventually, the pale light of dawn seeped through the tall, narrow, iron-barred window that looked out on the prison compound. Despite all the scratches on the window, all the etched graffiti and gang signs, Kane could still look out over the

Recreation Yard and see mountains looming in the near distance.

The housing unit officer—not Simpson—unlocked the door at 0615 hours. Kane debated taking a shower but decided against it. He didn't know if all those prison shower scenes in the movies were accurate or not, but he didn't feel like risking it. With luck, he would be out of this hellhole by tonight and would shower then. He washed up in the sink instead. His body ached from the beating he had taken in R&D, and bruises had started to blossom in a black-and-blue patchwork.

"Buenos dias, amigo," Pedro greeted him as he swung out of his bunk. "Sleep well?"

Kane answered honestly, "I slept like a man worried about getting a dick in the ass and a shank in the face."

Pedro laughed. "Hate to break the news to you, Kane, but in here, sometimes it's the other way around."

"Charming thought."

He dressed in his prison khakis. They were at least two sizes too small, but they served to accentuate his muscular frame, and he figured that couldn't hurt as he took his first walk among the general population. Broadcast the message loud and clear: *Mess with me, you're gonna get hurt.*

Then again, it could also make him a target for David-types looking to take down a Goliath and gain some prison cred.

As he followed Pedro down the hill, joining the flow of inmates converging on the dining facility, he felt hundreds of eyes on him. He sensed hostility, curiosity, ambivalence, and even some admiration, probably from prisoners who had heard that he'd tangled with Nazareno's enforcers and walked away the winner.

As they joined the line waiting to enter the chow hall,

Pedro pointed at a beautiful Japanese woman standing near the door. "That's Warden Ghastin."

"Not hard on the eyes, is she?"

"No, but if you stare too long, Nazareno will have those eyes gouged out of your head with a spork."

"Just need to talk to her, that's all."

"Be careful, *amigo*. That's all I can tell you."

As the line shuffled near the warden, Kane stepped over and said, "Excuse me, warden. Can I have a word?"

Up close, he could see the misery haunting her eyes. She kept her face stoic, but Kane sensed the pain just beneath the surface. "What is it?" she asked.

"I need to meet with you."

"I don't meet with inmates. If you have an issue, go through your counselor."

Lowering his voice, Kane said, "I'm not who you think I am. I can help you."

She gave him an appraising look, then said, "Back in line, inmate. This conversation is over."

He nodded respectfully, like a good, well-behaved convict would, and stepped back into line. He had reached out and thrown her a lifeline. Nothing more he could do right now. He just hoped she was smart enough to take it.

Inside the cafeteria, the sound of hundreds of yelling, shouting, cursing voices bounced off the concrete walls and created something close to bedlam. Kane suffered through the aural chaos as he grabbed his plastic tray. On the serving line, a white inmate with Aryan Brotherhood tattoos coloring his neck slapped a dismal heap of oatmeal onto his tray. Another server tossed him a stale cinnamon bun drizzled in some sort of white, sticky glaze that Kane didn't trust.

Pedro grinned. "Nothing but gourmet cuisine for us convicts."

"Better than starving, I guess," Kane said.

Pedro gave a noncommittal shrug. "Maybe."

They grabbed pints of milk from a plastic crate at the end of the serving line and waded back into the high-decibel roar of the chow hall.

Kane quickly deciphered how the inmates segregated the various factions. The Hispanics sat in the southeast corner. The northeast section was white-boy territory. The blacks owned the whole western side of the room, with subdivisions—Muslims, Bloods, DC Blacks, Crips, etc.—clustered in various sections. In the middle of the circus sat the motley misfits—the ones with no affiliation, the loners, outcasts, and pariahs.

Kane and Pedro headed for the middle.

As they made to sit down at a four-person table occupied by only one other man, a large white guy built like a linebacker with neck muscles that looked hard enough to shatter concrete, the convict waved them off. "This table's taken." His voice had the telltale rasp of too much whiskey and too many cigarettes.

Pedro turned away. "Sorry, man. We'll sit somewhere else."

But Kane wasn't in the mood to back down. Plus, he knew he needed to continue to establish his *don't-fuck-with-me* prison cred in case he got stuck in here for an extended period. Strength was respected, even feared; backing away would be seen as weakness.

"Doesn't look taken to me," Kane said, giving the man a challenging stare. He set his tray down on the table with slow deliberateness.

The inmate—the name tag on his shirt read H. Jackson—lowered his eyes to Kane's tray, then slowly raised his gaze back up to meet Kane's challenge. "You're gonna want to pick that tray up and move along, dipshit," he growled.

"Or what?" Kane retorted.

Jackson set down his plastic fork and bunched his hands into fists. "Or I'm gonna have to hurt you."

Pedro jerked his head toward another table. "C'mon, *amigo*. We can sit over here."

"Negative," Kane said. "I like this table better." He slid into the seat directly across from Jackson.

The rest of the chow hall had started to take notice of the drama playing out. When Kane sat down, catcalls cut through the din.

"Oh, no, he din't!"

"Damn! Honky got a death wish!"

"Look at the balls on dat sumbitch!"

For his part, Kane smiled coldly across the table and said, "I'm gonna sit here, mind my own business, and eat my breakfast. You so much as twitch wrong, and I'll punch you in the mouth so hard you'll be shitting out your teeth by nightfall. You clear, Jack?"

"I'm clear that you're a dead man." Jackson swept his arm across the table and knocked Kane's tray to the floor. "Right after I make you lick your food off the floor like a goddamned dog."

Kane reacted immediately, backing up his tough talk with even tougher action. Faster than Jackson could react, he pounced across the table and hammered a fist into the man's mouth. He felt his knuckles getting cut up, but he also felt at least two of Jackson's teeth rupture out of the gums and sluice down his throat on a river of blood.

Choking, Jackson staggered out of his seat and reeled against a concrete support pillar. His gagging noises sounded like a retching cat trying to cough up a nasty hairball.

Out of the corner of his eye, Kane saw the prison guards just leaning against the wall, watching with amused smirks on their faces, happy to have some morning entertainment.

He stalked over to Jackson and said, "Warned you." He slammed the edge of his palm across the inmate's throat. Not hard enough to rupture anything, but hard enough to make Jackson cough and sputter even worse.

Kane moved forward. He planned on grabbing Jackson's head and pounding it against the pillar until his lights went out, but a bellowing roar from behind him stopped him in his tracks.

"FIGHT *ME*, YOU BASTARD!"

Kane spun and found himself facing the biggest Mexican he had ever seen, and he had seen plenty of them. The man's jet-black eyes glared dark fire at him.

"Fuck off," Kane rasped. "I've got no beef with you."

"Well, I've got a beef with you, *cabron*. You took my brother's eye last night." He pulled a long icepick-style shank from a homemade sheath hidden inside his waistband. "Now I'm going to take both of yours."

Now that the guy mentioned it, Kane could see the resemblance to Tattoo from the night before. This guy—M. Santos, according to the name tag embroidered on his shirt—was much bigger, but the facial structure was similar. No doubt the guy was a piece of trash, but Kane could at least respect a man for trying to avenge his brother. Hell, he would have done the same thing.

Of course, that wouldn't stop Kane from putting him down.

He took out the survival knife he had taken from Santos' brother the night before. Another glance at the guards showed them still rooted in place, content to let the games play out and mop up the blood later.

He leveled his hard-eyed stare at Santos. "Sure you want to do this? Your brother danced with me last night and got carved up like a damn turkey."

"I'm not *mi hermano*."

"You'll bleed like him."

"Only thing gonna be bleeding is your ass when I stab the shit out of it."

Kane held his blade low. He missed his Ka-Bar, but this knife was good enough to get the job done. "Nazareno approve this hit?" He figured it couldn't hurt to throw the man's name out there.

"Nothing around here happens without Nazareno's approval," Santos growled. "Even a new fish like you knows that."

"Pretty sure I didn't ask his permission to fuck up your asshole brother last night."

Santos scowled. "He'll probably have your tongue cut out for that, but me, I just want your fucking eyes."

He charged.

Like a lot of big men, he moved with a distinct lack of grace. Bull in a china shop, all pounding thunder and grunting fury.

Kane stood his ground until the last possible second, then slid to the side with fluid speed, letting the human locomotive barrel right on by. As Santos' momentum carried him past, Kane reached out and let his blade carve a channel across the man's ribcage, slicing through his shirt to part the flesh beneath.

Santos lumbered around, wincing at the stinging pain in his side. Behind him, Jackson had finally coughed up his busted teeth. Holding his bloody mouth, he retreated into the crowd, wanting no part in the current battle. Probably going to visit the dentist.

"Walk away," Kane said to Santos. "You're too slow."

Santos roared an obscenity and performed his charging rhino routine again.

Kane sidestepped and ducked, dodging the wild, stabbing strike that Santos launched at him. The survival knife lanced out like a serpent's tongue and slashed open the man's muscular thigh.

Santos stumbled and slowed. He swung backward desperately and got lucky. His cinder block-sized fist snuck through Kane's blind spot and caught him upside the head like a heavy club. Bright lights starburst through Kane's brain as the back-fisted punch knocked him sideways into the mob that had gathered to watch the *mano a mano* deathmatch.

Despite his wounded leg, Santos crashed toward him like a rabid brontosaurus, lifting his boots to stomp the crap out of Kane, who was still crouched as he shook off the dizzying blow to the skull.

As Santos' boot came up, Kane drove his knife right through the rubber sole and out the top, impaling the convict's foot.

Santos howled in pain and tried to hobble away, but Kane had him trapped like a hooked fish. As the convict fell, Kane jerked the knife backward. The serrated spine ripped through Santos' foot, splitting it in half between the second and third toes.

The big man toppled like an axed tree as Kane powered to his feet. He drove the tip of his boot between Santos' legs with rupturing force. The convict's eyes started to roll back in their sockets as Kane leaped into the air and came down on the man's sternum with a savage knee-strike.

The thick bone cracked with a sharp snap like breaking ice.

Kane stood up, feet planted on each side of his opponent's damaged chest. The smashed balls and crushed sternum had jacked Santos' system full of pain, too much for him to handle. The convict was out cold. When he woke up, he wouldn't be happy.

If he woke up.

Kane stared at the pulsing artery on the side of Santos' neck. Maybe he should just finish the job. One quick slit and Santos' darkness would become permanent.

As if sensing the primal urges burning through his adrenalized bloodstream like a narcotic, the mob began urging him toward lethality.

"Kill him!"

"Ice the fucker, man!"

"Take him out!"

"No mercy!"

"Finish it!"

The murderous chants intensified into a deafening roar as the inmates stomped their feet and shook their fists and pounded their trays on the tables like makeshift tribal drums. Bloodlust scorched the air, a sharp electrical tang you could almost taste, like the aftermath of a lightning strike.

And then, as if someone had flipped a switch, the mob silenced itself. The seething mass of people parted, and a Hispanic man wearing white robes, sandals, and a crown of thorns tattooed on his shaved scalp stepped forward. He stared at Kane with the cold eyes of a cobra.

Kane stared right back. "Let me guess: you're Nazareno."

"In the flesh."

Kane gestured at Santos. "He one of yours?"

"One of my best."

"If that's what you call the best, you should really up your standards."

"So it would seem." A little smile played across Nazareno's lips. "Of course, I could try out a quantity over quality option. You might be able to handle my best fighters one on one or even two on one, but I'm curious what would happen if I ordered a dozen men to attack you at the same time."

"You keep throwing bodies at me," Kane said, "and I'll keep sending them to the hospital. If that doesn't get the point across that you really should just leave me the fuck alone, then I'll start sending some to the morgue."

"You can start with the one at your feet."

"Say what?"

Nazareno pointed at Santos. "Kill him."

Kane glanced down at the unconscious inmate, then back up at the drug lord. "Why?"

"Because I did not sanction this hit," Nazareno replied. "Santos knows better. Nothing happens in here without my permission. His actions cannot go unpunished, and I say that his punishment is death." He dragged a demonstrative finger across his neck. "Cut his throat and be done with him."

Just moments ago, Kane had considered doing that very thing, but now rebellion rose up within him. Even in a shithole prison like Black Bog, it would be a cold day in hell before he took orders from a sadistic drug lord.

With a look of disgust, as if Nazareno was somewhere lower than dog shit on the spectrum of things you didn't want to be near, Kane tossed the knife. It skidded across the waxed floor tiles and bounced off the man's sandals. "I ain't your bitch," Kane rasped. "You want blood, do it yourself."

A collective gasp ran through the crowd. Kane had no doubt that it had been a long time since anyone challenged Nazareno this way.

For his part, the cartel king seemed unfazed. He idly kicked the blade back across the floor. It came to rest next to Santos' head. "You would be doing him a favor," Nazareno said. "No matter how this plays out, in the end, Santos will die today. If I have to do it myself, he will be tortured first, an example made to show what happens to those who act without my permission. But if you do it, it will be quick." Nazareno smiled with all the mirth of a shark. "Consider it an act of mercy."

"Consider this my final answer." Kane kicked the knife back to him. "No."

The shark-smile vanished. "It is not wise to cross me, *cabron*."

"We'll see."

"I could have your *cajones* put in a blender while I set your eyes on fire."

"Where I come from, we call that date night."

"Keep cracking jokes," Nazareno said. "You'll be dead by dawn."

"That's what your shithead sheriff kept telling me yesterday," Kane replied. "And yet here I am, still standing."

"Enjoy your day," Nazareno said with exaggerated graciousness. "We'll talk later, after I've made some arrangements."

"Can't wait."

Nazareno snapped his fingers. Two men came forward and grabbed Santos' wrists as Kane backed away. They dragged him out of the chow hall with all the callousness and lack of dignity a butcher bestows upon a slab of beef. With one final, baleful, cold-eyed glance at Kane, Nazareno followed them out.

The noise level shot back through the roof as soon as the drug lord disappeared. Kane retrieved the survival knife. This time when he went to sit down at a table, nobody told him it was taken.

Pedro got him another tray of food and joined him. "You got brass balls, *hombre*, but you ain't much in the brains department."

They ate their breakfasts in silence. As they were finishing up, two correctional officers approached. One took out a pair of handcuffs while the other motioned to Kane. "On your feet, convict. Warden wants to see you."

Kane rose to his feet, his imposing six-foot-four frame towering over the average-sized guards. "No need for the cuffs, guys."

"Nobody sees the warden without cuffs. Do we look stupid to you?"

"Do you want me to answer that?" Kane asked sarcastically.

In hindsight, not his smartest move. The pissed-off guards cranked the handcuffs down so hard the metal bit deep into his skin, bruised the bone, and strangled circulation. His hands went numb in almost no time, but he didn't say a word or give any sign of discomfort. He just sucked up the pain. With any luck, the steel bracelets would be off in short order.

Each gripping his arm just above the elbow, the two officers escorted him out of the chow hall, over to the administrative building, and up a flight of stairs to a suite of executive offices. They led him over to a wooden door with a metal gold-on-black nameplate that read *Kumi Ghastin, Warden*. One of the officers knocked.

"Come in."

They opened the door and pushed him inside. "Here's the new guy you asked to see, ma'am."

"Thank you, officers. Please wait outside."

They stepped out, closing the door behind them.

Kane nodded at the beautiful but haunted Japanese woman. "We meet again."

Ghastin cut right to the chase. "You said you can help me. Tell me how."

"Can you take these cuffs off?"

"Of course, I can. But I'm not going to."

Kane couldn't blame her for not trusting him. As far as she knew, he was just a big, violent, predatory inmate trying to run a con game on her. So he took his cue from her and got right to the point.

He nodded at the phone on her desk. "Let me make a call, and all your problems will be over."

"What do you know about my problems?"

"I know enough. I know you're not really running this prison. Nazareno is, and if you don't play ball, your family is dead."

"That's not exactly a secret around here," she said. "Having that knowledge doesn't make you anything special."

Kane caught her eyes with his level gaze. "Trust me, Ghastin, I'm not who you think I am."

"Warden," she said.

"Huh?"

"Don't call me Ghastin. Inmates are only allowed to call me 'warden.'"

"I'm not a damn inmate," Kane snapped. "Give me that phone, and I'll prove it."

"And who are you going to call?"

"The Chairman of the Joint Chiefs." He gave her a little smile. "Or Hank, as I like to call him."

"You mean General Hank Carter?"

"Yeah."

Ghastin threw back her head and laughed. "Oh, that's rich," she said. "I've heard some whoppers from inmates before, but this takes the cake."

"It's the truth."

Something in his voice made her stop laughing. She stared at him with eyes narrowed and quietly said, "You've got sixty seconds to tell me exactly who you are and what you're doing in my prison. If I'm not satisfied with your answer, if I'm not convinced you're not lying to me, I'll have you thrown into Solitary so fast your head will spin." She glanced at the clock on the wall. "Sixty seconds. Start talking."

Kane realized his only chance was to tell her the whole truth. While glossing over the more secretive details, he quickly told her about Team Reaper and his leadership role on the strike force.

"So you see," he finished, "you let me call my headquarters, and they'll have General Jones on the phone in less than ten minutes. Once that happens, your problems disappear. This prison will be shut down by nightfall, and Nazareno will be buried in the deepest hole we can find."

As he talked, he saw the hope spring into her eyes at the revelation of his true identity. But by the time he finished his pitch, her fatalism had returned.

She slowly shook her head. "I can't risk it."

"You don't believe me?" Kane asked.

"That's not what I'm saying. I believe you are who you say you are, but you underestimate Nazareno's reach."

"I guarantee you that Jones is not working for some cartel cocksucker."

"I don't think he is," said Ghastin. "But if I let you make that phone call, Nazareno will know, and my husband and daughter will be dead long before you, your team, or the general can do anything about it."

"I can have your family grabbed up by a SEAL team in less than two hours."

She stared at him with pain in her eyes. "Nazareno has people watching my family at all times. I let you make that phone call, they'll be dead in less than thirty minutes."

"He's not God," Kane said. "He can't be everywhere at once. You let me make that call, there's no way he'll know."

"He's tapped into the prison phone system," she informed him. "And he's got men monitoring it around the clock."

Kane felt his frustration growing. "How about a cell phone?"

She shook her head. "All cell phone signals are jammed inside the prison."

"Dammit!"

"Sorry."

Desperation crawled around the edges of Kane's mind. This had been his shot, his chance to get the hell out of here. Now Nazareno's ruthless stranglehold combined with Ghastin's risk-averse mentality worked to shut that play down.

"You're really not going to let me make that call, are you?" he said, and it wasn't a question.

Face stricken, she shook her head. "I can't. I'm sorry, really I am...but I just can't."

"You know Nazareno is going to have me killed."

"In order to keep my family safe, I have stood by and watched many people die," Ghastin confessed. "I will regret your death, but I must do whatever it takes to keep my husband and daughter alive. I can't help you."

"Can't?" Kane growled. "I think you mean 'won't.'"

"Sorry." It was becoming a mantra with her. "I hope you can at least understand where I'm coming from."

Kane sighed and softened his voice. "Yeah, I get it, lady."

She called for the guards. Just before they came in, she said quietly, "Good luck, Reaper."

"Thanks," he said, then silently added, *I'm damn well gonna need it.*

TWELVE

Black Bog Federal Prison

Back on the prison compound, the guards took the cuffs off Kane's throbbing, raw-red wrists and sent him on his way. He headed back up to Delta Unit, noticing that the inmates gave him a wide berth. No surprise there. In the span of twelve hours, he had taken out four inmates and challenged Nazareno. Call it a shortcut to a badass prison rep.

When he ducked back into his cell, Pedro was lying on his bunk reading a dog-eared *Able Team* novel. Without taking his eyes off the page, he greeted Kane with, "Welcome home, *compadre.*"

Kane glanced at the two empty bunks. "Our cellies haven't come back yet?"

"Still being held down in medical," Pedro replied. "Why? You looking for another round?"

Kane turned on the faucet and splashed some cold water on his face. "Negative," he said, drying off with a towel. "I think I've kicked enough ass for a couple of days."

"You can say that again." Pedro put down the paperback and sat up on the edge of his bunk. "How'd it go with the warden?"

"Not as well as I hoped," Kane admitted. "Gonna have to go with plan B."

"What's plan B?"

Kane grinned. "Don't have one yet."

Pedro chuckled. "Well, at least you've thought about it."

The work-call announcement sounded over the prison's public address system a few minutes later, and Pedro shuffled off to his job in the recycling center. He had explained to Kane the night before that every inmate, save those excluded by Nazareno, had a work assignment. Some toiled as orderlies, some worked in the carpentry shop, some did the cooking in food service. The list of where they could force an inmate to work ran a mile long. They were paid anywhere from a penny to ten cents an hour, depending on the complexity of the assignment. Slave wages, Pedro called it, then muttered a curse in Spanish that had something to do with Uncle Sam getting sexually violated by a diseased mule.

Kane, being new—not to mention off the books—had no job assignment yet. As inmates filed out of the unit like obedient drones, he flopped down on his bunk, laid his head on a pillow that was a second cousin to a concrete block, and stared at the bottom of the bunk above him. It was painted a dreary buckskin tan, but there was more graffiti than paint, all sorts of signs, sayings, and symbols crudely carved into the metal. How many hundreds, maybe even thousands, of men had laid here before him, staring at the same carvings? How many had been innocent like him?

He closed his eyes and fought off a wave of despair. He couldn't let that emotion sink its talons into him. Couldn't go down that dark dead-end road. Despondency weakened a man; determination gave him power.

To ward off the feelings of hopelessness, he thought about Luna. Not the way he had last seen her, brutally robbed of life by an evil, badge-wearing man whom Kane still vowed to put in a body bag. He refused to think about her death other than to stoke the coals of vengeance simmering in his heart. When the moment came, those coals would fan into a flame so hot it would turn mercy to ash and ensure Sheriff Duncan Dunkirk died hard.

Instead, his thoughts focused on the night before she died, the one and only night they got to spend together.

He was not some young fool who believed in love at first sight, nor was he dumb enough to dismiss it when someone special came into his life, even for the briefest of moments. He remembered her vibrancy, her energy, and the bright spirit that had done so much to burn away the darkness that had engulfed him when their destinies crossed. He thought of her gentle touch, her silken skin, the fierce tenderness of their lovemaking.

He would remember her as a beautiful angel, not a broken plaything.

With most of the inmates out working, the cellblock —or housing unit, to use the proper jargon—was fairly quiet, and Kane took the opportunity to grab a power nap. He slept fitfully, his dreams full of blood and fire, death and destruction, dead teenagers and murdered women.

He jerked awake when his cell door swung open. He

came up off his bunk in one fast, fluid motion. His hand gripped the survival knife, tucking it just out of sight behind his right leg. If this was bad news coming into his room, they were going to catch seven inches of sharp steel right in the throat.

Kane was sick of playing nice.

But the visitor turned out to be Officer Simpson. Kane tossed the knife onto his bunk and made sure the guard could see his unarmed hands. "Morning, officer."

Simpson grunted at him. "Heard you're making a real name for yourself, Kane."

"It's prison. You're either predator or prey, right?"

"Something like that, yeah."

"Thought you worked the evening shift?"

"Doing a double," Simpson said. "Not that it's any of your concern."

"Right." Kane shrugged. "No reason for me to give a shit."

Simpson jerked a thumb over his shoulder. "Roll out. Nazareno wants to see you."

"He knows where I live."

"That's not the way it works around here, Kane."

"Maybe it's time for someone to change how things work."

Simpson sighed. "You're probably right, but not on my shift. You refuse to go see Nazareno, he'll send twenty MS-13 gangbangers in here to snatch you up. Being the big, beefy badass you think you are, you'll refuse to go quietly, and it'll turn into a full-blown riot. Goatsack and his pack of psycho trigger-pullers will roll in here and fuck everything up seven ways from Sunday, and I'll be left to clean up the goddamned mess." He paused and looked Kane right in the eye. "So do me a

favor, will ya? Just go see the man and save me a whole
lot of aggravation."

Kane detected the weariness and cynicism in Simpson's voice. "You on Nazareno's payroll, Simpson?"

Anger sparked in the officer's eyes. "No," he said,
"I'm not. Do you think I'd need to work a double if I was
on the take? But I happen to know how things work
around this cesspool. Even those of us who don't work
for Nazareno know better than to work *against* him."

"The only thing necessary for the triumph of evil is
for good men to do nothing," Kane quoted.

"Yeah, that's a real noble saying," Simpson said. "But
it don't mean jack-all in the real world where good men
are just trying to keep from getting their throats slit and
their families safe. You have no idea what kind of power
Nazareno has."

"Oh, I'm getting the picture," Kane said.

"So, will you go see him?"

"Point the way."

Simpson gestured toward the front door of the unit.
"Go outside, take a left, and follow the walkway until you
come to Alpha Unit."

"Do I need to report to the officer?"

"There ain't no officer in Alpha Unit. That's
Nazareno's home base."

Kane made a disgusted noise deep in his throat. He
couldn't believe how much of a stranglehold Nazareno
had on the prison. The corruption had to run seriously
high up the Bureau of Prisons food chain to pull off this
kind of total takeover.

Out in the fresh air, Kane breathed deeply. He hadn't
realized how stifling the housing unit was until he
stepped outside and got a face full of the breezes coming
off the surrounding mountains.

He strolled along the path toward Alpha Unit, taking his time, making Nazareno wait. He passed a couple of yard workers using short straw brooms to sweep up trash from the asphalt. They both lowered their heads and kept their distance.

The entrance to Alpha Unit was unlocked. Knowing attitude counted, Kane walked in like he owned the place.

A burly Hispanic with an inverted pentagram tattooed on his forehead immediately braced him. "Who the hell are you?"

"You know who I am," Kane replied. "So cut the scare tactics and take me to the guy who holds your leash."

Pentagram's eyes narrowed to glittering slits. "You calling me a dog, *cabron*?"

"Pretty much." Kane flashed a wolfish smile. "Now, be a good bitch and take me to your boss."

Right on cue, a knife appeared in the inmate's fist. Kane was starting to think they handed them out like toothbrushes. "You begging to be cut, asshole," Pentagram snarled.

Kane ignored the threat. "Cut the crap," he said. "You and I both know you can't do shit unless Nazareno says so."

Pentagram looked like he was about to say something else—probably some standard-issue Spanish insult—but an agonized scream pierced through the housing unit, reverberating off the walls like the echoes of the damned.

The enforcer glanced over his shoulder at one of the six-man cells on the lower right tier, then turned back toward Kane with an evil grin. "You and I can dance later, *cabron*. Right now, I think there is something you should see." He headed for the cell, clearly expecting Kane to follow.

Kane seriously considered turning around and walking out. It grated on him to be following the demands of a drug lord and his scumbag minions, but he also knew Nazareno commanded enough manpower to drag him here against his will. He preferred to stand on his own two feet.

He crossed the common area and stepped into the six-man cell.

It was like he had entered some kind of twisted hybrid of a luxury suite, a torture chamber, an abattoir, and a sublayer of hell.

The wall between two six-man cells had been knocked out, creating one long, spacious—by prison standards—thirty-five-foot by twelve-foot room. To Kane's right, plush rugs covered the tile floor. There were silk sheets on the bunk, covering a mattress at least quadruple the thickness of the one Kane slept on. Satin drapes adorned the window, which came equipped with blackout blinds. On the wall hung paintings that Kane didn't recognize but looked expensive. In keeping with Nazareno's Christ persona, Catholic iconography like crucifixes and Virgin Mary statues also served as decoration. Or perhaps they served a more devotional purpose. After all, Nazareno wouldn't be the first person to commit wickedness while claiming to serve God.

On the left, the room looked more like a regular cell —except the bunks had been removed, the floor sloped slightly downward toward a stainless steel drain, and a naked man hung by his wrists from a fire suppression system pipe. All the flesh below his knees had been filleted off, exposing a wet, glistening mess of musculature.

Nazareno, dressed in blood-splattered robes, stood beside the man, performing the same grisly operation on the right side of the man's face with an oversized butcher blade that looked better suited for carving beef carcasses than peeling off layers of skin.

It took Kane a few moments, but once he got a good look at the horrible face twisted into a rictus of pain, he recognized Santos, the convict he had tussled with in the chow hall a few hours earlier.

Leaning against the wall by the sink was another face Kane recognized. He felt his guts tighten. The man's presence here was bad news for Kane.

Nazareno turned to face his visitor. The blood droplets spattered on his shaved head gave the tattooed crown of thorns an eerily realistic appearance. The drug lord held the knife low by his side, blood dripping off the tip like a leaking faucet.

"We meet again, Kane." Nazareno gestured toward the mangled man hanging from the pipe. "Recognize our friend Santos? I told you that if you killed him, it would be better than what I would do to him."

Kane shrugged. "He's nothing to me, and if you wanted to prove you're a sadistic son of a bitch, you're wasting your time. I already knew that."

Nazareno smiled. "Well, I've been learning some things I didn't know about you," he said, "thanks to my special guest, Mr. Chance." He nodded toward the man leaning against the wall.

Kane looked at Eddy Chance, a white guy with dreadlocks, and wondered why karma was kicking him in the nuts right now. It was pure bad luck that Eddy was here in this shithole along with Kane.

Eddy Chance had survived an autofire blitz Team Reaper had launched in New York City that had exposed an alliance between the upper echelon of the DEA and a Colombian cartel with ties to a homegrown al-Qaeda cell. To kick-start the kill count, Kane had shaken down Eddy, a street-level dealer, for information, and then let him scurry away like a rat while they torched his bar. He'd been a lowlife nobody who Kane had seen no reason to kill at the time.

Hindsight being 20/20, that might have been a mistake.

Eddy crossed his arms and sneered at Kane. "Remember me, hotshot?"

"Sure," Kane grunted. "I never forget an asshole."

"Yeah? Well, this asshole just made sure you're screwed, dipshit. Consider it payback for what you did to my bar."

Nazareno said, "Eddy claims you are not who you appear to be."

"You believe everything you hear?"

"He was *muy* persuasive. Says you are a cop or narc or some kind of special agent."

"I'm just a nobody who got locked up for a crime he didn't commit."

"I believe you didn't commit any crime," Nazareno said. "But I do not believe you're a *peon*, a nobody. Your fighting skills alone prove that you've had extensive combat training."

"My past is my business," Kane replied. "But I'll tell you this—I'm not a cop."

"Prove it." Nazareno tossed him the butcher knife. Instinctively, Kane caught it, fingers gripping the rubberized handle. The drug lord backed away and gestured at Santos. "If you're not a cop, finish him off."

Kane briefly considered going after Nazareno with the blade. Just kill the bastard right here and now. But it would be a suicide play. This was not one of those times where executing the head snake meant the rest of the vipers would slink off. No, if he cut Nazareno's throat, he would be ripped apart within minutes. The drug lord commanded a small army. They would pull his arms off and use them to play softball, then yank his head off his spine and play a game of soccer with it.

Damn straight, Kane wanted Nazareno dead, but he didn't want to die doing it. He wasn't above sacrificing himself for the greater good if that was what it came down to, but a kamikaze blaze of glory was the last resort, not his first option.

Nazareno seemed to read his thoughts. An amused smile tugged at the corner of his lips. "Trust me, Kane, you wouldn't even get close."

Kane stared hard at the drug lord. "Another time, another place, maybe we'll find out."

"There won't be another time or another place if you don't finish off Santos and prove to me that you're not a cop."

In the end, Kane did it. Not to convince Nazareno of anything—thanks to Eddy Chance, the cartel king knew he was some kind of law enforcement, and nothing Kane did would change that—except to put the tortured son of a bitch out of his misery. He had no idea what crimes Santos had committed, but whatever they were, they didn't merit being skinned alive. Kane wasn't above torturing a bad guy when necessary, like when he needed information fast. But this? This was nothing but sick sadism.

Kane stepped close, careful not to slip on all the blood greasing the floor. He could hear Santos' shallow breathing, the whimpers of pain convulsing deep in the convict's throat. The lid had been sliced off his right eye, making it bulge in grotesque agony. His hacked-up lips moved in a whispered plea to Kane.

"Kill...me."

Kane granted his final wish, slipping the knife into his ribcage. The sharp blade punched between the curved bones and stabbed into Santos' frantically-beating heart. He stiffened at the metallic penetration and shuddered like a pinned moth, then his muscles slowly relaxed as Kane withdrew the knife. The life pumped out of him in a red river, and the light quickly faded from his eyes. His head slumped onto his chest as he took his last breath.

Kane turned to Nazareno. "Satisfied?"

Eddy came off the wall and stepped toward them. "I'm telling you, Mr. Nazareno, this guy's some kind of special agent or something. He had some bitch with him, and if you can find her—"

Kane's hand moved in a blur, the butcher blade a silver streak as it sliced through the air and then through Eddy's throat. His windpipe and jugular slit wide open, blood sprayed from the wicked gash as the dreadlocked drug dealer stumbled backward, bounced off the wall, and slumped to the floor in a sitting position next to the toilet, gurgling his last.

Kane didn't waste time with a snappy post-mortem one-liner, instead settling for a simple, "Fuck you, Eddy," as he glared down at the fresh corpse. He should have left Cara out of this.

Nazareno smiled. "You're racking up quite a body count in a short amount of time. Then again, you probably have hundreds of notches on your gun-belt, being the leader of a covert anti-cartel strike team."

Kane kept quiet. Nazareno already knew too much. Talking wasn't going to help anything.

"Give me the silent treatment if it makes you feel better," Nazareno said. "But I can see the surprise on your face." He plucked a towel off a hook on the wall and wiped the blood off his face and scalp. "Trust me, Kane— or should I call you 'Reaper?'"

Kane's jaw clenched. How the hell did this son of a bitch know all this?

"I like 'Reaper,'" Nazareno said. "Let's go with that. So trust me, Reaper, when I tell you that my reach is vast and I own people in high places. I will admit I do not have all the details, but I do know that you are part of some black ops team that wages war on the cartels."

Kane pointed at Santos. "Then why go through the theatrics of having me kill him?"

"Merely curious to see if you would do it."

"They call me Reaper, not Mother Theresa."

Nazareno tossed the towel on the floor. No doubt some boot-licking—or rather, sandal-licking—lackey would pick it up and wash it later. "That's *muy bueno* to know because if you want to stay alive to see another sunrise, you will have to kill again. And again. And again."

"What are you talking about?"

Before Nazareno answered, the door opened and Goatsack, along with several members of his team, entered the cell.

"Take him," Nazareno ordered. "Put him on ice until *esta noche*."

"What happens tonight?" Kane asked, although he already had a good idea.

As Goatsack and Breezy stepped forward to flex-cuff his wrists, Nazareno replied, "Since you enjoy killing bad guys so much, we're going to give you the chance to do exactly that. Tonight, you fight in the Pit."

"Kill or be killed," Goatsack growled.

"To the death," Breezy said.

"No mercy," Big Belly added.

"Yeah," Kane rasped, "I get the fucking idea."

As he felt the plastic loops slip over his hands, Kane thought about resisting, putting up a fight, making these assholes earn their keep. He quickly discarded the idea. There was no way to win. He would get in his licks, break a few limbs, and maybe snap a neck or two if he got lucky. But in the end, between Goatsack's crew and Nazareno's gang, he would be subdued and beaten. His body still ached from last night's welcome-to-Black-Bog beat-down, so adding bruises on top of bruises didn't seem like a smart play. He would need all his strength to survive the Pit tonight; better to conserve his energy now.

As Goatsack and Breezy escorted him out of the cell, Nazareno called, "Enjoy the rest of your day, Reaper. I'll see you tonight."

Over his shoulder, Kane tossed him a bared-teeth wolf-smile and replied, "Just remember, asshole, they don't call me Reaper for nothing."

THIRTEEN

Vesper Lake Sheriff's Station

Sheriff Dunkirk set the phone back down in its cradle as Paul entered the office, which was really just a glass-enclosed cubicle in the back corner of the station.

His sole surviving son plopped down in one of the two chairs arrayed in front of the desk. He looked like he had been crying, but he also looked sweaty.

"Where have you been?" Dunkirk demanded.

"Banging Jailbait."

"Where?"

"Back room of Baldy's."

Dunkirk said, "That little slut is gonna give you an STD one of these days. For God's sake, Paul, she's been with damn near every guy in a fifty-mile radius."

Paul sniffed and shrugged. "I wanted to forget about Nick."

"Did it work?"

"For about sixty seconds, yeah, it worked great."

Dunkirk shook his head again, but he understood Paul's need to do something—anything—to not think about his brother's death. Hell, he was being hypocritical because he had screwed the shit out of Jailbait last night in the back of the Bronco, but there was no reason to tell Paul that. He had done it for no other reason than to stop the pain inside. He felt nothing for the girl, nor she for him, but he didn't care. For the better part of an hour, he had taken from her exactly what he needed.

But it hadn't lasted. By the time he'd crawled into the shower, the grief had pounced on him again, Nick's ghost haunting his mind. He couldn't believe his son—the only one worth a damn, although he almost never said that to Paul—was gone, snuffed out by a lucky bullet from a stuck-up whore who thought she was better than them.

Nick was now laid out on a mortician's slab at McCulley's Funeral Home on Church Street, funeral scheduled for the day after tomorrow. No point in waiting to bury him. Wasn't like there were going to be carloads of friends and family rolling into town to pay their respects. His wife had run off to Manitoba with some neck-bearded lumberjack shortly after Paul was born, and the other relatives had never factored much into their lives. Partly because they were so isolated up here in the mountains, partly because Duncan Dunkirk was a mean, ornery son of a bitch who nobody wanted to be around.

Made scheduling a funeral real easy.

Paul pointed at the phone. "Who were you talking to?"

"Nazareno."

"What'd he want?"

"Just letting us know the Pit is open tonight."

"We going?"

"You want to?"

Paul shrugged. "Nick always liked the Pit fights."

"That cocksucker Kane is fighting." Dunkirk leaned forward in his chair and rested his elbows on the desk. "Turns out he's some kind of spec-ops federal agent."

Paul's eyebrows shot up. "Federal agent? Shit, we fucked with a fed?"

"Relax. Nazareno's got it covered."

"Still..." Paul looked worried.

"Do you want to go tonight? Watch him die with your own eyes?"

"Yeah. Yeah, let's do it for Nick. If that damn fed hadn't come to our town and got Luna all hot an' bothered, Nick would still be alive."

Dunkirk didn't bother pointing out that if Paul and Nick had just left Luna alone, Kane wouldn't have messed with them, and Nick would still be alive. Let him blame Kane for his brother's death. The delusion provided him with a focus for his rage and grief.

"Go home and get some rest," Dunkirk said. "Meet me back here tonight at seven-thirty."

"Seven-thirty." Paul grinned. "Watching Kane get killed tonight is gonna be fun."

Yeah, Dunkirk thought. *Killing is always fun, as long as you're not the one getting killed.*

* * *

Black Bog Federal Prison
2030 Hours

. . .

Kane stood in the "arena" as the mob roared, hungry for blood.

The Pit turned out to be the prison's old textile factory, which had once manufactured backpacks and canteen holders for the U.S. military, until mandatory sourcing laws changed and Uncle Sam found cheaper manufacturers on the free market. The industrial sewing machines and fabric-cutting tables had been stripped out and sold off, leaving the hangar-sized building empty.

When Nazareno seized control of the prison, he'd had the factory retrofitted into a makeshift coliseum. Portable sports bleachers, enough to seat eight hundred people, formed an octagonal ring in which the combatants battled. Racks of weapons—clubs, axes, knives, machetes, spears, etc.—hung on the walls. Loudspeakers were suspended from the exposed steel rafters.

All this had been explained to Kane by Goatsack. He and his SORT team had escorted Kane from Alpha Unit directly to the factory and spent the rest of the day guarding him. It had given Kane a chance to get to learn the individual team members' personalities as he listened to them grumble and grouse. Not that it mattered; he still fully intended to kill them all.

"This is some bullshit," Yippy had snapped. "Yesterday we're gunning down bitches, today we're babysitting."

"Least you ain't got blue balls," Big Belly had said. "Hey, Goat, really wish you had let me nail one of them girls yesterday before we smoked 'em."

"Reaper looks bored." Sirius had waved at Kane. "Hey, Reaper, you okay with getting diddled by Big Belly here? It'll help pass the time and take care of his blue ball problem."

Kane hadn't bothered responding.

The team swapped war stories, told dirty jokes, boasted about sexual exploits, and played cards. Around noon, Red Cent and Happy went out and fetched some pizzas the team scarfed down like a school of piranhas attacking a monkey that fell in the river. They didn't offer Kane any, ignoring his growling stomach.

When the feast ended, Goatsack came over with a couple of crusts and tossed them on Kane's lap like a master offering scraps to a mongrel mutt. Kane's hands remained flex-cuffed in front of him, but he was able to pick up the crusts and get them to his mouth. Beggars couldn't be choosers, and he needed the fuel for the upcoming fights.

Goatsack perched on the bleachers nearby and studied him. "You really some kind of badass fed, Reaper?"

"Not officially, no."

"Black ops?"

"Something like that."

Goatsack shook his head. "How the hell did you end up in here, Reaper?"

"Long story."

"I've got the time if you're interested in telling."

"I'm not."

"Figured as much." Goatsack stood up.

"Hey," Kane said.

"Yeah?"

"You were a good man once, right?"

Goatsack pondered that, then replied, "Yeah, I guess I was. A long time ago."

Kane nodded. "I'm gonna do you a favor and kill you quick."

Goatsack burst out laughing. "I appreciate that,

Reaper. I really do." He shook his head, still chuckling. "Damn, man, but I like your style."

They spent the afternoon napping, Kane included, resting up for the evening's blood-sport. Dinner turned out to be Chinese takeout. They gave Kane half an eggroll and the dregs of the pork fried rice.

Duck crumbled a fortune cookie in front of him and made a big show of reading the slip of paper. "Hey, Reaper, I've got your fortune right here. It says, 'You're fucked.'"

The team had a good laugh at that one.

Goatsack took him to the bathroom and let him drink some water out of the faucet and use the toilet. "Almost game time, Reaper."

"Wasn't sure I was gonna make it," Kane said. "Thought I might die of boredom first."

Around 8:00 p.m., some of Nazareno's posse showed up to open the main doors so that the spectators could filter in and fill the bleachers. Within minutes, the quiet of the day gave way to the bloodthirsty noise of the night.

The Pit was ready for some rock 'n' roll carnage.

Men wove through the crowd, taking bets. The loud-speakers blared to life, and some kind of reggae-infused heavy metal blasted through the factory like a sonic cannonball. Even that paled in comparison to the thunderous roar of the crowd.

Goatsack motioned for Kane to stand up, then snipped off his flex-cuffs. "Get ready," the SORT leader said. "Nazareno will be here any minute now, and then this party will really get started."

"The warden come to this shitshow?" Kane asked.

"Ghastin? You bet. Nazareno makes her come." He

chuckled at the double entendre. "She'll be right by his side like a good little pet."

As if on cue, the Nazarene Dragon appeared, wearing a robe so dazzlingly white that it had to be bleached. Six hard-eyed men swarmed around him, including Pentagram, all sporting the distinctive tattoos of the murderous MS-13 gang. All carried machetes, and all looked more than ready to use them. No, not just ready—*hoping* to use them.

To his left and slightly behind, heeling like a well-trained dog, walked Kumi Ghastin. Her eyes locked with Kane's for a brief moment, then slid away. Her hair was damp as if she had just showered. Kane suspected he knew why she had needed one.

Try as he might, Kane just couldn't bring himself to hate her.

The same could not be said for the men on Nazareno's right.

The sight of Sheriff Dunkirk and his son Paul sent hot rage seething through Kane like molten lava. He clenched his jaw, teeth grinding together as he stared at the men who had murdered Luna, wondering if there was any way he would get a chance to kill them tonight.

The sheriff spotted him, flashed a toothy grin, and mockingly dragged a finger across his throat to remind him of how Luna had died. Because of his repetition tic, Paul mirrored his father's actions.

Kane welcomed the hate he felt for the two men, and the anger and fury their presence spawned. He let it pump into his bloodstream like fuel and fill his veins like an adrenalized narcotic. That hate, that rage, would keep him alive tonight.

He would live so that he could see the Dunkirks die.

A section of the bleachers had been reserved for

Nazareno and his entourage. Once they were seated, a tall, skinny black man walked into the center of the octagon with a wireless microphone in his hand. He had long, slender fingers like a concert pianist.

The ring announcer raised the mic to his lips. As the last note of the heavy metal music faded, the announcer bellowed, "Mad dogs and motherfuckers! Welcome to the Pit!"

The mob roared, the cacophony echoing and reverberating and rolling off the concrete walls and metal roof.

"Are you ready for blood?" the announcer shouted.

This roar was even louder than the last. A jet engine could have fired up in the next room and nobody would have heard it.

"You know the rules! Three rounds! Last man standing lives to die another day!"

More screams and howls and shouts of approval. The throng began to stomp on the metal bleachers, kicking into a well-known rhythm and chanting a famous rock anthem with altered lyrics.

"We will, we will, KILL YOU!"

The announcer spun three hundred and sixty degrees, leg cocked in some weird dance move that looked like a combination of the moonwalk and the hokey-pokey. Clearly, the guy loved playing to an audience. Had probably been a DJ in his pre-incarceration life.

"Now listen up, y'all." His voice boomed from the loudspeakers. "We have a newcomer tonight. Bastard came in like a wrecking ball and has been stacking up bodies since his boots hit the compound. You can call him a newbie, you can call him a cherry, you can call him the new fish on the block...or you can just call him by his motherfucking name." With a flourish, he pointed a bony finger at Kane and shouted, "John 'the Reaper' Kane!"

The crowd erupted. Word of Kane's combat prowess had spread through the prison like wildfire, and they were all expecting him to bring the pain tonight. They began chanting his name.

"Reaper! Reaper! Reaper!"

Kane wasn't fooled into believing they actually liked or respected him. They simply expected him to unleash the carnage they craved, and for that, they would cheer him on.

The announcer motioned for silence, and the mob complied.

"His opponent, the current reigning champion of the Pit," he pointed at the inmate as he stepped down from the bleachers and entered the octagon, "is the man we call 'Lumberjack!'"

It wasn't hard to figure out where the convict's name had come from. A black knit cap perched on his head, thick tufts of red hair sprouting from underneath. His bristly ginger beard hung all the way down to the middle of his barrel chest, which was clad in a sleeveless red-and-black checked flannel shirt that left his bulging biceps exposed. His jeans were tucked into calf-high steel-toed logging boots.

Lumberjack glared across the ring at Kane and snarled, "I'm gonna split you open like a rotten log, asshole."

The crowd roared its approval at the trash-talk.

The announcer raised the microphone to his lips again. "As the reigning champion of the Pit, Lumberjack gets to choose which weapons they will fight with tonight."

"Axes," Lumberjack said. "Gonna chop this fucker down like a tree."

An inmate wearing a black t-shirt with the word

Armorer stenciled in white letters on the back walked into the ring holding two double-bladed axes. He tossed one to Lumberjack and one to Kane, then scurried back out of sight.

Kane hefted the weapon, getting a feel for its weight and balance. The hickory handle was worn smooth. He took a test swing, making sure to keep a tight grip. The wood slid against his palm slightly. Not enough to cause concern, but if the handle was slick with blood, weapon control might become a problem.

Nothing he could do about it. This was the hand the gods of war had dealt him. All he could do now was play the game.

"You know the rules!" the announcer shouted. "One man dies! One man lives! THIS IS THE PITS!"

The skinny man moonwalked out of the ring. Kane had to give him style points. The guy knew how to fire up a crowd.

There was no bell to signal the start of the death-match. As soon as the announcer exited the octagon, Lumberjack bellowed a roar that would have made Godzilla proud and charged across the ring. He swung the axe like a baseball bat, aiming to hit a homerun on Kane's neck.

Kane saw that while Lumberjack might be big, he was also slow.

He easily ducked the blow and the axe whistled over his head. He fired an elbow into Lumberjack's flank, connecting just above the hipbone but missing the ribcage. He cursed silently. He'd been hoping to break a rib and make it harder for the man to maneuver.

He powered upright before Lumberjack could bring the axe around for another swing. Gripping his own axe just below the double-bladed head, he jabbed his opponent in the face. Not enough force to punch through bone, but the honed edge split Lumberjack's nose open like a sliced pear. Blood drizzled into his beard, staining the bristles a much darker shade of red.

Lumberjack staggered backward, clutching his hacked-up face. He looked surprised as hell to be bleeding.

Kane hooked a heel behind the man's ankle and sent him to the ground. As he fell, Kane raised the axe and brought it slamming down in a hard, vicious chop.

Lumberjack landed on his back and raised a hand to ward off the blow.

Kane's axe struck him between the middle and ring fingers, shearing all the way through to split his forearm open halfway down to the elbow. Blood exploded from carved flesh and severed tendons.

Lumberjack howled in pain, his bloody mouth forming a large, perfect circle.

Ripping the axe free, Kane swung again, using that circle as a target.

The axe scored a bullseye, silencing the howl in a sickening crunch of bone.

The whole fight had barely lasted thirty seconds.

Kane pulled the axe out of Lumberjack's bisected face, brains dripping from the blade, and stared up at Nazareno in the bleachers. "That the best you got?" he rasped.

The crowd had lapsed into stunned silence following his rapid destruction of the fearsome Lumberjack. Now it erupted into hoots and hollers. Their tongues took up his name and turned it into a primal chant.

"Reaper! Reaper! Reaper!"

There was a new champion in the octagon.

Nazareno did not look pleased.

The announcer stepped forward and raised the microphone to his lips. "Did *not* see that coming, y'all. Lumberjack went down, and I mean *hard*. Damn fool fell like a chain-sawed tree." He cupped his free hand behind his ear. "Can I get a 'Timmmmmmberrrrrr?'"

The mob responded with vigor and enthusiasm.

"TIMMMMMMBBBERRRRRR!"

A couple of inmates hustled into the ring and dragged out Lumberjack's body, leaving behind a crimson smear on the floor like slug-slime.

"Next up," the announcer said, "is the man who don't need no nickname, 'cause his real name is already badass. Tommy Gunn!"

The blond-haired, chisel-jawed inmate who climbed down out of the stands and entered the ring lacked the bulk of Kane's previous opponent. Gunn topped out at only six feet tall, giving Kane a clear height and reach advantage.

But as he sized up his new foe, Kane recognized the danger lurking beneath Gunn's deceptive surface. His muscles might not bulge with 'roid-rage intensity, but their lean power could prove deadly. Kane also expected Gunn to be much faster on his feet than Lumberjack.

"As the current prince of the Pit, Reaper gets to choose the weapons for this match." The announcer looked expectantly at Kane.

There were plenty of exotic and oddball weapons arrayed on the racks, but Kane stuck with the familiar. "Knife."

The armorer appeared with a bucketful of blades. Not chintzy, makeshift prison shanks, but real, honest-to-goodness knives, including several tactical options.

Kane preferred a Ka-Bar, but he didn't see any, so he selected a Schrade SCH9 with a 6.4" drop blade and a weight of only sixteen ounces. With its blunted nose, the Schrade worked best for chopping and slicing rather than stabbing thrusts. Kane tended to be more of a slasher than a stabber, so that didn't bother him.

Gunn selected a SOG SEAL Pup Elite, a full-tang knife with a partially-serrated edge. The handle sported a deep diamond pattern for a better grip. It was a few inches shorter than Kane's blade but weighed just five and a half ounces—light and lethal, just like the man wielding it.

The announcer shouted his pre-fight shtick. "You know the rules! One man dies! One man lives! THIS IS THE PITS!"

The crowd roared encouragement, but neither man rushed to engage. Instead, they circled each other warily. Every twenty seconds or so, Gunn feinted, but Kane refused to take the bait. He also refused to make the first move. He had all night. The onlookers started demanding action, with loud boos coming from the assembled mob. Kane didn't give a damn. He would dance to his tune, not theirs.

Gunn proved to be less patient. As the crowd started calling them pussies, he came in fast, looking to score first. He feinted for the tenth time, started to draw back as usual, and suddenly lunged forward in a fake-out attempt. As Kane had suspected, he was quick. His blade flicked out like a silver serpent's tongue.

Held low, Gunn's SOG went for a gut strike, trying to tear a hole in Kane's lower abdomen. He came close, but close only counted when you were playing with grenades, not knives.

Kane spun away from the stab, the blade just kissing his shirt. He tried to punch Gunn's jaw with his left hand but only succeeded in delivering a glancing blow to the neck that did no damage.

He brought up his right knee, catching Gunn's elbow and popping his arm up into a horizontal position. He tried to thrust his Schrade underneath the outstretched limb and into the vulnerable armpit, but Gunn dropped his arm in time to block the blow.

With his knife deflected downward, Kane let momentum carry the blade across Gunn's kneecap. A shallow wound, not much worse than a shaving cut, but it still meant Kane had drawn first blood.

Gunn went for payback with a wild slash. Kane jumped back out of range, and the SOG caught nothing but empty air.

The crowd started chanting again—*"Reaper! Reaper! Reaper!"*—as he went on the offensive. Knife-fighting was not his specialty, but his skills were well above average. Gunn countered better than expected, but within minutes, his arms were cut to shreds. He managed to deny Kane a killing blow, but his forearms looked like they had been run through a threshing machine. Blood dripped like rain all over the floor.

That blood almost cost Kane his life.

He spotted an opening that would let him shove the Schrade into Gunn's belly. After that, it would just be a matter of slitting him open and letting his insides come out.

He stepped forward to make the kill...and his foot slipped on the blood.

It was like stepping on spilled grease.

He recovered quickly, his boot only sliding a few inches, but it was enough to make him miss his opportunity. Worse, it left him momentarily vulnerable.

Gunn was no chump fighter, and he seized the

moment. Seeing Kane off-balance, he bulled forward, knife slashing. The blade caught Kane high on the left shoulder and sliced a burning path of pain down across his collarbone. Nothing deep and certainly not fatal, but too close a call for Kane's comfort. A few inches higher, and the SOG would have sunk into the side of his neck and severed an artery.

As he retreated from the slashing blade, Kane's left hand shot out, fingers wrapping like steel bands around Gunn's wrist. Using the man's forward momentum against him, Kane rolled down onto the floor, slammed his boots into Gunn's stomach, and executed a tactical rear somersault that sent the convict sailing over his head.

As Gunn crashed down on his back with spine-jarring force, Kane regained his feet and attacked. Before his opponent could recover, he stepped forward, dropped to one knee, and drove his blade hilt-deep into Gunn's belly. He immediately dragged the knife upward until he hit bone.

The crowd's savage roars of approval drowned out the agonized groans from Gunn. As bluish-gray loops bulged from the gaping wound, the inmate reached down to hold them in, fingers fumbling with the slippery coils spilling out onto the floor.

Kane quickly ended Gunn's pain by cutting his throat.

Primal energy crackled through the building as the mob once again took up the chant.

"Reaper! Reaper! Reaper!"

Kane rose as Gunn's gutted corpse twitched at his feet. He despised being forced to kill for sport, but it was the only way to survive. He either killed or died. The crowd screamed for blood, and he would give it to them —not because he wanted to, but because there was no other choice. He would give no quarter, show no mercy, until he gained his freedom. When he was free, he would avenge Luna's death.

He fixed a cold-eyed stare on the Dunkirks seated next to Nazareno. The sheriff and his deranged son were dead men walking, and they didn't even know it. Kane would crawl out of hell to kill them if that was what it took.

The corpse-removal cadre swept in and dragged the very dead Gunn out of the octagon.

Right on cue, the announcer stepped forward. "We always knew Tommy Gunn had guts, but leave it to Reaper to show them to us!"

The crowd yelled and shouted and pumped their fists in the air.

"One more fight," the skinny man announced. "Who will be tonight's final challenger for Reaper?"

Nazareno stood up.

An absolute hush fell over the mob.

The drug lord descended from the bleachers and entered the octagon, careful not to put his sandaled feet down in any of the spilled blood.

Kane glanced up at Kumi Ghastin. The warden looked stunned. He understood how she felt. He could hardly believe it himself. What would make the Nazarene Dragon come down here and fight him to the death?

Nothing, as it turned out. Nazareno had no intention of fighting him. But he did have other plans, and they were almost as shocking.

He took the microphone from the announcer. "Is everyone enjoying the show?"

The rafters rocked as the mob expressed its enthusiasm. Nothing like eight hundred bloodthirsty men screaming, "Hell, yeah!" at the top of their lungs to make the walls rattle and shake.

"For our final showdown, we have a special treat for you," Nazareno declared. "A bona fide grudge match."

He walked over to Kane, who still had the knife in his hand. He experienced another flickering temptation to just stab the drug lord in the face and call it a night, but it passed immediately. He would never make it out of the octagon alive. The crowd would tear him to pieces.

Standing next to Kane, Nazareno pointed up into the stands at Paul Dunkirk. "Tell us, Reaper, what that man did."

Paul looked stunned to suddenly be the center of attention.

"He raped and murdered a woman I cared for," Kane said.

"You want to kill him? Eye for an eye, tooth for tooth, that sort of thing?"

"Damn straight."

"*Excelente,* because you are going to get your chance."

Up in the bleachers, Paul's face turned white and stricken.

"That's right, *hombres,*" Nazareno said to the crowd. "Tonight's final contest will be a vengeance match between Reaper and the man who killed his woman. To the death, with no mercy given!"

The mob erupted into absolute bedlam. They stomped and cheered and shouted, their enthusiastic roar shaking the building like the thunder of the apocalypse. *This* was next-level entertainment as far as they were concerned, and they loudly expressed their appreciation.

Sheriff Dunkirk, Paul trailing close behind him like a shadow, shoved his way through the raucous crowd and stormed into the ring. "What the hell do you think you're doing, Nazareno?" he demanded.

"Spicing things up," the drug lord replied. "Adding a personal component to the Pit fights."

"I work for you," Dunkirk said. "I'm on your side. You *need* me out there to run your operations. My son doesn't fight for the amusement of these dirtbags."

"Dirtbags," Paul echoed.

Nazareno stepped in close, his voice dropping to a hiss that didn't even carry to the bottom row of the bleachers. "That's right, you work for me, which means you do what you're told, or you'll find yourself rotting at the bottom of the bog. And you're not on my *side*, Dunkirk. You just like my money. You're a *mercenario*, not a partner." His thin lips peeled back in a predatory smile. "And while it's true that I need someone on the outside, that someone doesn't have to be you. You're expendable, Dunkirk. Nothing more than a *peon*, and don't you dare forget it."

"This is crap, Nazareno, and you know it."

"You know it," Paul repeated.

"Your son fights," Nazareno stated. "That is the end of it."

"Dammit, man! I just lost a son yesterday!"

"That was your fault, not mine. Your sons roughed up a *chica* and took a beating for it, but they couldn't just leave it at that. No, like a bunch of *tontos*, you had to go mess with the man, rape his woman, and cut her throat."

The sheriff looked dumbfounded. "How the hell do you know all that?"

"I've told you before that I know everything that happens in this town. It's *my* fucking town."

"Yeah, well, that stuck-up little bitch had it coming."

"Had it coming," Paul agreed.

Seething with rage, Kane nearly ripped their throats out then and there.

"Maybe she did, maybe she did not." Nazareno shrugged. "That is not my concern. What *is* my concern is that by giving 'that stuck-up little *puta*' what you say she had coming, you pissed off a man who happens to be the head of a black-ops task force with just one mission: destroy the cartels and anyone associated with them."

"How the hell was I supposed to know that?" Dunkirk whined.

Nazareno ignored the question. "You fucked with this man and then dumped him here. You stirred up a shit-storm and then tossed it in my lap for me to deal with."

"Like I said, how was I supposed to kn—"

Nazareno cut him off. "I will deal with it, but not until you have paid the price for your stupidity." He pointed at Paul. "He fights, or I will have you both chopped into pieces an inch at a time. No more conversation. Make your choice."

"C'mon, man!" Dunkirk gestured at Kane. "Paul doesn't stand a chance against this bastard."

"Make your choice," Nazareno repeated.

During the exchange between the drug lord and the sheriff, Kane watched the color return to Paul's face and the fear leave his eyes. His jaw clenched, and his hands curled into fists. "Let me fight him, Dad," he growled. "Let me kill him for Nick."

"He'll destroy you."

Paul shook his head. "Not today, he won't. He can fight for that stupid whore, and I'll fight for my brother. When it's over, I promise you Kane will be burning in hell."

The look on the sheriff's face made it clear that he knew his son didn't stand a chance. It would take a miracle for Paul to survive, and God wasn't in the habit of wasting His miracles on murdering rapists.

Sheriff Dunkirk looked at Nazareno again. "Why are you doing this to me?"

"I told you. You dumped shit on my doorstep. Now you pay the price."

"Something tells me there's more to it than that."

Nazareno's eyes flashed with dark, hostile fire. "You thought you could run guns out of my town and not tell me?"

"That's what this is about? Hell, Nazareno, we can square that up right now. I'll cut you in for fifty percent of the profits. Hell, buddy, make it sixty."

Nazareno shook his head slowly, like a cobra trying to hypnotize its prey. "I am not your *companero,* and I do not get cut in on deals. I am the one who does the cutting, and you are about to learn that some lessons cut deep." He stepped back, raised the microphone to his lips, and shouted, "They fight! To the death!"

Looking distraught but accepting his fate, or rather, his son's fate, Sheriff Dunkirk returned to his seat in the bleachers.

Paul stripped off his shirt and tossed it aside. Sweat beads glistened in the tangled nest of his chest hair. If Kane had his way, that sweat would soon be mixed with blood.

Nazareno whispered something to the announcer as he handed him back the microphone. The skinny man nodded and stepped into the ring. "All right, you mad dogs and motherfuckers! Get ready for the main event! Man to man, *mano a mano*...with no weapons!"

The crowd thundered its approval.

"That's right," the announcer shouted. "Reaper and the sheriff's son will battle each other using nothing but tooth and claw. One fights for a woman. One fights for his brother. They both fight for VENGEANCE!" He thrust his fist into the sky in a rock star pose and screamed, "You know the rules! One man dies! One man lives!" He held the microphone out to the mob. "Give it to me!"

Eight hundred spectators roared, "THIS IS THE PIT!"

The announcer moonwalked out of the octagon again —Kane wondered if the skinny guy knew how to bust any other dance moves—and the war began.

Except it wasn't much of a war.

More like a beat-down.

With Luna's face at the forefront of his mind, Kane demolished the man who had violated her. He opened up with a hard, looping right cross that struck Paul flush on the jaw and sent him reeling sideways. He followed up with a short, sharp punch to the ribs.

Paul managed a weak swing that didn't even come close. Kane punished him for his pathetic fighting skills by hammering his already-broken nose. Cursing and snorting in pain, Paul staggered backward. Kane chased him like a lion stalking a crippled antelope. His left hand feinted a jab. Paul fell for the fake, moving to block, and Kane instead sank a vicious blow deep into the bastard's belly, doing his damnedest to drive his fist all the way through to the spine.

The air exploding from Paul's lungs sounded like a blacksmith's bellows. He backed away, retching and gasping like a beached fish as he struggled to reclaim his ability to breathe.

Kane grabbed him and pivoted, rolling the man over his hip in a judo throw. Paul flipped through the air and landed on his back.

Anger burned through Kane's veins. He wanted Paul

Dunkirk dead for what he had done. Spurred by vengeance, he stormed over to the fallen man and raised his boot to stomp Paul's face into a broken, bloody mess.

Desperate not to die, Paul managed to move his head just enough. Kane's boot missed a direct hit and instead raked down the man's left cheekbone, tearing open the skin before hitting the floor.

Paul grabbed the boot, pulling hard, trying to bring Kane down.

The rage boiling Kane's bloodstream abruptly turned ice-cold. He reached down, took hold of Paul's left arm, and with a savage pull and twist, popped it from its socket with the harsh sound of ripping tendons. As Paul howled in pain, Kane stretched out the arm like that of a criminal about to be crucified, then jerked it back against his knee. The bone snapped like a dried twig, and the jagged ends burst through the skin.

Then Kane broke his other arm. Even the bloodthirsty mob winced at the sharp crack, although they continued to yell encouragement as he systematically decimated Paul Dunkirk.

Kane didn't need encouragement. All he needed to do was think about Luna.

He broke both of Paul's legs as well, stomping on his knees until they resembled crushed eggshells.

Completely crippled, Paul thrashed his head from side to side, words blubbering from his lips, begging for mercy.

Kane towered over him, a stone-cold pillar of rage and revenge. "Did Luna beg for mercy, you son of a bitch?"

He kicked Paul between the legs as hard as he could.

Again.

And again.

And again.

Until he was damn sure nothing remained of Paul's manhood except pulped meat.

When he finally stopped kicking, breathing heavily from exertion, the thunder of blood-red rage in his ears gave way to the roar of the crowd.

"Kill him! Kill him! Kill him!"

A primal rhythm, a chant for carnage, the mob hungry for the *coup de grace*.

Paul had passed out after the third kick to his ruptured balls. Kane now knelt beside him and clasped his head in his hands, ready to deliver the sharp, savage twist that would snap his neck and shoot vertebrae fragments into his brainstem. Ready to claim his vengeance.

Ready to kill.

"Kill him! Kill him! Kill him!"

Kane's muscles tensed.

At the last second, he looked up into the bleachers and saw Nazareno watching him. With a cold, cruel smile, the Nazarene Dragon held out his hand with his thumb raised, like a Roman emperor granting a gladiator permission to finish his opponent in the arena.

Like blood from a slit vein, Kane felt the kill-lust bleed out of him. Taking Paul Dunkirk's life for the sake of avenging Luna was one thing, but taking it because a dirtbag drug lord told him he could left Kane feeling cold and empty.

Kane knew he might be signing his death warrant, but he refused to dance to a cartel king's cutthroat tune.

He rose to his feet, letting Paul's head fall from his hands.

The crowd hushed into stunned silence.

Nazareno stood up and pointed at Paul. "Kill him!" he commanded.

"He'll never walk again," Kane replied. "He'll never rape another woman. It's enough for me."

"I don't care if it's enough for you, *cabron*. I said, kill him!"

Kane turned and spat, then looked at Nazareno again. "Not gonna happen."

Someone in the crowd shouted, "Reaper's a pussy!" and everyone laughed. Then they began chanting his name again.

"Reaper! Reaper! Reaper!"

They continued chanting as Nazareno descended into the octagon. Stepping close to Kane, he snapped, "Enjoy the glory while it lasts. Tonight you're a champion. Tomorrow you'll be a corpse."

"Maybe," Kane said. "But you'll always be a piece of shit."

Sheriff Dunkirk appeared, face twisted with fury. "You son of a bitch," he snarled. "What did you do to my son?"

"Turned him into a crippled eunuch," Kane replied. "You're lucky I let him live." His lips peeled back from his teeth in a cold, wolfish smile. "When your turn comes, I won't be so nice."

"I'd say let's do it right here and now, but I need to get my boy to the hospital." Dunkirk looked at Nazareno. "You mind?"

The drug lord nodded and gestured to the body-removal crew, who darted in, picked up the unconscious Paul, and carried him out. With a baleful glance that brimmed with all the hate in the world, the sheriff followed them out.

"You fight again tomorrow night," Nazareno informed Kane. "Four on one. They will have weapons, you will not." He smiled, all shark-like and toothy. "Sleep well tonight, Reaper. Tomorrow, you die."

"Been hearing that for two days now," Kane said. "You guys suck as prophets."

"Everyone's clock runs out eventually."

"You'd do well to remember that, asshole."

"You talk a lot of *mierda*, and frankly, it bores me," Nazareno said. "Time for bed. Enjoy your breakfast tomorrow." He turned away with a chuckle.

Leaving Kane to wonder what the hell he meant.

FOURTEEN

Black Bog Federal Prison

The next morning, Kane woke up when he heard the metallic clang of the brass key hitting the lock. Usually, the unit officer unlocked the door and rambled on down the tier, releasing the inmates from their cells.

But today, his cell door swung open and Goatsack rolled in, accompanied by three of his men: Red Cent, Happy, and Goodbye.

"Up and at 'em, Reaper," Goatsack growled. "Time to rise an' shine."

Pedro rolled over in his bunk, took one look at what was going on, and faced the other way again. He was smart enough to know that whatever was going down, he wanted no part of it.

Kane threw off his blanket, swung out of his bunk, and stood up. He towered over Goatsack like Goliath looming over David. Of course, the black, pump-action, synthetic-stock Remington 870 Tactical Express shotguns all four SORT members carried served as twelve-gauge equalizers.

Goatsack looked relaxed, but his boys seemed jumpy, fingers tense on the triggers. Wouldn't take much for them to start blasting. Kane knew the Remington 870 Tactical Express featured a two-round magazine extension, upping the shotgun's capacity to seven, meaning there was a whole lot of buckshot for them to blast. Inside the cell like this, they wouldn't even need to use the XS Ghost Ring sights. It would just be point-and-shoot close-quarters splatter.

So Kane kept his movements slow and his tone agreeable. "You boys here to take me out for breakfast?"

"Oh, you're going out," Goatsack said. "But not for breakfast. In fact, no breakfast for you today."

"Unless you like dead meat," Red Cent snickered.

"Pretty sure most meat is dead before you eat it," Kane said.

Red Cent stopped snickering and frowned. "Shut your smartass mouth before I make you deep-throat a twelve-gauge."

Kane got dressed, and the SORT team took him outside. No flex-cuffs this time, but they did put him in leg shackles. They lifted his pant legs and slid down his socks to slap the cold steel directly against his skin. They were tight, grinding painfully against his ankle bones when he walked, but he said nothing. Complaints would just get the shackles cranked down even tighter. Better just to shut his mouth, grit his teeth, and suck it up.

The early morning sun was just cresting over the mountains that rose above the prison to the north and east, the rays not yet heating up the autumn briskness. The men's breaths plumed in the crisp air like dragon smoke.

The team led Kane through the compound guard shack, bypassing the chow hall, and took him down a long, dingy corridor by keying their way through two steel doors. The last door opened onto the loading dock area, and Kane saw they were approaching the sally-ported rear gate of the prison.

Goatsack keyed his radio. "Control, open the slides."

The first gate of the sally port rumbled into motion, retracted by a concealed winch-and-track system, sliding open wide enough to let them enter the rear gate. There was a small guard shack converted from a Conex shipping container, but it appeared unmanned, the windows dark.

The first gate closed behind them, then the second gate powered open just enough to let them through, reaffirming that they were being monitored by cameras, presumably from the control center. As soon as they had exited, the gate shut again.

Kane found himself standing on the potholed, frost-heaved, asphalt road that circled the perimeter of the prison. He knew heavily armed patrol trucks roved the road twenty-four/seven year-round, but right now, either by accident or design, there was no sign of them.

But there was another truck, a Toyota pickup that had seen better days. On the ground behind the vehicle were two dead bodies.

Kane recognized them because he had killed them both.

Lumberjack and Tommy Gunn.

The fallen opponents of the Pit.

He turned to Goatsack. "What the hell is this?"

"Body disposal detail," the SORT leader replied. "Load 'em in the back of the truck."

"That's it?"

"Not by a long shot. But that's the start."

Kane shrugged and got to work. With four shotguns trained on him, it wasn't like he had much choice. Firepower was always a great persuader.

Grunting with effort, he grabbed the cold, stiff corpses and chucked them into the cargo bed. No reason to be gentle; they were dead.

The task completed, he looked at Goatsack. "Now what?"

"Now we take them down to the bog." Goatsack gestured with the muzzle of his Remington toward the back of the truck. "Get in."

Accompanied by Goodbye, Happy, and Red Cent, Kane climbed into the back of the truck, not an easy thing to do while wearing leg irons. The three SORT operators kept wary eyes—and weapons—on him. Kane pointedly ignored them and stared at the nearby mountains. He would have stared at his feet to express his disinterest, but he didn't feel like looking at dead men's faces. Especially when one of those faces had a giant axe-hole in it.

Goatsack climbed behind the steering wheel. After a short quarter-mile drive down the perimeter road, he veered off to the left, tires rumbling onto a gravel drive that snaked down an incline before flattening out to reveal the prison's firing range.

To the left of the range, Kane saw the black waters of the bog lapping at the eroded banks, where exposed tree roots tangled together like a nest of hibernating copperheads. Bright sunbeams struck the water but failed to penetrate, ricocheting off it as if they had struck some kind of force field. The surface looked like an oil slick.

Kane wondered how many dead bodies rotted beneath those strange waters. Dredging up the bog's secrets would be like dragging a horrible nightmare to the surface, all decaying flesh and algae-stained bones.

Goatsack cut the engine and exited the truck, slapping the side panel. "All right, Reaper, move your unlucky ass and haul those two stiffs down to the water."

"Then what?" Kane asked. "Your guys gun me down?"

"Pretty much. Fill you full of buckshot and toss you in the bog."

"I appreciate the honesty."

"I like your style, Reaper, so I'm just keeping it real with you. Besides, you knew it had to end this way, right?"

"Thought Nazareno wanted me to fight in the Pit again?"

"He changed his mind," Goatsack replied. "You challenged him, and Nazareno knows the best way to deal with challengers is to put 'em down hard and fast. Sure, he'd like to play with you in the Pit some more, but he can't afford to have you beat the odds and survive another night. People might start thinking you're a bigger badass than he is, and we just can't have that kind of crap floating around."

"Yeah, that'd be a damn shame."

"Not gonna lie to you, Reaper," Goatsack said. "Nazareno wants you to die hard. Said to hold you down, shove a shotgun up your ass until the barrel disappears, and then pull the trigger."

"Sounds unpleasant."

"Hardcore unpleasant, and frankly, it's not my style, so I'll make you a deal. Take care of these bodies for me —basically, we just cut 'em open and dig out the guts so they don't fill up with gas and bob to the surface—and in return, I'll kill you quick. No twelve-gauge enema. Just one shot, back of the head. You won't feel a thing, I promise."

"How the hell can you promise that? You ever been shot in the back of the head?"

"You know what I mean, man."

Red Cent griped, "For god's sake, let's get this show on the road. I hate dead-body detail."

"I second that," Goodbye agreed. "This sucks donkey balls."

"I'll third it," Happy chimed in.

"No, what you'll all do is shut your damn mouths," Goatsack snapped. "For the money Nazareno pays us, you'll eat the snot out of a dead man's nose if that's what the boss wants."

"Uh, yeah, that's gonna be a big negative," Goodbye said.

"Yeah, ten-four on what he said," Happy agreed. "That ain't happening."

Red Cent shrugged. "Guess it would depend on how long the guys' been dead. I mean, as long as it wasn't extra crunchy..."

Goatsack looked at Kane and shook his head. "See the morons I have to deal with?"

Kane ignored the banter and said, "I need a knife."

"For what?"

"Those bodies aren't gonna gut themselves."

Goatsack's arched eyebrows showed his surprise. "Thought you'd put up more of a fight, Reaper."

"A man's got to know when the fight is lost."

"That makes you a wiser man than most." The SORT leader gestured toward the bog. "Drag them down to the water, and then I'll get you a knife."

Kane hopped off the truck, stumbling slightly, ankles numb from the shackles strangling his circulation. He reached into the cargo bed, grabbed Lumberjack's ankle, and dragged him out of the truck. The dead man landed in the dirt with a thud. Kane hauled him down to the edge of the bog, then repeated the process with Tommy Gunn's corpse.

Standing over the human carcasses, Kane pointed at his leg irons. "Any chance of getting these bracelets off? Make it easier to work."

"Bet it would," Goatsack replied. "Also make it easier for you to jackrabbit."

"You've got four guns on me," Kane said. "How the hell am I going to run?"

Goatsack shook his head. "Nice try, but not happening. Leg irons stay on."

"Gonna take me longer."

"We've got time." The SORT leader pulled a folded Spyderco from a sheath on his belt and tossed it to Kane. "Get to work."

Kane gritted his teeth and buckled down to the gruesome task at hand. He worked slowly, not because he wanted to linger over what basically amounted to field-dressing a human, but because he needed his captors to get bored. People who were bored tended to grow complacent and lower their guards, and that was his only chance of surviving the next thirty minutes.

He gutted Lumberjack's corpse first, feeling no shame for retching as the vile odors roiled out of the abdominal cavity when he slit the body open from pelvis to sternum.

Even Goatsack backed off a few meters, taking his left hand off his shotgun to press it over his mouth. "My God, that's foul."

"Dead man's guts," Kane said, taking shallow breaths

through his mouth to minimize the stench. "They're not supposed to smell like roses."

He rolled the body onto its side to let the internal organs slide out, taking his time. Goatsack didn't even waste time telling him to pick up the pace. Probably figured he was simply in no hurry to get to his own execution.

Goodbye hopped up and perched on the Toyota's lowered tailgate, letting his legs dangle. "That's some nasty shit right there." He set the shotgun down next to him and waved a hand in front of his nostrils.

Happy slung his shotgun over his shoulder and hopped up next to him. He took out his cellphone and began playing some game that sounded like an electronic slot machine. He wasn't paying Kane a lick of attention, solely focused on hitting the jackpot.

Tommy Gunn's corpse proved easier to butcher since Kane had practically disemboweled him in the Pit the night before. By the time he was done widening the slit, Red Cent was sitting on the ground, ankles crossed, leaning against the truck's rear tire. His shotgun laid on the ground beside him.

Yeah, Kane thought, these guys might have been top-tier operators at one point, but easy living and victims who didn't fight back had rendered them soft and careless.

He dumped Gunn's guts out and swiped the back of his hand across his forehead to flick off the beads of sweat dappling his brow despite the cool morning air. "You want to do an inspection before I toss these guys in the water?" Kane asked Goatsack.

The SORT leader ambled over, oblivious to the fact that he was walking to his death.

The whole time he had been desecrating corpses, Kane had kept his movements deliberately slow and nonthreatening, lulling his four guards into a false sense of security. When people see slow-moving objects, they subconsciously anticipate the object will remain lethargic. They do not expect them to suddenly explode into high speed.

But that was exactly what Kane did.

Goatsack was smart enough not to walk within arm's reach, but even that turned out to be too close.

Kane burst into fast, violent motion. He leaped forward, shackles biting into his ankles. His left hand swept out and knocked aside the shotgun. At the same time, his right hand drove the gore-stained knife up under Goatsack's chin. The point punched through the windpipe, severed the jugular, and stabbed through the back of his tongue.

The SORT leader didn't even have a chance to cry out, silenced by cold steel and the hot blood clogging his throat.

Kane left the knife stuck in Goatsack's neck. The attack had taken less than three seconds. It took him just one more second to flip the Remington 870 around so that the muzzle pointed at the other three SORT boys clustered around the Toyota.

Red Cent reacted the fastest to Kane's sudden attack.

He also died the fastest.

"Oh, shit!" the SORT operator yelped, grabbing for the shotgun on the ground beside him.

Kane pulled the trigger and sent his first blast of buckshot right into Red Cent's face, blowing it to mush. His instantly-dead body slammed against the truck tire as his soul discovered that Nazareno's blood-money didn't spend in Hell.

With his leg irons on, Kane couldn't run and seek

cover, so he didn't even try. He just stood there, right out in the open, a pissed-off giant with a hot-blasting shotgun, and dumped the remaining rounds into Goodbye and Happy as fast as he could pump the slide.

Both men died hard, chunks of flesh and bone exploding everywhere as a half-dozen shells of double-ought buck ripped them to shreds. The savage impacts blew the two men off the tailgate and into the cargo bed. Their heads, necks, and chests looked like crimson confetti.

Kane refocused his attention on Goatsack. The SORT leader was on his knees, spasming fingers grasping the knife handle jutting from beneath his jaw like an obscene growth.

Kane thumped the butt of the shotgun into his forehead, knocking him flat on his back. Staring down at Goatsack's terrified gaze, he felt nothing. The man deserved to die. Black Bog Federal Prison was hell on Earth, and Goatsack was one of the demented demons who allowed the devil to thrive.

"You should have let me go," Kane rasped, reaching down to grab the handle of the Spyderco. "Told you I wasn't someone you wanted to fuck with."

He ripped the knife sideways, slashing Goatsack's throat wide open. Blood jetted into the bog to stain the black water red. The murderous SORT commander died far more quickly than he deserved.

Kane knew he had to move fast. Even in a prison as deeply corrupted as Black Bog, that many shotgun blasts were sure to draw attention. It wouldn't take long for people to come down to the firing range to investigate. He needed to make his escape before they showed up.

He patted down Goatsack's twitching body, found the

cuff key, and ditched the shackles. His raw, abraded ankles hurt like hell, but they would hold.

He slung the Remington 870 over his shoulder and stripped the bodies of all their shells. The Spyderco went into his pocket. Next, he helped himself to Goatsack's duty belt, complete with its holstered Sig-Sauer P228 9mm pistol and two spare magazines. They were topped off with hardball ammunition rather than the hollow-points he preferred, but beggars couldn't be choosers. He just hoped the guns and ammo would survive the coming baptism because he needed to get out of here fast, and the fastest way to freedom was straight across the bog.

He didn't waste time thinking about it, just put his plan into action and dived into the brackish water.

He swam toward the opposite bank with broad, powerful strokes. He tried not to think about all the dead, decomposing bodies beneath him. At one point, a submerged branch snagged his ankle, and he imagined a skeletonized hand, fingers stripped to the bone by what-ever carrion-eaters lurked in these stagnant depths, reaching up to drag him down into a watery hell.

Kane wasn't given to flights of fancy, but he had no doubt restless ghosts called this godforsaken place home.

He kept expecting to hear shouts of alarm behind him, but he reached the other side of the bog without his escape being discovered. He pulled himself out of the foul water and clambered up the bank by using roots and rocks for handholds, and found himself on the aban-doned train tracks that skirted the edge of the prison.

The railroad ties had started rotting. Weeds, browned and dying by the cool kiss of autumn, choked the gravel bed. To Kane, it looked like the road to Heaven.

He turned east toward the mountains and began following the steel rails toward freedom.

FIFTEEN

Mad Mike's cabin

Miles back in the forest, Mike didn't hear the klaxon wail of the prison's alarm system alerting the village of Black Bog and the town of Vesper Lake that there had been an escape. He didn't know that under Nazareno's orders, the lid had been clamped down and no notifications made to the US Marshals. He didn't know that Warden Ghastin, directed by her drug-lord master, had only activated the five surviving members of the SORT team—plus a pair of bloodhounds from a local tracker—for the manhunt. No State Police roadblocks, no helicopters circling the rugged terrain with infrared sensors, no hundred-man grid searches.

Mike didn't know that Nazareno had notified the kill squads seeded throughout Vesper Lake—twenty-four cartel *sicarios* in all—to be prepared. He had also called Sheriff Dunkirk and advised him that there was little doubt Kane would come for him.

No, Mike's first hint of brewing trouble was when Beta's ears suddenly shot up and a low, rumbling growl formed in the back of the wolf's throat. The beast padded across the wooden floor planks on silent feet and took up a position near the door, head lowered, hackles raised.

Mike put down the cookbook he'd been reading and picked up his AR-15. "What is it, boy?" He moved to take up a position against the wall beside the door. "Somebody out there?"

Beta rumbled a warning deep in his throat again.

Mike nodded. Yeah, they had a visitor. He wondered if they were lost or just had a death wish. Thanks to his cannibalistic reputation, not too many people wandered this way. Nobody wanted to find out if his filed-to-points teeth were just for show.

He reached for the door handle and looked at Beta. "Ready, boy?"

The wolf stood poised, muscles tensed, ready to spring.

Mike yanked open the door. "Get 'em!"

Beta launched himself forward like a one-hundred-and-thirty-pound fur-covered missile.

Mike slammed the door closed before it could be breached, then spun toward the nearby window. He listened for the bestial snarls that would signal Beta's clash with whoever had been foolish enough to wander into their territory.

But instead, he heard the wolf yipping excitedly.

Mike looked out the window and saw Kane crouched and Beta wiggling like a happy puppy as he scratched his ears and rubbed his head. The wolf's tongue lolled out and scraped across Kane's stubbled cheek in a sloppy dog-kiss. Kane chuckled and sleeved away the saliva.

Mike noticed that Kane was covered in grime and sweat and dressed in prison clothes.

Shaking his head, he opened the door. "Well, well, look who came back."

Giving Beta one more pat, Kane rose to his feet. "Need your help, Mike."

"I'll just bet you do, judging from the looks of you."

"Sorry to come here, but I don't have a lot of options."

Mike nodded. "Don't worry, I know more than you think." He jerked a thumb over his shoulder. "Come on in, have some tea, and we'll get it all sorted out."

* * *

Kane had expected his escape to be discovered within minutes, but luck had been on his side this time, and it was a full half-hour before he heard the alarm start blaring. By then, he had followed the railroad tracks until they veered south toward Lake Placid, at which point he'd abandoned them and struck off into the mountains.

Given the illicit nature of the prison, he didn't expect a full-scale manhunt to be launched. That would bring too much attention. Instead, Nazareno would depend on the remaining members of the SORT team and his kill squads to hunt him down. Also, unless he was sorely mistaken, they would have no choice but to bring in dogs. It was their only chance of running him to ground.

It took an hour, but sure enough, he heard hounds baying in the distance.

He had taken no particular precautions to avoid leaving a scent trail, knowing it would be worthless. No wading through streams or sticking to rocky ground. Tricking a bloodhound was not as easy as the movies made it look. In fact, it was damn near impossible. If properly trained, and with an experienced human tracker/handler, the dogs eventually sniffed out their quarry. Diversionary tactics were just a waste of time.

He stuck to the harshest terrain he could find. That would at least wear out the hounds and slow them down a bit. Of course, the tradeoff to this tactic was that it slowed his progress too.

He kept moving, his peak physical conditioning meaning he rarely had to rest, and when he did pause, it was rarely for more than a couple of minutes. He slaked his thirst in the streams, cupping his hands in the cold, clear water.

The swim in the bog had washed the blood off his hands physically but not metaphorically. Some deaths left their mark on him more than others, like the teenager he'd been forced to shoot a week ago, kicking into motion the sequence of events that had led him here. But Kane knew that he would never regret killing Goatsack. He might always remember doing it, but his conscience would remain clear.

He'd headed for Mad Mike's cabin because he needed someone intimately familiar with these woods. Someone who could help him ambush his hunters. He needed to shake the heat off his trail and whittle down the odds so he could focus on cutting the cartel cancer out of Vesper Lake. He owed Luna that much, and he refused to back down.

Plus, he still had a sheriff to kill.

Sitting at Mike's table and sipping blackberry moonshine with the tomahawked skull keeping them company, Kane brought the hermit up to speed. He kept his words short and succinct. They didn't have much time.

Mike took it all in and then nodded. "Hell of a tale

you got there, Kane. So your plan is to stroll into town like a modern-day Wyatt Earp and start blasting until all the cartel cocksuckers are dead?"

"Pretty much, yeah. But I need to get these assholes off my back first."

"How many men, you figure?"

"Five would be my guess, plus a tracker and dogs. Nazareno knows I plan on hitting Vesper Lake, so I doubt he'll pull any of his soldiers out to run around in the woods."

"Only tracker around these parts is a local guy, half-Mohawk, named Abhijit. Folks just call him Abe. Lives in a shack in a swamp about ten miles north of here. Only got one eye. Lost the other one during a stint in state prison."

"What'd he do time for?"

"He's a kiddie toucher. Forcibly raped an eight-year girl behind a casino dumpster."

"So, he's a piece of shit."

"Damn straight, but he's got a pair of bloodhounds that could sniff out a ghost underwater." Mike rubbed his beard thoughtfully. "You're as good as found, pal."

Kane nodded, accepting his fate. "Guess it's time for me to start hunting *them*," he said. "I'll backtrack, then cut over the ridge so I don't lead them to your door."

"What's wrong with my door?"

"Nothing. Just don't want to bring you any trouble."

"Spare me the noble warrior crap," Mike replied. "Just make your stand here."

"I can't."

"Why not? Bullets aren't getting through those log walls, there's no basement so they can't hit us from below, and we've got an attack-trained dog if they somehow manage to breach. I mean, maybe it's not the Alamo, but it's your best option."

Kane grinned. "Everybody died at the Alamo."

"Okay, bad example, but you get my point."

"Yeah, I get it," Kane said. "But what's in it for you?"

"Maybe I'm just a Good Samaritan."

"Or maybe you could just tell me what you want."

Mike drummed his fingers on the table, studying Kane, clearly wanting to say something but not quite sure if he should. Finally, he sighed and said, "When this is over, there are going to be a lot of dead bodies lying around."

"Yeah, so?"

"I want you to let me take care of them."

"Wait, are you saying—"

Mike cut him off. "And I don't want you to ask me any questions."

War makes for strange allies, Kane thought. Aloud, he said, "Deal."

Mike raised his glass of moonshine. "A toast, then. To killing bad guys and fine dining."

"Cheers." Kane clanked his glass against Mike's while thinking this was the strangest damn thing he'd ever drunk to.

The molten-lava moonshine scorching his throat made Kane think of something. "You know, they could just set the cabin on fire and burn us out."

"They'd have to get pretty close to pull that off," Mike said. "And we could just pick 'em off from the windows when they tried."

"There's going to be at least five or six of them. They rush us, we might not be able to get them all before they start the cabin cooking."

Mike smiled wickedly. "Trust me, Kane. When they get here, there won't be five or six of 'em. Now here's what I need you to do..."

SIXTEEN

Black Bog / Mad Mike's cabin

Breezy still couldn't believe that Goatsack—not to mention Happy, Goodbye, and Red Cent—was dead. But not one to miss an opportunity, he also wondered if he would get a pay raise from Nazareno now that he had been promoted to SORT leader. Sure, he would miss his fallen brothers, but fattened coffers never hurt anyone. Besides, he had no doubt that Goatsack, rest in peace, would approve of him going mercenary in the midst of his melancholy. Grief and greed made for perfectly fine bedfellows.

Of course, he wouldn't have to worry about his new position or whatever enlarged bank account might follow if he didn't take down Reaper. Nazareno had made that crystal clear. "You find him, you kill him, and you bring me his head. If you fail, I will slaughter your entire family, all the way down to second cousins. Am I clear?"

Perfectly clear, Breezy had assured him. After hooking

up with Abhijit, or Abe, the one-eyed half-breed tracker, and his two hounds Cutter and Duke, Breezy had led Yippy, Big Belly, Duck, and Sirius into the woods to hunt down their prey. The dogs had made short work of identifying where Reaper had emerged from the bog, and the chase was on. Abe estimated Kane had no more than an hour's head-start on them.

Nazareno had ordered four of his *sicarios* to stand guard at Ernie Foxx's residence, anticipating that Kane might seek shelter there. Another four had been dispatched to Cripple Creek Camp to make sure he didn't try for his Jeep. Four more men had set up a roadblock at the intersection of Wolf Pond Road and Route 86, cutting off the only road out of town.

That still left a dozen cartel hitters prowling the streets of Vesper Lake, locked and loaded and ready to kill.

Breezy didn't see any way for the man called Reaper to survive this. Then again, they had underestimated him before. He had survived multiple prison attacks. He had survived the Pit. He had escaped and left a quartet of hard-assed operators dead in his wake. Clearly, the man had an unnatural talent for beating the odds and staying alive.

Expecting Kane to lead them through rough terrain, the SORT team had kitted themselves out lightly. Big Belly whined about wearing his Kevlar, but they knew Kane was armed, so Breezy took no chances. Now was not the time to sacrifice protection for comfort.

They all carried Sig-Sauer P228 pistols on their hips and opted for M-4 carbines instead of the shorter-range Heckler & Koch MP-5 submachine guns. Breezy's M-4 had a 40mm M203 grenade launcher mounted beneath the barrel, a non-agency-approved modification. He carried four rounds slotted into loops on his vest: two high-explosive rounds, one CS round, and one buckshot round. In other words, a grenade for damn near every occasion.

The hounds strained at their leashes, noses flush with the scent of their quarry, eager to run him down. Abe handled them easily and his dark eye roved in its socket, scanning the ground. Kane's spoor was so obvious that even Breezy could see it. Looked like the bastard wasn't even trying the usual rocks-and-streams tricks. Probably knew it was pointless.

Breezy couldn't wait to get his hands on the son of a bitch. Nazareno wanted his head, but before he chopped it off, Breezy intended to make Kane pay for what he had done. Goatsack, Red Cent, Happy, and Goodbye had been his brothers in arms, and he would avenge them. *Blood for blood, boys. I got you.*

"He's bleeding," Abe announced.

Breezy stepped up beside him. "Where?"

The tracker pointed at the ground. Breezy saw it immediately. Little splatters of blood on the leaves, spaced a foot or so apart.

"We don't even need dogs for this," he said. "We can just follow his blood trail."

"Just like tracking a wounded deer," Duck commented.

Abe shrugged. "I'll head back if you think you can handle it from here." He grinned, exposing tobacco-stained teeth that looked like they hadn't seen a dentist in at least four decades. "Got me a date with Jailbait tonight."

"Ain't she a bit old for you?" Yippy asked. "Thought you liked 'em young, you sick fucker."

"You wanna dunk your junk, you gotta take what you can get."

"What you can get," Breezy growled, "is get going. Make those mutts earn their keep."

"Oh, they earn their keep, all right." The tracker grinned again. "I love these dogs."

The way he said it made Breezy's skin crawl.

The half-breed loosened up on the leashes, and his hounds surged forward.

Then the earth opened up and swallowed them. Hanging on tight to the leashes, Abe was dragged down with them.

The SORT team rushed forward to see what the hell had happened.

"Holy shit," Big Belly said. "It's a goddamned punji pit."

The hole in the ground was approximately eight feet in diameter and six feet deep. The depth was fitting, given that the pit was meant to be a grave, full of sharpened wooden stakes that jutted up from the bottom like stalagmites. A thin screen of twigs and leaves and dirt had concealed the trap until the hounds, following Kane's blood trail, had collapsed the camouflaged cover.

Both hounds were dead, impaled. One had caught a spike directly under the jaw and up into the brain. The other had been punctured right through the heart. Neither death was pretty, but both had been relatively quick.

The same could not be said for their owner.

Dragged in by his falling dogs, Abe had fallen face-forward into the punji pit. One spike had shattered his teeth and torn out his cheek. Another had punched into his belly and burst out his lower back, just missing the spine. A third stake had impaled him right through his pelvic girdle. He thrashed like a hooked worm as blood poured from his gruesome wounds.

"Damn," Yippy muttered. "Can't say the sick fuck didn't deserve it, but that's still a hard way to die."

Breezy turned away. "Somebody put him out of his misery."

"Won't Reaper hear the shot?" Big Belly asked.

"So what? Not like he doesn't know we're coming for him."

"Good point." Big Belly drew his Sig and pumped a 9mm mercy round into the back of the tracker's skull.

"Yippy," Breezy said, "take point."

"Why me?"

"Because you've got the best eyes."

"They sure are pretty." Big Belly made kissing noises at the sniper.

Breezy scowled. "Cut the crap, you hear me?" He glared at the team. "Make no mistake, boys, if we fuck off out here and don't take shit serious, we're going to die in these damn woods."

Big Belly hung his head and shuffled his feet. "Sorry, boss."

"Don't be sorry. Be smart." Breezy looked pointedly at Yippy. "Watch out for fucking traps. Where's there's one, there's bound to be more."

That turned out to be the damn truth. They found the next one a quarter-mile away.

Yippy snorted derisively. "Kane doesn't think we're actually dumb enough to fall for that, does he?"

The blood trail had taken them into a thick copse of pine trees, threading along a narrow game path that was barely wide enough for an anorexic rabbit, let alone a team of geared up Kevlar-clad operators. But hell, if Kane had pushed his way through this shit, they could too.

Right where the path cut between two huge boulders, a giant log hung suspended above the trail. A rope crossed the ground at ankle height, poorly camouflaged by some cut pine boughs. Trip the rope and the log would smash down, crushing whoever had triggered the deadfall trap.

"That's some rinky-dink, amateur-hour bullshit," Duck sneered, turning to the left. "Come on, boys, we can circle around the rock and pick up the trail on the other side."

With Duck leading the way, followed by Yippy, Big Belly, and Sirius—Breezy brought up the rear—the SORT team stepped off the path and snaked their way along the far side of the boulder. The trees grew tightly together here, branches interlocked into a tangled, snarled mess that they simply had to bull their way through. Vines and creepers and thick underbrush added to the misery.

Feet practically invisible in the ground vegetation, Duck never saw the tripwire.

Nor did he see the M18A1 claymore mine strapped to a nearby tree, hidden by a cluster of dead leaves mocked up to resemble a squirrel's nest.

When the mine detonated, seven hundred steel balls shot out at a velocity of nearly 4,000 feet per second, propelled by the layer of C-4 explosive inside. The lethal storm was designed to spread until it was over six feet high and fifty yards wide, scything a devastating swath through any enemy forces unlucky enough to be caught in the kill zone.

Being in closer proximity, this blast didn't have a chance to maximize its terminal spread. But it didn't matter, because the SORT team was a close, tight formation as they forced their way through the brambles and thorns.

KANE: TOOTH & NAIL   265

Bunched together like lambs to the slaughter.

Bringing up their six, only Breezy survived the carnage.

The explosion shook the woods. He watched his men evaporate right in front of his eyes, shredded into red mist in a single heartbeat. One second they were all hunched and moving slowly; the next, they dissolved into a crimson slurry. Blood, flesh, and bone splattered the boulder like some caveman's gruesome abstract painting.

Breezy recoiled in horror, jaw hanging open so wide that a swarm of flies could have dive-bombed down his throat. With very little remaining intact above their waists, the dead men's lower torsos tumbled to the ground, legs kicking spastically like horror props in a zombie flick.

"Sirius," Breezy breathed as if saying their names would somehow bring them back. "Big Belly... Yippy... Duck... Oh, God, no!"

Wasted breath. They were all beyond prayers now. Probably already partying it up in Hell and telling Ol' Scratch to get the fuck off their throne.

Only thing left to do for him now was get some payback.

As the last man standing, he owed them that much.

Breezy threw back his head and howled at the morning sky, a primal scream full of grief and rage and vengeance. Then the scream evolved into a name as he bellowed a challenge into the mountain air.

"Reeeeeaaaaapppppppeeeeeeerrrrrr!"

* * *

Even from inside Mike's cabin, Kane heard the call. Just as he had heard the gunshot—"Misfire or mercy bullet," Mike had surmised—and a short time later, the thunderous blast of the mine detonating.

Kane said, "Sounds like somebody is royally pissed off."

"I'd rather he was dead," Mike replied. "Looks like at least one of them got lucky and dodged the claymore."

At Mike's suggestion, Kane had doubled back on his trail. Using the Spyderco, he had opened a cut on his forearm deep enough to make the blood drip steadily. Mike showed him the location of the punji pit—one of several antipersonnel devices the hermit had rigged—and they had carefully laid the "mock" blood trail right across the screen.

They had used the same trick to lead Kane's pursuers to the giant boulders, then head-faked them with the deadfall trap to divert them into the range of the claymore.

Kane had asked him where the hell he'd gotten a claymore.

"eBay," Mike had deadpanned. "Amazon was out of stock."

"You really don't like people much, do you?"

"Nothing says fuck off like an M18," Mike had replied.

Now, as the challenging cry of his enemy echoed through the woods, Kane walked over and picked up the Remington 870 off the table. He'd given the shotgun a good cleaning while they waited for the SORT team to stumble into their traps, and he expected it to function properly. Being a semi-auto fan, Mike didn't have any shotgun shells lying around, so Kane would have to make do with the ones he had pilfered from Goatsack and the others down by the bog. They hadn't been submerged that long, plus the plastic casings and tight primers meant the shells were generally able to withstand water. No guarantees, but it was all he had, so no point in fretting about it.

He also cleaned the Sig P228 and the pistol's spare magazines, clearing them of any grime and gunk the bog might have deposited during his foul-water swim to freedom.

He double-checked to make sure there was a shell in the Remington's chamber and that all the mags had been topped off, then headed for the door.

"Where you going?" Mike asked.

"Hunting," Kane replied. "I can handle whoever's left."

"Maybe so, but why bother sneaking around in the woods when you know the son of a bitch is coming here?"

"Like I said before, no reason to bring trouble to your doorstep."

"And like I said before, you can spare me that hero crap."

"I'm no hero."

Mike ignored the byplay. "Listen, we pretty much know that whoever is left out there will hit this cabin. Stay here until they show up, and once you've got their position locked down, if you want to go out there and play Rambo, have at it. But there's just no damn good reason to go hunting blind."

"Just trying to keep you from getting shot at."

"I'm not some little girl who needs saving," Mike said. "Stay here, and let them bring the fight to you. To *us*. Because I guarantee that if I get that fool in my sights, I'm popping holes through his boiler room."

Kane stopped arguing and gave the hermit an affirming nod. Mike might be strange—hell, he might even be a cannibal—but he was still a badass. Any man who willingly took up another man's fight deserved respect.

They watched and waited. Time ticked by, with the inexorable carving away of seconds that turned into minutes. Beta sensed the adrenalin in the air, the tension, the elevated alertness, and paced around the cabin, ears pricked.

Twenty minutes later, the front window exploded as automatic fire blew shattered glass into the cabin.

"Looks like they found us." Mike grinned. "Let's get this party started!" He moved to the window, spun into the opening, and rattled off a full-auto six-round burst from his AR-15—clearly not a civilian model—into the trees. Then he moved back behind the wall and looked at Kane. "Just letting him know we're here."

"Having fun?" Kane asked wryly.

"Gotta admit, it's more exciting than my usual day."

Kane peered around the edge of the busted window, studying the terrain through a triangular shard of glass that still clung to the frame like a broken tooth. It took him a minute, but he spotted the shooter positioned behind a large white birch tree approximately one hundred meters away. Despite all the other trees surrounding the cabin, the gunman possessed a clear line of sight to the front of the cabin. It was a narrow lane, but a skilled operator didn't need the tactical version of a four-lane highway to score kill shots.

"Got him," Kane said. "But he's out of shotgun range."

Mike hefted the AR-15. "Can you nail him with this?"

"Is it combat-zeroed?"

Mike shrugged. "If you mean, does it generally hit what I aim at, then yeah, sure, it's combat-zeroed."

Another burst from the shooter thudded into the logs around the window.

"Reaper!"

Kane recognized the voice. It was the SORT member they called Breezy.

"Reaper! Get your ass out here!"

Mike looked puzzled. "Who the hell is Reaper, anyway?"

"Let's just call it my prison name," Kane said.

"You were only inside for two days, and you caught yourself a nickname?"

"Guess I made an impression."

Another burst knocked the rest of the glass out of the window. Shards skittered across the cabin floor. Beta danced out of the way, careful where he put his paws.

Kane figured Breezy's rifle—most likely an M-4—sported a scope, which accounted for his long-range accuracy. Kane could borrow Mike's AR-15 and *rat-a-tat-tat* away, but he would just waste ammo. That far out, with open sights and his target concealed behind a large tree, it would take a stroke of luck to bury a bullet in bad-guy flesh.

He needed to shorten the distance, close the gap, maneuver himself into shotgun range. Then he could blow the bastard away with a couple blasts of buckshot.

"Reaper!" Breezy yelled again. "Come out here and take your medicine, or I'll burn the place down around you!"

"Ha!" Mike shouted back. "Like to see you get close enough to pull that off!"

A moment later, Kane heard a *whump* noise that he recognized. "Shit, he's got a grenade launcher."

A moment later, a 40mm grenade sailed through the window, bounced on the floor, and slid under the table. It immediately started hissing white smoke.

Mike asked, "Is that what I think it is?"

Kane nodded. "He's trying to gas us out." Already, the fumes were starting to sting his eyes and burn his throat. While he was trained to fight through the effects of CS gas, Mike would be incapacitated if they stayed in the cabin.

"Reaper!" Breezy yelled. "The next one's HE!"

He didn't have to explain what that meant and the repercussions. An M406 High Explosive round launched inside the cabin would take them all out, courtesy of its five-meter kill-zone and 137-meter casualty radius. Even if they somehow managed to survive the blast, they were guaranteed to suffer serious damage.

With the CS gas fogging up the interior and Mike hacking like he was trying to cough up a lung while tears streamed down his face from the gas's debilitating effects, Kane knew it was time to abandon the cabin and take the fight outside.

"We need to get out of here," he said to Mike. "Can you lay down some cover fire?"

Coughing fiercely, half-blinded with tears, Mike nodded and stumbled over to the window. He immediately started cranking off rounds in Breezy's direction.

Kane barreled out the door. He half-expected to catch a bullet as soon as he exited, but Mike's cover fire kept Breezy pinned down.

Kane dashed twenty meters to a pine tree and crouched behind the trunk. He was still outside effective shotgun range.

Mike's magazine ran dry.

As soon as the hermit stopped firing, Breezy leaned

out from behind his cover and triggered a three-round burst that tore into the pine tree. Splinters exploded everywhere, but Kane knew the 5.56mm slugs couldn't punch all the way through. As long as he stayed right here, he was safe.

Problem was, he couldn't stay right here.

He had a man to kill.

Putting thought to action, he tucked the Remington tight to his shoulder and whipped out from behind the tree, firing as he did so. He kept pumping and firing as he moved aggressively forward. Shredded pine needles, leaves, bark, and wood filled the air with organic debris as load after load of buckshot ripped the hell out of everything in its path.

None of it reached Breezy, but it damn sure kept him pinned down behind his birch tree.

Fast-actioning the shotgun, Kane bought himself enough time to move forward another forty meters. Only fifty meters separated them now, putting him at the outer edge of the shotgun's range. From here, a buckshot blast had a fifty-fifty chance of a terminal takedown. Not great, but better than nothing.

When the Remington ran dry, Kane slid behind another pine tree, this one even wider than the first. Even his broad shoulders fit behind it. He racked the slide, ejecting the last spent shell. He immediately began thumbing fresh shells into the breech as fast as he could, expecting Breezy to attack while his weapon was empty.

Autofire from Mike's AR-15 rang out as he tried to provide more cover fire, but the bullets zipped all over the place. Clearly, the rifle was not steady in the hermit's hands. Kane knew Mike had to be just about completely overcome by the CS gas. The fact that he was still firing at all proved the man's grit, but the wild, erratic salvo failed to keep Breezy at bay.

As he slotted another shell up the tube, Kane heard Breezy's M-4 chugging rounds. He felt the vibrations as the bullets pounded into the tree, but he held fast. The pine was plenty big enough to absorb some punishment.

Kane clicked the last shell home and racked the pump-action to lift the first round into firing position, but before he could launch another attack, he heard the *whump* again.

Shit!

The tree might be able to stop bullets, but it wasn't going to stop a high-explosive grenade.

Fueled by desperation, knowing his chance of survival had just been shaved down to a sliver, Kane bolted from the cover of the pine. He just managed to clear six meters when the mini-bomb slammed into the tree and detonated.

He dived to the ground as shrapnel and debris buzz-sawed the air above him. The force of the explosion smashed into him like an invisible fist and tossed him even farther, rolling him like a rag doll across the forest floor. Somewhere during the tumble, he lost the shotgun.

He slammed to a stop against an old stump, taking a painful blow to his already bruised ribs. His vision swirled in a crimson kaleidoscope, and it took him a second to realize blood from a scalp wound dripped into his eyes. As he wiped it away, his ears rang like a son of a bitch, muffling sounds like he was underwater.

He struggled to his feet. He felt like he'd been hit by a runaway bulldozer, but at least he was alive. For now, anyway. That would change when Breezy showed up to ventilate him with a couple dozen bullets.

Kane's hand clawed for the Sig Sauer P228 holstered

at his side, secured in place with a thumb-break retention strap. Smoke from the explosion drifted through the trees, mixing with the floating dust and debris to turn everything into an artificial fog. He got the gun out, but it was damn hard to hold. Shrapnel had lacerated his right forearm and blood had run down onto his hand, making his fingers slippery.

He dropped to one knee and switched the pistol to his left hand. Blinking away the blood, he scanned the woods, narrowed eyes trying to pierce the smoke, looking for his enemy.

A sound caught his attention. Mike, followed by Beta, stumbled out the cabin door, coughing and gagging and clearly half-blinded. Thick streamers of snot spewed from his nostrils as the gas wreaked havoc on his sinuses.

Breezy's carbine barked a double-tap, and Mike spun to the ground.

"Damn it!" Kane snarled. "Mike!"

The hermit didn't move, just laid there in a lifeless heap.

But the act of shooting Mike had betrayed Breezy's position. Glimpsing the man's movements through the dissipating smoke, Kane raised his pistol and rapid-fired five rounds. Just to keep the bastard occupied. Just to let him know he wasn't dead yet.

Come and get me, you son of a bitch.

The fog had started to clear from his skull, just like the smoke was clearing from the woods. While he was hardly in prime fighting condition—two days of beatdowns and prison brawls had seen to that—he still felt more in control of himself than he had a minute ago.

He rose from his knee and moved to his left, not wanting to stay in one position any longer.

Bullets stitched a line at his feet, tearing divots in the dirt.

Breezy stepped through the last dregs of smoke like a weaponized wraith emerging from the throat of hell, his M-4 locked on target.

Kane gauged the distance at about sixty-five meters. Normally not impossible with a handgun, but it would take serious luck to score a kill shot with an unfamiliar pistol while shooting left-handed.

"Put it down, Reaper," Breezy called. "I can drill you from here, and you know it."

Kane hesitated while his eyes scanned the woods. Then he dropped the pistol. Partly because he knew Breezy was right. Partly because he knew something Breezy did not.

Kane's hand crept toward his pocket, thinking about the Spyderco. If Breezy came close enough, the knife might be his last chance to walk away from this death-match, or to at least go down fighting.

But the SORT soldier caught the movement and snapped, "Keep your hands where I can see them, Reaper."

Kane complied, holding his hands out to the side to show he was unarmed. His gaze flicked past Breezy for a moment, then refocused on the gunman. Breezy stalked forward, the M-4 tucked tight against his shoulder, the muzzle aimed at Kane's center mass. That was how most law enforcement operators were trained to shoot—just go for the middle, no fancy headshots.

By the cabin, standing watch over his fallen master, Beta let out a series of growl-barks, letting Kane know he was in imminent danger.

Tell me about it, boy.

As he closed the gap, brittle leaves crunched so loudly

under Breezy's boots that the noise temporarily eclipsed all other sounds in the woods. Tucked behind the scope, the gunman zeroed in on Kane with laser-like focus.

He pulled up twenty meters away, too close to miss when he cut loose with the carbine, too far away for Kane to make some kind of desperation play.

"I could have just nailed you from back there," Breezy said. "But after what you did to my brothers, I owe them more than a long-distance kill. They died hard, and I want to look you right square in the eye when I get payback and blow you to hell." A cold, cruel smile twisted his lips. "Got any last words you want to get off your chest before I drill some holes in it?"

"Yeah," Kane said. "Your situational awareness sucks."

Breezy scowled. "The hell are you talking about?"

"Behind you."

"Nice try, motherfu—" He choked off the words as a huge shadow fell over him.

Kane watched as Gasper the grizzly rose up on his hind legs behind the SORT gunner. As Breezy had been stalking Kane, the bear had been stalking Breezy. Drool slobbering from his muzzle, Gasper opened his jaws and bellowed a roar that shook the woods. Raised by and acclimated to humans, the grizzly had not avoided the gunfire like a regular bear. Hell, to Gasper, gunfire probably just meant man was in the area. And man meant a fresh meal.

"*Oh, shit!*" Breezy turned to face the beast, trying to swing the M-4 into play.

The grizzly's massive right paw lashed out. Dark claws tore deep, digging ruts across Breezy's chest and ripping apart his bicep. The M-4 tumbled to the ground.

A second later, a vicious swipe from the bear's left

paw slashed open the man's belly, spilling his guts onto the ground. Breezy staggered back, his innards unspooling as he tried to retreat from the savage attack.

The grizzly didn't let him suffer. Even as Kane debated picking up the pistol and delivering a mercy round to his enemy, Gasper swatted him in the side of the skull, tearing it off his shoulders like a rotten pumpkin. Blood fountained from the ragged stump as the decapitated head tumbled across the dead leaves.

With his prey dead, the bear dropped back down on all fours and stared at Kane. No huffed threats or snarls of dominance this time; the grizzly just stood there and stared with those dark, primal eyes. It was so quiet that Kane swore he could hear the heavy thumping of the beast's wild heart.

Kane wasn't near the bear's kill, but he still backed away, making it clear that he offered no challenge and made no claim on the corpse. All he wanted to do right now was check on Mike and then head into town to terminate the rest of the bastards who had it coming.

Gasper lowered his head and shuffled forward, seemingly unconcerned about Kane's presence. Maybe he remembered their encounter up on the knoll. Maybe he remembered that Kane posed no threat. Or maybe he just figured there wasn't a whole lot Kane could do to stop him.

The grizzly batted Breezy's corpse a couple of times, then sank his teeth into the thick shoulder muscle next to the spine. He picked up the body as if it weighed nothing, then turned and walked away. Maybe he would come back for the head, maybe he wouldn't. Kane didn't plan on sticking around long enough to find out.

He remained motionless as the bear disappeared into the woods with his fresh kill. With the beast gone, he could now hear his own heart pounding. He dragged in several deep breaths, cooling the adrenalin pumping hot through his veins.

It had been a rough few days, with several near-death scrapes, but he was still standing. Call it luck, call it a warrior's stubborn refusal to go down, call it whatever you liked—Kane was just damn glad to be alive. He hustled back to the cabin as fast as his battered, bruised, and bloodied body would let him.

Beta whined nervously as Kane knelt beside Mike, who was sprawled face-down in the dirt. He could see blood on the hermit's buckskin jacket, but when Kane rolled him over, Mike's eyes popped open and he grinned. "Is it over?"

Kane grinned back. "Yeah, it's over. Faking it?"

"Playing possum," Mike confirmed. He probed at the bloody hole high on his upper right arm. "Bastard winged me, nothing more than a flesh wound. I figured, no reason he needed to know that. Let him think he nailed me."

"Good play." Kane helped the hermit to his feet and pointed at the injury. "Want me to stitch that up?"

"This little scratch?" Mike waved his hand dismissively. "Not worth bothering with. Besides, don't you have some more asses you need to kick?"

"Yeah, I'm not done stacking bodies yet."

"Then you'd best get going."

Kane nodded. "Mike, I can't thank you enough."

"Don't start any mushy-man crap with me, Reaper. That's not how we do it up here in the mountains." He held out his hand. "Just shake my hand, pet the dog, and be on your way."

Kane clasped his hand firmly. "Fair enough, Mike."

Then he reached down and scratched the wolf behind his ears. "See ya, boy."

He retrieved the shotgun, then gathered up Breezy's M-4. There was only one magazine, half-depleted, with a 40mm buckshot grenade slotted into the launcher. Not enough to take on the whole town, but it would get him started. When he ran out of bullets, he would keep fighting with his bare hands until he ripped Nazareno's cartel cancer right out of Vesper Lake.

As he walked away, Mike called, "Hey, Reaper?"

"Yeah?"

"Give 'em hell, buddy."

"That's the plan, friend," Kane replied. "That's the fucking plan."

SEVENTEEN

Dribble Creek Camp

Kane approached the cabin, or rather, what was left of it, from the east, circling wide when he was still a half-klick out and climbing the steep backside of the hillock. With the ground rising eighty feet at a thirty-five-degree angle and nothing but a natural barrier of sharp rocks and twisted deadfalls at the bottom, it was the last direction from which the sentries would be expecting him to appear.

He knew Nazareno had positioned men up there. He could hear them, swapping sexual-escapade stories in Spanish and laughing coarsely. Their loud conversation covered any sounds he made as he crept up the slope.

It was hard going and he lost the shotgun along the way, biting back a curse as it slipped from his hands and skidded down the slope. He held his breath as it banged against the rocks at the bottom, not sure if the sentries would be alerted or not. But they just kept on cackling and one-upping each other with dirty jokes, oblivious to the danger creeping up on them.

Descending back down the steep incline to retrieve the Remington was too risky, so he left it where it fell. He continued to climb, clawing his way to the top using roots and rocks for handholds. Sweat and dirt covered his clothes by the time he peered over the edge and saw the burnt wreckage of the cabin, the charred timbers looking like collapsed heaps of blackened bones. He thought about Luna's immolated remains buried beneath the cold ashes and let the grim thought stoke the fires of his fury.

Peering across the flat crest of the hillock, he spotted his Jeep, squatting low on four flattened tires. The hood gaped open, torn wires and tubing dangling in mechanical disembowelment. Behind the Jeep was the kill squad's ride, a bright orange Hummer H2 pickup truck sporting blacked-out windows, a lift kit, knobby off-road tires, and a heavy-duty brush guard that looked sturdy enough to go head-to-head with a rabid rhino.

Nazareno's quartet of killers sat at the picnic table playing cards and drinking beer. Their rifles leaned against the benches, within arm's reach but not exactly at the ready. They clearly thought this was a stupid assignment, that there was no way in hell Kane would come back here.

Time to prove them wrong.

Dead wrong.

One of the cartel soldiers got up from the table with a crude comment about having to "drain the *serpiente*" and headed for the outhouse.

There was nothing slick or tactical about Kane's strike. It was all direct, hard-hitting, blunt-force trauma.

He simply powered up over the edge with a primal war cry and began killing them.

He triggered the M203, and the 40mm buckshot grenade slammed into the lower spine of the sentry going to take a piss. The explosion sent twenty metal balls through the target, blowing apart everything between his pelvis and sternum and ripping him in two. His upper torso went spinning in one direction while his bottom half toppled the other way.

His three *companeros* barely had time to react to their comrade's sudden death before Kane blew them all to hell. The M4 carbine cycled on full-auto as he swept the muzzle back and forth. The 5.56mm rounds cut them down where they sat, punching lethal tunnels through their twitching bodies. Blood spewed into the air like a hot red blizzard.

The last spent cartridge spat from the ejection port. Kane could feel the heat coming off the fast-fired gunmetal. Yeah, things were getting hot around here, and they were only going to get hotter before he was done.

He gathered the sentries' weapons—FX-05 Xiuhcoatl assault rifles, which proved that Nazareno favored his soldiers enough to provide them with Mexican military hardware—and stowed them in the back of the H2. The keys dangled from the ignition, and since they had ruined his ride, it seemed only fitting that he would steal theirs.

Even better, a closer inspection of the truck revealed bullet-resistant windows, Kevlar-lined door panels, and run-flat tires. Not a true armored vehicle, but the tactical upgrades would come in handy when he rolled into town on his kill-'em-all mission.

Before he left, Kane walked over and stood at the

edge of the burnt wood and rubble. He allowed himself a few quiet moments of reflection before he resumed his hell-bent-for-leather rush toward revenge.

Luna's spirit lingered here as if she had known he would come back to say goodbye. He could feel her ghost, a warm, vibrant presence that seeped past his skin and bones to find his soul. He would never know what he had meant to her, but he knew what she had meant to him. He had come here burdened by a cross of death, and she had been the angel who let him lay that burden down—and in doing so, had died.

His salvation had cost Luna her life.

Kane knew that even the strongest men must sometimes weep, and he felt no shame at the tears coursing down his cheeks. He might die today, or he might live another fifty years, but no matter what, he would never forget her.

"Rest in peace, Luna."

Then he turned away, the warmth of her spirit replaced by the steely coldness of his fury.

No more tears.

Now it was time for blood.

* * *

Black Bog / Ernie Foxx's house

Foxx was sitting on his front porch with an old double-barreled sawed-off shotgun braced across his knees when Kane rolled up in the Hummer. Foxx had not been a young man for quite some time, and he looked like he had aged at least ten years since Kane had last seen him two days ago when Sheriff Dunkirk had murdered his wife and killed his cat.

As the H2 halted, Foxx glared daggers at it, more hate on the old man's face than Kane had seen in a long time. It took him a moment to remember that the windows were blacked out, so Foxx couldn't see inside the truck. The old man naturally assumed some cartel cockroach sat behind the wheel.

When Kane lowered the window, Foxx's face didn't exactly light up, but he definitely looked less miserable. "Well, I'll be damned," the old man exclaimed. "John Kane, as I live an' breathe. Figured you'd be buzzard food by now."

"I'm a hard man to kill."

"Nice ride you got there. To the victor goes the spoils?"

"More like dead men don't need a Hummer." Kane exited the truck and walked over to Foxx. "How you doing, Ernie?"

"Buried wife number two yesterday." He waved a hand at the field next to his house. "I just put her out back, along with Doofus. Figured she'd rather be here than in some cemetery surrounded by people she barely knew." A tear snuck out and slid down his cheek. He quickly thumbed it away and peered up at Kane. "That make sense to you?"

"Sure, I get that."

"Anyway," Foxx continued, "I just finished a bottle of Jim Beam, went downstairs to get my daddy's shotgun," he hefted the cut-down blaster, "and was thinking about joining her."

"Killing yourself won't bring her back."

"Not trying to bring her back," Foxx replied. "Just

don't want to live without her." He smiled fondly through the pain. "Even if she did have a fat ass from all those doughnuts."

"So you eat some buckshot, and Dunkirk gets away with what he did? That's your plan?"

"You got a better one?"

"Yeah," Kane said. "Help me kill the bastards."

"How you figure on doing that?"

"I'm going to ride into town and shoot every cartel asshole I see. When that's done, I'm going to find the sheriff and make him wish he'd never fucked with me."

"Easy as that, huh?"

"Didn't say it would easy," Kane replied. "Just said that's the plan."

Foxx pondered it for about five seconds. "Well, my plan was to die right here on my porch with the back of my head splattered all over the front door, so I guess I can tag along with you and die in a blaze of glory instead."

"I don't plan on dying."

"We'll see," Foxx said, then asked, "Whattaya got for guns?"

"One M4, one Sig, and four FX-05s."

"Impressive," Foxx grunted. "Especially for a man who just broke out of prison this morning. But I can do better." He stood up and turned toward his front door. "Follow me."

Kane trailed him through a cluttered kitchen and down a set of stairs that led to the basement. Foxx flicked a switch and fluorescent lighting buzzed to life, illuminating enough firepower to kick-start World War III and enough ammunition to survive the apocalyptic aftermath.

Kane picked up an FN SCAR rifle and whistled appreciatively. "Quite the arsenal you've got here."

"Just don't ask me where I got it all."

"Wasn't planning on it."

Kane spotted a shelf with three claymores on it, along with a clutch of fragmentation grenades.

Foxx saw him looking and said, "Used to have four of those claymores, but some bastard broke in and stole one this past summer. Helped themselves to an AR-15, too."

A little smile tugged at the corners of Kane's mouth as it became clear where Mad Mike had acquired the mine they'd used to decimate the SORT team.

Foxx gestured around the room. "Anyway, welcome to my armory and help yourself."

Kane pointed at a futuristic rifle resting in a bench cradle. "I see you've got a Barrett M95."

"Best sniping system in the world, if you ask me," Foxx replied. "Want to borrow it for this shindig?"

Kane shook his head. "Wrong tool for this job."

They spent the next twenty minutes selecting their weapons and loading magazines. Then, each burdened by a duffel bag full of deadly hardware, they went back outside and climbed into the H2. Kane took the wheel, and Foxx rode shotgun.

Or more accurately, "Rode Uzi." The matte-black Israeli submachine gun rested in the old man's lap, a full magazine in the well and a round in the chamber.

As the H2 rumbled down Wolf Pond Road, Foxx warned, "There's a roadblock up ahead. They've got the road going into Black Bog and Vesper Lake blocked off."

"How many?"

"Four, last time I checked."

"They'll never know what hit 'em," Kane said, then explained to Foxx what he wanted him to do.

As they rounded the bend, Kane saw the roadblock. Two orange H2 pickups, identical to his own, were positioned nose-to-nose across Route 86. They even boasted official sawhorses, painted yellow with black stripes and emblazoned with VLPD in reflective stenciled letters.

A quartet of cartel soldiers leaned against the Hummers. They showed no signs of alarm as Kane rolled toward them. Why should they? The windows were blacked out and the bright sunshine reflected off the windshield, bouncing the rays back into their eyes so they couldn't see inside the truck's cab. They just assumed it was the team from the cabin coming back down.

Sometimes assumption doesn't just make you an ass. Sometimes it makes you dead meat.

As Kane stopped at the junction of Route 86 and Wolf Pond Road, Foxx exited the Hummer, stepped around the open door, and came up firing across the hood with his Uzi screaming full-auto rock 'n' roll.

The four cartel hitters performed spastic death-dances to the lethal tune, thrashing and twitching as Foxx hosed them down with 9mm hollow-points. Blood burst from the ragged holes ripped through their heads, necks, and chests, and they all hit the ground in lifeless heaps. They wouldn't be getting up again.

Foxx swapped the spent magazine for a fresh one, then hopped back in the Hummer. He smiled, and Kane would have bet good money that it was his first smile since his wife and cat had died.

"Now that's what I call grief therapy," Foxx said. "God, that felt good."

"Ready for a repeat?"

"You know it."

Kane turned onto Route 86 and slammed the pedal to

the floor, heading for a showdown with the rest of Nazareno's gunners and Sheriff "Double D" Dunkirk.

If Kane had his way, the "D" would soon stand for "Dead."

The Hummer peeled rubber in smoking black strips as the truck surged forward, engine roaring like a hungry beast as they rocketed down the highway to hell.

EIGHTEEN

Vesper Lake

As the H2 rumbled over the railroad tracks that marked the edge of town and thundered toward the main drag, Kane spotted cartel gunmen roaming the street and parking lots like an occupying army, FX-05 rifles in hand. There was no sign of civilians; no doubt, the townsfolk had been ordered to stay locked down in their homes upon penalty of death.

That made this assault much easier since it reduced the chance of collateral damage. No innocents to get caught in the crossfire.

The cartel soldiers paid little attention as he rolled into town. Like the roadblock Kane and Foxx had decimated minutes before, they all thought the orange Hummer was one of their own.

Three gunners stood on the curb by the gas station. Kane slowed down as they drove by. Foxx rolled down the window and yelled, "Catch, boys!" as he tossed them an M67 fragmentation grenade.

The middle guy actually caught the green metal sphere as Kane stomped on the gas pedal, accelerating away. In the rearview mirror, Kane saw the blast tear him to pieces while the lethal shrapnel scythed through the men on each side of him. The force of the detonation flung them through the air like rag dolls. By the time they hit the ground, they were nothing but bloody sacks of human garbage.

Four men grouped outside of Baldy's grocery store turned toward the explosion, and three men across the street in the bank parking lot mimicked them. They all saw the H2 revving down the road toward them, but all seemed unaware that the truck contained the threat. Their heads swiveled like startled chickens, searching for the source of the blast.

As they raced by, Kane thrust a Heckler & Koch MP-5 submachine gun out the window and emptied a thirty-round magazine into the cartel bastards at the bank. Next to him, Foxx did the same thing with his Uzi to the boys at Baldy's. Their bodies doing awkward, blood-spewing pirouettes, the men crumpled to the ground, dead or dying.

The two gunners stationed at the liquor store caught on that the H2 barreling toward them wasn't friendly. They raised their FX-05s and began firing salvos at the truck as it devoured the asphalt, coming right for them.

Foxx flinched as slugs caromed off the windshield, but Kane didn't bat an eye. He knew the glass would give way once enough rounds had hammered it, but they weren't there yet, and the cartel hitters were firing wildly. They missed as often as they connected. Through the bullet-spalled windshield, he saw a few rounds gouge into the hood and hoped like hell they didn't screw up the engine. He would continue this war on foot if that's what it came down to, but he'd rather not.

He wasn't interested in offering the enemy a fair fight. He just wanted to turn them into maggot food.

The two cartel soldiers lacked trigger discipline and exhausted their mags rapidly. As they fumbled to reload, Kane punched the gas harder, making them believe he was going to race right on by and leave them choking on his exhaust fumes.

But it was a head-fake. At the last second, he whipped the wheel to the left and smashed the Hummer into the pair. One disappeared beneath the knobby tires with a short scream and a wet crunch. The other tried to jump to the side but got rammed by the brush guard. The blow shattered his pelvis and sent jagged bone shards razoring through his bowels. He spun through the air like a scarecrow in a windstorm and crashed through the front window of the liquor store.

Kane cranked the wheel again, slicing the Hummer's back end around as he guided the truck through a hundred-and-eighty-degree tire-smoking turn to put it back on the street. He stomped the gas pedal to the floor, and the H2 surged forward like a war machine hungry for more blood.

The lake appeared on the left. Two gunmen crouched on a dock with a moored motorboat, rifles spitting fire as the Hummer tore down the road. Directly across from them, two more—the last two, if Kane's intel was correct —cut loose from the alcove of an accountant's office. Clearly, the two kill teams hoped to take them down with a crossfire play.

Foxx quickly slapped a new magazine into Kane's MP-

5 and handed it over. He had already refreshed his Uzi. "Let's get some!" he yelled.

Despite the danger, Kane couldn't help but grin. The old man was having the time of his life.

The gunners were getting their range. Bullets banged into the weakening windshield. Kane thrust the HK out the window and triggered a six-round burst. Despite still being eighty meters out, he got lucky, and one of the men flipped backward into the water as a round cored through his forehead.

Foxx cut loose with his Uzi, blistering through half the magazine, but the 9mm slugs sparked off the brick wall of the office. The two hitters ducked back into the cover of the doorway to avoid the short fusillade, then leaned back out and resumed firing.

The H2 had closed the gap. The three remaining targets poured autofire onto the windshield. Integrity compromised, the glass let a bullet punch through, and it drilled Foxx in his upper left arm. He lurched in his seat, crying out in pain.

Kane glanced over. The arm hung crooked, clearly broken. Looked like the slug had snapped the bone in two. No doubt it hurt like hell, but there was nothing they could do about it right then.

Kane put his eyes back on the road. "You gonna make it, Foxx?"

"It's just an arm," the old man said through pain-clenched teeth. "God saw fit to give me two, and the other one still works just fine." As if to prove his point, he started firing the Uzi one-handed as they drew abreast of the accountant's office.

One of the men died where he stood, his chest turned into a sieve. The other bolted from the doorway, making a break for better cover. Foxx shifted his aim and caught the runner in the left hip. The Uzi's rising muzzle stitched bullets right up the man's ribcage, and he face-planted on the sidewalk with his heart and lungs torn to shreds.

Nazareno's squad of killers had been whittled down to one.

The sole survivor cooked off the rest of his FX-05's magazine, punching a line of holes in the side of the Hummer as it sped past. The Kevlar door panels prevented the bullets from penetrating.

Kane tried to get lucky one more time, firing the MP-5 left-handed. But the cartel gunner dodged to the left and the slugs chewed into the dock, tearing up splinters from the pressure-treated wood.

As Kane stomped the brakes and whipped through another one-eighty, ready to make a second run-and-gun ride down the gauntlet, he saw the gunman jump into the motorboat, toss off the line, and shove the throttle forward. The boat, a Glaston GT160 with a 75HP engine, leaped forward, leaving a trail of churned foam in its wake as it raced for the far side of the lake.

Kane jumped out of the H2, opened the back door, grabbed the M-4 carbine with the grenade launcher attached, and fed a high-explosive shell into the breech, courtesy of Foxx's armory. He snapped the weapon up to his shoulder, aimed, and fired.

The boat was only a hundred meters out, well within range for someone as experienced as Kane. He dropped the HE round right inside the vessel, and the explosion tore the boat apart, along with the cartel soldier. Sparking wires fused with shredded fuel lines and the wreckage burst into flames, a funeral pyre for the last of Nazareno's native-country henchman.

Kane canted the carbine over his shoulder as his eyes

drifted away from the burning boat to the sheriff's station on the opposite side of the lake. As he watched, Dunkirk exited the front door and climbed into his Bronco. The sheriff raced out of the parking lot, clearly in a hurry. The sound of squealing rubber carried all the way across the water.

The son of a bitch was trying to get away.

"Oh, hell no," Kane growled. He tossed the M-4 into the back seat and slid behind the wheel. "Put your seatbelt on, Ernie." He snapped his own into place.

"What's going on?" Foxx asked, dragging the safety belt across his chest with his right hand and clicking it home.

"Dunkirk's making a run for it."

"What're you gonna do?"

"Cut him off."

The Hummer shot forward, eating up the pavement. Across the way, the Bronco turned the corner around the northwest end of the lake. A few seconds later, Kane skidded around the northeast corner, back end fishtailing for a moment before he brought it back under control.

The road along the back side of Vesper Lake consisted of a quarter-mile of two-lane dragstrip-straight stretch of asphalt. As the Hummer slid around the corner and blocked Dunkirk's escape route, the Bronco slowly rolled to a halt. Kane pumped the brakes and the two trucks squared off, engines rumbling.

Kane knew the next few moments would be terminal. One of them was going to die. He tightened his grip on the steering wheel, determined it would not be him. Determined to make Dunkirk pay for murdering Luna. Determined to have his revenge.

The Bronco shot forward, oversized tires digging into the road.

Kane responded by punching the pedal to the floor. The H2 rocketed down the middle of the road like a heavy metal beast.

"Yee-haw!" Foxx yelled. "Get some!"

Kane could barely see through the damaged windshield, but he didn't care. He could see enough to aim the Hummer at the Bronco's grill, and that was all that mattered. Wind howled into the cab and scoured his grim face.

He didn't even think about hitting the brakes. He would bash head-on into the Bronco if that was what it took to destroy Dunkirk. He throttled the steering wheel like it was the sheriff's throat, anger and adrenalin pulsing through his veins.

The Bronco raced toward him, two enemies playing a high-speed game of chicken.

Kane knew they had reached the end of the line. One way or the other, it all ended right here, right now. Dark emotions injected themselves into his bloodstream. He stomped even harder on the gas, trying to push the pedal through the floorboard. The two trucks hurtled toward each other on a collision course, closing the gap fast. The wind whipped Kane's eyes as he steeled himself to die with his enemy in a twisted, fiery wreckage.

Dunkirk blinked.

At the last possible nanosecond, the sheriff jerked the wheel to the left. The Hummer flashed past, missing the Bronco by scant inches.

Kane's pulse pounded as he slammed on the brakes. Turning to look over his shoulder, he saw the Bronco veer out of control, careening into the entrance of the Cammeaux Logging Company on two tires. The rear end slewed around and then the tires bit into the gravel, sending the truck into a roof-crushing roll. Metal crunched and glass shattered as the Bronco came to an abrupt bone-jarring halt against a pile of logs.

By the time Kane turned around and drove back to Cammeaux's, the sheriff had managed to crawl out of the wrecked Bronco. His hat was missing, and blood streamed down his face from multiple lacerations. He looked like he had gone twelve rounds with a merciless heavyweight boxer.

He still managed to climb to his feet and start to run.

As Kane exited the Hummer, a roughneck crew of loggers who had been feeding limbs into a large wood chipper picked up heavy logging chains and headed toward him. They all dropped the chains and backed away when Foxx hopped out and aimed the Uzi at them.

"Back up, boys, and mind your own damn business," the old man growled. His broken left arm dangled at his side, blood dripping from the bullet wound. "This ain't your party."

Kane had selected a Desert Eagle .44 for this dirty work. It was an older model, not the modern Mark XIX L6 edition he had brought with him from Texas, but it still bucked in his fist just fine when he leveled it at the fleeing Dunkirk and pulled the trigger. The Magnum thunder sounded like the roar of an angry god.

The bullet struck the sheriff in the back of his right thigh and powered through with enough force to shatter the femur. The leg buckled and Dunkirk pitched forward, his already-battered face scraping through the gravel.

Kane walked over and picked up one of the logging chains, eight feet of linked steel clenched in his fist like a metal whip. Behind him, the rumbling noise of the wood chipper made it hard to hear anything but the roar of his vengeance-fueled blood pounding in his veins.

The sheriff managed to climb to his feet, all his

weight supported by his good leg. As he turned to face
Kane, he clawed his Glock out of the holster and tried to
bring it into play.

Kane lashed out with the chain. The steel links struck
Dunkirk's wrist and crushed the fragile bones like
hammered ice. His fingers spasmed open in pain, dropping the gun to the ground.

Kane whipped the chain forward again with a sharp,
snapping strike. The metal links coiled around the sheriff's neck like a constricting snake. Dunkirk reached up
and clawed at the steel noose with his good hand,
hopping on one leg as Kane dragged him forward until
they were standing just two feet apart.

Kane got right down to business. "Got anything to
say, asshole?"

Dunkirk's left eye had swollen shut from getting
banged up in the crash, but his right eye glared raw hate
at the man who had wrecked his world. "Yeah, I got
something to say," he said, blood oozing from the
corners of his mouth to trickle down over the chain
wrapped around his throat. "Fuck you, fuck this town,
and most of all, fuck that bitch Luna." A vile, mocking
laugh escaped his battered lips. "Oh, yeah, that's right.
We did."

Kane's jaw clenched as he stared into the face of the
monster who had raped and murdered an innocent
woman. He had come to this town to figure out if he
could still kill, if he *should* kill. Now he knew the answer.

He could and he should because as long as men like
Dunkirk and Nazareno existed, somebody had to hunt
down and exterminate the wicked. When the crimes and
the sins demanded the dispensation of lethal justice,
there had to be men willing to answer the call.

With a primal roar, Kane spun and jerked the chain

with every bit of his considerable power, lifting Dunkirk clean off his feet. Dropping low, Kane leveraged his back muscles to send the sheriff flying over his shoulder.

Face-first into the wood chipper.

Dunkirk managed one short scream that was abruptly cut off by the grisly sound of powerful blades chopping into flesh and bone. The machine sucked him in and dissolved him into mincemeat. His legs thrashed frantically as a crimson slurry spewed from the chute.

Foxx let out a low, appreciative whistle, then broke out in a huge grin. "Rest in pieces, you son of a bitch."

Kane turned and headed back to the truck.

Foxx called, "Hey, John?"

"Yeah?"

Foxx saluted him with the Uzi. "Thanks, my friend."

Kane nodded. "You've got your town back. Time to rebuild and make it a home again."

"How about you?" Foxx asked. "Time to go back home?"

"Not yet," Kane said grimly. "One more thing I have to do."

NINETEEN

Black Bog Federal Prison

As Nazareno stepped onto the prison recreation yard, he slipped on his mirrored aviator shades to block out the bright sunlight reflecting off the sand and concrete. Two MS-13 enforcers walked beside him, while another pair brought up the rear.

The sunglasses served a second purpose: they prevented the minions from seeing the doubt and concern staining his eyes. Reaper had been on the run for over ten hours now, and all of Nazareno's cronies had gone silent shortly after noon. Breezy and the SORT team had never returned. His kill squads had failed to report in. Sheriff Dunkirk was missing in action.

Was it possible? the drug lord wondered. Could a single man dismantle everything he had built here? Had one *bastardo* crippled his illicit kingdom? On the one hand, it seemed utterly impossible. On the other, it seemed like that was the stark reality he now faced.

Nazareno knew of two *sicarios*, twin brothers, based out of Tijuana who specialized in hunting down hard-to-find targets. They swore no fealty to a singular cartel, but operated as freelancers, shadowing their way through the narcotics underworld while working for whoever paid them their considerable fee. They did not come cheap, but they had never lost a target.

Nazareno nodded, happy to have reached a decision. He would call the twins and pay them handsomely to track down John "Reaper" Kane and kill him. Then he would have them kill every member of Kane's family, starting with second cousins and carving their way up the family tree. Not quite as satisfying as cutting the *bastardo's* balls off himself, charring them with a blow-torch, and making him choke on them like roasted chest-nuts, but Nazareno could deny himself personal, hands-on gratification as long as Kane ended up in a coffin.

Yes, the drug lord thought. *You can run, Reaper, but you can't hide.*

He reached up and wiped away the beads of sweat dappling his freshly-shaved scalp.

A moment later, his crown of thorns tattoo exploded as a .50 BMG bullet impacted his skull with over ten thousand foot-pounds of force and left nothing above his neck except a few fragments of his lower jaw. His enforcers all recoiled as they were sprayed with wet, sticky muck.

Just like that, the Nazarene Dragon was dead.

* * *

Twelve hundred meters away, concealed on a rock ledge on one of the mountains overlooking the prison, Kane lay prone behind the Barrett M95 sniper rifle and

watched through the Vortex Viper PST scope as
Nazareno's headless body hit the ground. He smiled.

"Burn in hell, motherfucker."

He climbed to his feet and started the long walk back
down the mountain.

Now it was time to go home.

EPILOGUE

Team Reaper Headquarters
  El Paso, Texas

Kane leaned back in the swivel chair and stared up at the large monitor as the President of the United States shook his gray-haired head and said, "Damn, Reaper, that is one hell of a story."

President Jack Carter had been briefed by General Hank Jones and General Thurston twelve hours earlier, right after Kane got back to headquarters. Protocols had immediately been activated to deal with the situation, but the President had wanted to talk to Kane one on one and hear the tale in the words of the man who had lived it.

"Sure is, sir. Emphasis on '*hell*.'"

"Turned out Nazareno's corruption extended all the way up to the Director of the Federal Bureau of Prisons," Carter said. "I believe he's en route to the supermax as we speak. He's going to go from running the system to being an involuntary guest of it."

"What about Warden Ghastin?" Kane inquired. "She's not an evil person. Everything she did was to save her family."

On the monitor, President Carter frowned. "I hear you, Reaper. Really, I do. But she ordered people to be murdered."

"Nazareno had men watching her husband and daughter. Did she have a choice?"

"There's always a choice," the President said, "and Warden Ghastin made some bad ones. She has to answer for what she did."

"With all due respect, sir, that's fucked up."

"I don't disagree with you," Carter replied. "So, I'll make sure she gets a lenient sentence and gets to serve her time at a camp instead of a penitentiary." With honest regret in his voice, he added, "That's the best I can do, Reaper."

"Fair enough." Kane leaned forward in his chair and folded his hands on the table in front of him. "Did you get a chance to think about my request?"

Carter nodded. "The Presidential Pardon paperwork is being drawn up. Your friend Pedro is a free man."

Kane grinned. Best news he had heard in a long time.

"Also," the President said, "we located his daughter. Pedro isn't just getting out of prison, he's getting a family reunion."

Kane's grin widened. That was even better news. "Thanks. I appreciate everything you've done."

"You made a promise, son. I'm just helping you keep it. Least I can do, given everything you've done, and everything you went through."

They exchanged small talk for a few more minutes,

then President Carter signed off to tend to the next national crisis on his schedule.

Kane left the briefing room and wandered outside. High clouds streaked the Texas sky as the setting sun set the heavens on fire.

The team had welcomed him back this morning, but now they were gearing up for their next mission. There was equipment to stow, weapons to check, and intelligence to analyze. They would deploy rapidly, meaning there was no time to focus on his return, and Kane was thankful for that. He was glad to be back, but he didn't need anyone to make a big production out of it.

Right now he was alone, but not lonely.

He stood there and stared up at the sky as it darkened from orange to red to purple. As the stars began to scatter themselves across the celestial tapestry, he heard light footsteps approaching.

An arm slid around his waist, and he looked down at Cara. "Hey," she said softly.

"Hey, yourself." He slipped an arm around her shoulders. Their touch was somewhere between friendship and love, just like their relationship.

"I'm getting ready to go wheels-up," Cara said. "But I wanted you to know that it's good to have you home, Reaper." She paused. "And this *is* your home. I hope you know that."

"Yeah, I do."

She stepped in front of him and put a hand on his chest. Even decked out in combat gear, ready to tangle with the latest cartel threat to pop up on Team Reaper's radar, she was still achingly beautiful. Kane didn't know what the future held for them, but he hoped that one day they could sort it out. Maybe when all the bullets and blood finally came to an end.

In other words, maybe never.

Her eyes searched his face. "Did you find what you were looking for?"

He nodded. "Yeah, I did."

She lightly brushed her lips against his. "Glad to hear it."

She walked away, off to kick some cartel ass, leaving Kane alone again.

His thoughts turned to the other woman who had managed to pierce his emotional walls. Luna would forever haunt his heart. You never forget an angel. Destiny had brought him to her, broken and scarred, and she had healed his pain and reminded him of who—and what—he was.

A warrior.

He vowed to never forget again.

A LOOK AT: KANE: CENTER MASS (FEAR THE REAPER 2)

BY BRIAN DRAKE

THE REAPER IS ON THE HUNT.

In a deathtrap of an abandoned drug lab in Caracas, John Kane and a unit from SEAL TEAM 6, discover a new threat to the free world. Heroin flows out of Afghanistan into Africa and then to Europe and the Western Hemisphere. Word comes down from On High; eliminate the cash cow funding the Taliban. With Prejudice...

Following the trail to a deserted island in the Arabian Sea, Kane unleashes hell on a group of drug runners only to uncover a shocking secret--China is a silent partner in the illicit operation. Pursuing the narco-terrorist network, Kane enters war-torn Africa. Hunting the Chinese connection, Reaper begins an elimination run that quickly brings the body count to staggering proportions.

But no plan survives contact with the enemy. If Kane wants to survive he's going to have to start putting bullets on target...

"There is no let up from the first page until the end.""

AVAILABLE DECEMBER 2024

ABOUT THE AUTHOR

Mark Allen was raised by an ancient clan of ruthless ninjas and now that he has revealed this dark secret, he will most likely be dead by tomorrow for breaking the sacred oath of silence. The ninjas take this stuff very seriously.

When not practicing his shuriken-throwing techniques or browsing flea markets for a new katana, Mark writes action fiction. He prefers his pose to pack a punch, likes his heroes to sport twin Micro-Uzis a la Chuck Norris in Invasion USA, and firmly believes there is no such thing as too many headshots in a novel.

He started writing "guns 'n' guts" (his term for the action genre) at the not-so-tender age of 16 and soon won his first regional short story contest. His debut action novel, The Assassin's Prayer, was optioned by Showtime for a direct-to-cable movie. When that didn't pan out, he published the book on Amazon to great success, moving over 10,000 copies in its first year, thanks to its visceral combination of raw, redemptive drama mixed with unflinching violence.

Now, as part of the Wolfpack team, Mark Allen looks forward to bringing his bloody brand of gun-slinging, bullet-blasting mayhem to the action-reading masses.

Mark currently resides in the Adirondack Mountains of upstate New York with a wife who doubts his ninja skills because he's always slicing his fingers while chopping veggies, two daughters who refuse to take tae kwon do, let alone ninjitsu, and enough firepower to ensure that he is never bothered by door-to-door salesmen.